MW01681024

PUSH YOUR LUCK

19

BLADES & BLOOD

PUSH YOUR LUCK

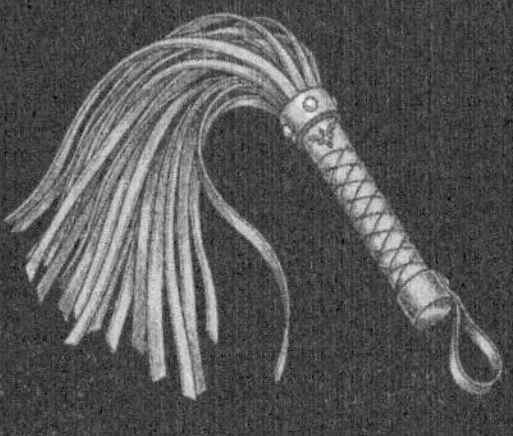

T.K. DRAKE

Push Your Luck
Blades & Blood Book Two

Contact Info: www.tkdrake.com

Cover design by Sandra Maldo (Maldo Designs)
Editing by Jenny Sims (Editing 4 Indies)
Interior Formatting by Alt 19 Creative

ISBN: 979-8-9995185-6-9 (paperback)
ASIN: B0GX35N34H (ebook)

First edition: June 2026

10 9 8 7 6 5 4 3 2 1

For those who understand that the most
dangerous woman in the room
is the one who is loved...
...and obeyed.

CONTENT WARNING

Please note that this is a sexually explicit romance with dark themes. Please visit www.tkdrake.com for a detailed list of content warnings and kinks. Your mental wellbeing is incredibly important to us! We can always be reached at tkdrakeauthor@outlook.com with any specific concerns or questions.

AUTHOR'S NOTE

Thank you for reading *Push Your Luck*! Whether you're new here, reading after reading the *Sinclair Affairs* series, or continuing your *Blades & Blood* journey, welcome! Writing our debut series was the realization of a lifelong dream, and those characters will stay with us forever. Blades & Blood is borne from our love of hockey and dark romance. The characters we've met while writing this book have brought us immense joy, and we hope they inspire the same in you!

Push Your Luck is book two in a five book series but can be read as a standalone.

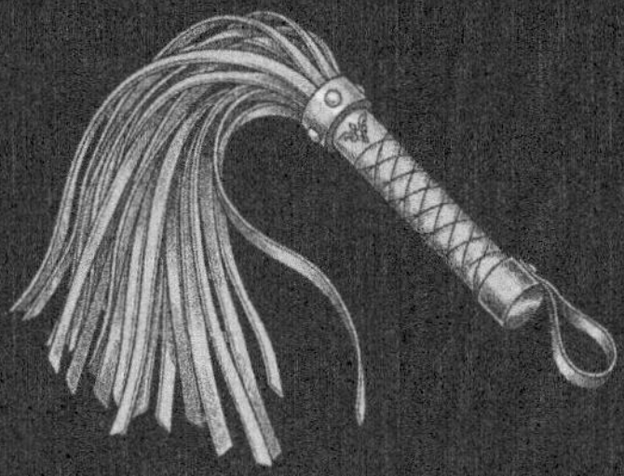

CHAPTER 1
Mila

"YOU HAVE TO keep practicing with your left hand as soon as you're cleared for physical activity. Otherwise, anyone who looks at you will notice your weakness immediately, and you'll be toast."

"I know, I—"

"The sniper rifle won't learn to shoot itself. Now that the season's over, I expect you at the range seven days a week. Sorry, Ellie. He has to get better. Maybe you can float in the pool while he trains?"

My future sister-in-law perks up from where she's sprawled on the couch. "That sounds amazing. I want to cook for all the guys, too. I'll finally get a chance to hone my barbecue skills."

"Your agility needs work. You won't have Misha, but Rusev will be here."

"Yes, he and I have plans to—"

"The council might give you some pushback on some of your planned changes, but honestly, they're probably so happy to have a penis in charge again that they might go easy on you."

"I've met with them already, and we—"

"Don't forget about the meeting with the lawyers either. Now that you're getting married and expecting, you have to update a lot of that shit."

My brother finally loses his patience with my reminders and takes off his glasses, covering his face with his hands. "I *promise,* Mila. You've taught me well, and so has Misha. Like you said, I have Rusev and all the other guys staying with me, and you're only a text away. Sasha sent me a fucking *shared* note on my phone, for crying out loud. He's already got like twenty checklist items on there for me to complete! I can do this."

Sighing, I glance at the woman who's actually in charge of Teddy's schedule. Ellie's a born-and-raised Mafia princess, just like I am. Although she hasn't been trained with the same expectations as I was, she's shrewd and knows the business inside and out. We aren't *merging* our Thunder Bay operations with the Santori family, per se, but business will boom for both of us now that we're bound by the blood of the baby she carries.

"*I got this,*" she mouths in answer to my raised eyebrows, and I breathe a sigh of relief. Before I can add on to my to-do list for my brother, the alarm on Misha's phone blares that it's time to leave for the airport. Once he says his goodbyes and grabs the last of our bags, I'm left alone with Ellie and Teddy. When we met, *damn,* only six months ago? It feels like a lifetime...

When we met, I resented him for existing. The one thing he has no control over. I wanted to hate him for inheriting the Bratva that I've poured my blood, sweat, and tears into for almost every one of my thirty-nine years on earth. He didn't even *want* this, and he got it for no damn reason except the thing dangling between his legs.

That was then, though. The man who showed up was smart, funny, and just a decent fucking human. It was impossible to hate him, even if he put us all through hell by entangling himself with the only daughter of one of our rival families. That worked out for the best, though, so maybe he's a good-luck charm. I hope the Thunder Bay branch of the Taranov Bratva thrives under Teddy and Ellie's leadership. My niece or nephew deserves to inherit a first-rate legacy, not some low-budget operation.

Teddy gets up first, awkwardly approaching me as if he's considering moving in for a hug. Instead, he runs his hand through his hair, then offers it for a handshake. "We're going to miss seeing you. I'm sure I'll be bugging you with texts and calls before you've even landed in New York."

"I can't believe I'm saying this, but I'll miss you too. I've gotten used to kicking your ass in the training gym. Without you around, I'll have to go back to showing Misha who's boss."

My best friend and right-hand man doesn't come back inside, but he does flash me a one-fingered salute from where he's leaning in the doorway.

"Look, I know Misha's going with you, and you'll have a ton of people around you at the compound, but if you ever need anyone, my grandma said to remind you that you can always video call her. I know she's traveling for most of the summer, but she'd love to hear from you."

"I appreciate that. Maybe we can have virtual lunch one day. I need to know more about your awkward tween phase where you were obsessed with that one television show. What did she say it was?"

"Ugh, no."

"Gargoyles! He had a crush on the hot, animated gargoyle," Misha calls from the hall, chuckling before reminding me we're on a schedule. "We gotta go, moya tsaritsa."

Ellie stands up for a hug before I give Teddy one last fist bump on my way out. Just before we reach the elevator, he manages to get on my nerves one last time.

"Hey, Sis—"

"You know I hate when you call me—"

"You know who's already asking me about when you're moving?"

"I swear to God, Teddy—"

"Your number one fan, Thatcher Prescott!"

"Remind me why we aren't having any fun in the city tonight before we have to start work tomorrow?" Misha stuffs his face with the last of his trail mix before moving on to gummy candy. He's always said the altitude makes him extra hungry, so we have to plan accordingly. We ran out of snacks on a business trip once, and I've never been around anyone so unpleasant.

"Well, for starters, the compound has a hangar and a runway. No need for an airport."

"Fanshmy," he says around a mouthful of candy.

"Yes, very fancy. There's also the fact that Ivan has graciously agreed to leave his home and loving family to show us the property and formally introduce us to the leadership team. It would be poor form to refuse just to get hammered in the city the night before. We'll have plenty of time for that after we settle in."

Settle in. When my world crashed down around me six months ago, and Teddy arrived to reluctantly abscond with my birthright, it seemed my training to *run* a Bratva branch would go to waste. Then when my cousin Ivan decided he wanted to step back, along with his heir, Sasha, he asked if I'd be interested in moving to New York and taking over his operation. Sasha helped show Teddy the ropes in Thunder Bay, Ivan helped with the legal aspect and assured me there was no male-only clause in their branch's bylaws, and the rest moved quickly.

Technically, this is an upward move. A *promotion,* if I had a normal career. It's a bigger area to operate, a larger property, and a much more lucrative investment portfolio. I waited for melancholy to hit when I finalized my move away from the home I've known for the past fifteen years, but…nothing.

It's a job. Something to fill my life until I die. Luckily, in that regard, it's a pretty damn all-encompassing job. No time to be sad, or anxious, or any of that shit. And no time to wallow in thoughts and memories, which is for the best. I work or work out eighteen hours a day, with every moment accounted for, and that's the way I like it.

If anything, I should be able to enjoy the weather in New York more than in Florida. I'm not built for the heat, and I stood out like a sore thumb everywhere we went. Jet-black hair, pale skin, broad shoulders, and my favored all-black outfits…not to mention a lot of men in Florida are *short.* Nothing says "want to be fuck buddies" like a guy looking up at your double chin from a few inches below.

No, my six-foot-tall pale ass is meant to be hauling lumber in a Siberian winter.

But I'm not going back there. Never.

So New York it is. This should be a relatively quick takeover, including a meet and greet, and then we can get to work. I have Misha to help smooth over any initial bumps in the road, and we'll do what we've always done. *Survive and thrive.*

CHAPTER 2

Thatcher

THE FINAL HORN sounds, and just like that, another hockey season is officially over. We lost in the first round of the playoffs, but after the finals, we always have a few practices before parting ways for the summer. It's impossible not to join the guys in a cheer of relief at the prospect of some much-needed time off.

"Alright, alright, stop skating around like a bunch of cheerleaders and get your asses in the showers! Dunbar, stop bellyflopping on my ice like a goddamn walrus," Coach yells. "You sure aren't acting like you want time off. Where's all that groaning I heard at the beginning of practice?"

We head to the locker room, but the commotion worsens as the guys talk over each other, telling their plans for the break. For once in my life, I shut the fuck up. Because for once, I don't have any plans. Instead, I just listen to everyone else.

"We're going to England for a month. My daughter is convinced that she's a real princess, so we're going to show her some castles."

"Aw man, we went through that phase too. Actually, there are some way better countries in Europe if you're just wanting to see castles—"

"We had our eyes on an all-inclusive resort in the Caribbean, but our kids begged us to go to Disney. Most magical place, my ass. Whoever coined that obviously never went with two preteens in the middle of summer."

"Hey, you leave the mouse alone. It's magical, and you know it!"

"Lisa and I are doing a Mediterranean cruise. You know, for someone who keeps trying to convince us to start a family, you sure aren't making it sound fun. I'll take my wife all to myself, especially in a bikini by the pool."

"What about you, Sunshine? Any big plans?"

"Sunshine?"

"Thatcher?"

"Ow, what the—" Something smacks me in the forehead, and the offending item lands at my feet, stench trailing in its wake. "Whose nasty-ass socks are these?"

Bubba Jones cackles like a hyena and wiggles his toes. "Next time I ask you a question, get your head out of the clouds and answer it!"

"What was your question, *asshole*?"

"What are you doing during the break? Any big plans, playboy?"

"Oh, um, just going to the Hamptons."

"Hell yeah, I hear the parties there this time of year are insane."

"They are. I swear the women there are fucking feral in the summer. It's like they get away for a while and lose their damn minds. You know, I have plenty of extra room if you want to come stay sometime."

Bubba ruffles my hair and laughs. "I bet it's wild. Maybe in my last lifetime. Natalie hates all the parties and stuff. We're going to an all-inclusive resort in Jamaica."

Oh yeah, I forgot he got married this year. "That sounds nice, too."

"Yeah, it sure as hell sounds nice," Milton shouts from across the room. "Just wait until you have kids and you end up in a theme park."

"I'm sure Nat would like that too." Bubba smiles lazily, then looks back at me. "Anyway, enjoy your bachelor time in the Hamptons. I think this might be one of the last years you'll be single. Someone is bound to snatch you up soon."

"Nah, I'm not ready for all that yet. You and Nat enjoy Jamaica, though."

One by one, the guys get their things and clear out of the locker room, saying their last goodbyes. As the team captain, I'm always the last man out. Finally alone, I take one last look at the empty room and turn out the light.

I'm usually counting down the days until the offseason, but I can't say I'm looking forward to it this time. No, two months with nothing to fill my days but alcohol and sex just isn't doing it for me this year. It's not like Teddy partied with me before, but I always had someone to go home to. I would spend my weekends at my parents' house in the Hamptons, live it up, then go back to the city and spend my days with him.

In fact, hanging out with Teddy and his grandma Muriel has been the only time in my life that I felt like I had a family. I haven't seen my own parents in months, and even though I'll be in *their* home in the Hamptons, I won't see them there either.

No, Dad and Mommy Dearest are probably gallivanting about in Europe somewhere right about now. As far back as I can remember, they'd leave in the summer to embark on their own adventures while I was left back in the city, or in the Hamptons, with whichever nanny was in rotation at the time.

Their absence led to some killer parties over the years. My friends all thought I was the luckiest guy in the world to have so much freedom, but I hated it. They got to come get drunk or high for a weekend, then go back to their loving family during the week. I would hear about their vacations and imagine what my parents and I might be up to wherever they were at the moment. Perhaps we would take a tour of the catacombs in Paris, a wine tour in Portugal, or even attend one of the contemporary operas my parents rave about, where the actors sing while standing in trash cans.

At least they're still in love. I think. I knew plenty of people whose parents couldn't stand each other. The Upper East Side was filled with infidelity, so much so that it was assumed to be the standard. It never sat right with me, though. Maybe that's why the idea of settling down with someone hasn't ever appealed to me.

Why have one woman when you can have them all?

Except, after so many years, they all turn into the same boring woman. Maybe that's why Teddy was never into it, and it worked out for him. He met his soulmate, Ellie. Those two could make someone with the hardest of hearts believe in love.

Someone like me.

For the first time in my life, a month away with one woman who loves me sounds better than the countless faceless women I'm used to. Too bad nobody's waiting for me at home except my empty bed.

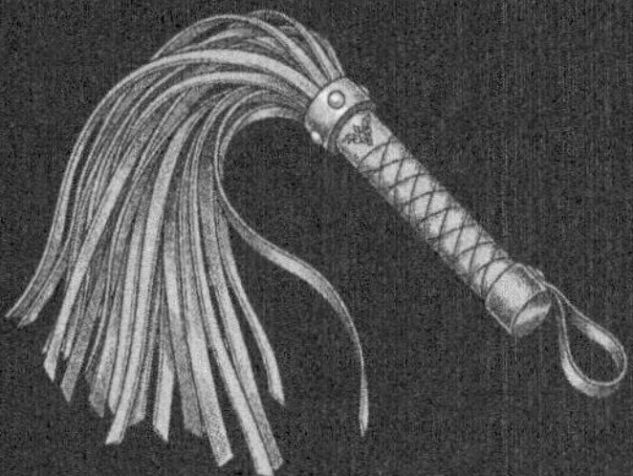

CHAPTER 3
Mila

"AND THIS IS the owner's suite." Ivan pushes open french doors and reveals the ugliest bedroom I've ever seen. "It's been empty since my brother passed away. I already had my own rooms and never felt inclined to move, and then, well, I started spending less and less time here after Blanche and I… Anyway, you're welcome to occupy any of the suites, but this is the largest and has the best view."

He continues, but all I can think about is the *fucking red latex*. It's everywhere in this wing of the house. The garish shade spans from the rug to the walls to the furniture. Even the ceiling wasn't spared, with velvet surrounding a mirror that hangs directly above the four-poster bed.

I've had my fair share of "red room" experiences, but it's a gauche aesthetic for a bedroom, especially in a house this big. The suite doesn't even have the equipment to make it a practical room for *real* kink. The bed frame looks domineering, but there aren't any metal reinforcements to attach restraints. A stripper pole is tucked into a corner of the room, but it's plain. I don't see any hooks dangling from the ceiling to hang a swing. *Or a bad boy who's gotten himself tied up.* There's a large red velvet chair in front of the bed, but no furniture ergonomically designed for more *strenuous* positions.

It seems like the owner of this suite wanted to feel like they're kinky, while fucking like every other vanilla loser out there. I shouldn't say *loser.* That kind of sex life is absolutely fine for most people. But most people don't run underground operations that could take out small countries. I learned early on that a simple fuck was never going to be enough for me. I need the power, the pain, and the absolute submission of my partner. Which means I need to add an *actual* kinky room somewhere in this mansion and make my own suite livable.

I rub my temples, making a mental note to add the owner's suite to the ever-growing list of renovations around the place. It's not a complete disaster. The bones of the house are solid, with traditional designs and layouts that have aged well over the years. Luckily, whoever got their hands on the place didn't have enough time to do *too* much damage. It's mostly surface-level renovations that will need to be done, so some fresh paint and furniture and my interior designer should have this tacky mess sorted out soon.

Not that redecorating is at the top of my list. There seems to be a never-ending list of tasks that precede making my new house feel like home. I knew taking over a larger branch of our family's Bratva would be hard, but I underestimated how much work it would involve by a long shot.

For starters, the transfer of power from Ivan to anyone would be a chore, but it's going to be especially hard, considering my gender. I'm up for the task, though. I can put any one of these men on their asses in a matter of seconds and outmaneuver them all politically. I just need the time to prove to them that I'm worthy of their loyalty.

That's just the emotional aspect. Their business operations are much different from how we ran Thunder Bay. Ivan ran through everything with me, and while there are some details I like, I'm going to need to tweak things to my standards. Apparently, Ivan only took over as the Pakhan from his brother Pavel a few years ago. He showed me records of the nightmare he walked into, and the improvements he's made in a short time are impressive.

We have a tight timeline for this merger, and it's barely enough time for a complete handover, even if everything goes perfectly. Ivan has agreed to visit as much as he can to make the transition as painless as possible, which means I'm going to be here a lot more than I planned. I was naive to think that I'd be able to travel back and forth between Thunder Bay and New York to check on Teddy. No, I won't be able to make a trip to Florida for at least a month with the mess I have to clean up here. Panic threatens to take hold, but with a deep breath and the reminder that he married into a whole-ass Mafia that will protect him, I find my resolve just as Ivan takes his leave.

"Alright, I'll let you settle in. I'll be back soon, but if you need anything, just reach out. My wife Blanche and I will be in the city, so I should be able to get back with you quickly."

"Thanks, I'm sure we'll manage just fine. I'll see you in a few days."

Ivan leaves, but I'm not sure how much "settling in" I'll be able to accomplish in this gaudy sex den. *So much latex...* At least it's easy to clean. *Although...* That thought lights a fire under me, and I decide to find the housekeeping staff instead of moping. Even if it takes some time to re-decorate, the least I can do is make sure the room's been drenched in bleach.

"What do you think, moya tsaritsa? Up to the challenge?" Misha knocks the back of my chair and hands me a cup of tea before sitting down across from me.

Sipping my tea, I observe my dearest friend through the steam. "Oh, please. This is nothing."

"It's not going to be as easy as it was under your father, you know. You had his protection and years to build rapport with the men. We barely have enough time to earn these guys' trust, and when Ivan leaves for good—"

"I said *I'll be fine*," I snap.

Any of my other men would cower, but not Misha. He raises a brow at me and smirks, daring me to continue with my attitude, knowing how much I hate to lose my composure. I roll my eyes, pulling a laugh from him before continuing, this time with a softer tone.

"Go ahead, tell me what you think of it all."

He sets his tea down and leans forward to prop his elbows on his knees. "I think we've got our work cut out for us, and I don't think we should let our guard down. *But* I also think you can do it. Ivan ran this place well, or as well as he could after inheriting his brother's mess. From what I've gathered, his men are loyal to him, which means he's a good leader. Not so different from you and your father. I think you'll inspire them in a similar way as your predecessor. And if they give you any trouble, I'll kill them."

"We've talked about this. You can't do that," I laugh, but I know he means it. He's protected me since, well, for decades now. Through thick and thin.

"I can and I *will*, moya tsaritsa."

"Whatever you say, moya sila. What did you think of the house?" I laugh again as Misha chokes on his tea.

"It's fine. I think the house is the least of your worries right now."

"Yeah, you're just saying that because you got the pretty blue room that seems to have gone untouched by whatever red latex demon threw up on the rest of the place," I grumble.

Misha reaches out to grab my hand, pulling my gaze to his. "We can do this. *You* can do this. If you could make it out of Russia all those years ago, you can do anything."

He's right. This is paperwork. It's clinical and administrative, and while yes, it can be annoying, it's not a big deal in the long run. It's not life and death; it's just stepping up once more to become the leader I was born to be. I'll prove myself, regardless of what it takes.

CHAPTER 4

Thatcher

"JESUS, SUNSHINE, WE'VE been looking for you."

"Yeah, man, how big is this place? We had no idea *this* was what you got up to in the offseason."

Shit. It's one of our rookies and an equipment guy, and I'm too drunk, *and high,* to remember either of their names right now.

"Hey, guys, I'm glad you made it! Everyone is usually off on their own vacations as soon as the season ends."

"Well, you clearly have plenty of friends who love to party even without the team, man. Listen, we're gonna head outside. I think I heard something about a wet T-shirt contest. We'll catch up before the night's over, yeah?"

A nod and a fist bump are all it takes to send them on their way. I must be more fucked up than I meant to be if I can't even remember a guy's name after playing an entire season of hockey with him. Although I have had some traumatic experiences recently. My best friend got traded off my team, we lost in the NHL playoffs, the same best friend inherited a Russian Mafia and almost got killed, and now he's in love and knocked a girl up.

There's a word for it. Not Mafia... Plucking another champagne flute off a passing tray, I admire my handiwork. Everyone is shiny in metallic fabrics tonight, and you can smell the hedonism in the air. My postseason Hamptons parties are legendary, even if my teammates usually don't show. Not even Teddy would show, usually skipping them to go hiking with his grandma. *It's fine. It's not everyone's scene.*

"Hey, Thatcher, thanks for inviting us."

Squinting, I can make out blonde twins in skimpy metallic bikinis. They do seem very thankful, based on the hard nipples showing off through the fabric. I don't remember inviting them, though. If only their faces weren't so blurry.

"You're very welcome, ladies. I'll see you soon. Excuse me."

Moving through the sea of people enjoying the DJ, I head for my favorite escape. The second-floor balcony overlooks the pool and the ocean, and since it's off-limits to party-goers, it's the perfect place to take a quick break. Sometimes, I'll bring whoever's caught my eye for the night up here, but tonight, maybe I can use it to take a better look at the crowd and find someone. Nobody's struck my fancy yet.

Fuck, life is good. The twinkle lights glisten as people splash in the water, the DJ is playing a mix I requested, and every inch of my parents' Hamptons house is filled with luxury and pretty people enjoying themselves. I'm not sure where my parents are, not that it matters. They never liked this house anyway, and I've never heard a peep from them about any of the parties. One year, every chandelier got shattered, and when I came back a week later, it was like the party had never happened.

They literally couldn't care less.

"There's our fearless leader! Captain Prescott, please grace us with your presence, oh great one!"

Another person I don't know has grabbed the mic for the outdoor area and spied me on my balcony. He's a fat fucker, maybe some Wall Street wannabe from the city, and I wish he hadn't seen me. As I move to the railing to smile and wave at my adoring public, I notice the woman by his side. Tall and with a toned back, black hair braided down her back. *No way.*

"Cannonball! Cannonball!"

She turns, revealing that she's just another stranger, and I shrug off my blazer and slacks to reveal the neon pink Speedo I custom-ordered just for tonight. It takes every ounce of awareness I have, but I manage to step onto the railing and balance, toes hanging on for dear life as I stand above the pool.

"Hear ye, hear ye. Who summons your Lord Prescott?"

The crowd goes wild. I've never jumped from here to the pool before, but it's not too far. I think. Before I have a chance to lose my balance, I leap for the pool, and the warm water welcomes me without injury.

What a time to be alive.

"You're lucky no one got hurt."

The burly fireman stares at me as if I *purposely* set my condo in the Upper East Side on fire.

"I agree that we're all lucky, but I'm not sure I appreciate your tone."

He doesn't respond, but does pull out a melted lump from his pocket. *Shit.* That definitely looks like one of my favorite candles. I'm pretty sure I blew them all out before I left for the Hamptons.

"Regardless, nobody's gonna be back in this building for a while. Smoke damage is the main problem. Once we finish our investigation, we'll turn it over to the remediation company. I believe your father has already been in touch with the insurance. Have a nice day, Mr. Prescott."

My father?

Right on cue, my phone lights up with a call from a contact that usually never graces the screen. If he's calling, this can't be good. I've barely answered the phone when his curt tone makes me feel like I'm five years old again. Or three, or ten, or sixteen…

"Good evening, Thatcher. I see you've finally managed to actually render one of our properties uninhabitable." *God,* he loves reminding me that they own everything.

"Hello, Father. It seems there was an incident, but I'm not sure I can be held responsible just yet—"

"Save it. The fire chief already sent a picture of the candle to the insurance company." He sighs heavily and mumbles something to, I assume, my mother in the background. It always sounds something like "can't believe we didn't abort," but I've never been able to make it out clearly. "This is disappointing, even for you."

If only he knew how little his disappointment meant to me at this point.

"Well, I'll go back to the Hamptons, I guess, until—"

"No."

"Okay. Well, can I stay in the brownstone at—"

"No."

"What do you mean no?"

"Your mother and I have discussed it, and this is beyond the realm of what we're willing to tolerate from you. The goats on the roof of the country house should have been enough, but we've given you too many chances. You're on your own to figure this one out. You can get a hotel or finally buy your own property."

"A hotel? For months?"

"At least until you purchase something. It'll be good for you to get into the real estate game, anyway. It's past time. We've got to be going. Have a good night."

With that, my loving father is out of my life again, probably for at least a few months. Staring at the still-smoking hulk of my condo building, I mull over my options. I can definitely get a hotel and try to buy something, but I'd really rather move back in here. The location is perfect, and I have, well, *had* it decorated just the way I liked.

I hate hotels. Even the most luxurious in the world feel lifeless when you're there alone, listening to other people come and go, laughing with their lovers or their families. Traveling with the guys, I at least have a roommate. But if I'm in a hotel alone, I'll get up to no good. I know myself.

The guys! There's no way every single teammate is out of town for the summer. Surely someone has to be around.

"Sorry, man. We're in Italy for the month."

"Jesus, Sunshine. The whole condo? Yeah, we're out West with the wife's family."

"Nah, bud. Back in Canada for the offseason."

"Can't, Sunny. I'm going back home to Norway to propose."

Sailboat trip, baby due any day now, backpacking through Japan… It seems like my teammates are cooler than I gave them credit for. Not a single one is available to put me up. Scrolling through my phone, I find the group chat that I somehow got added to after the party. The Wall Street guy got my number, and all his little buddies who were at the party wanted to send me texts of thanks. Hundreds of notifications later, I've scrolled past pictures I really didn't want to see before they're all cleared. Might as well put these guys to use.

"Anybody have somewhere I can crash for a month or so? Fire." There. A simple enough request to people who have drunk more champagne and eaten more caviar on my dime than a month's rent would be. My parents' dime, I guess, but tomato tomahto.

The regretful denials flow in just as quickly as they did when I reached out to my teammates, and as the sun sets, I realize I might have to impose on my dearest friend and his pregnant wife. Maybe I can stay at their estate and follow his scary, hot sister around some more.

"Hey, man, sorry to bother you." I give Teddy the whole spiel, but I can tell by the end that he's overwhelmed between his whole being-The-Godfather thing, plus getting ready to be a real father. He offers his grandma's place, but mentions she isn't there. Apparently, she went on a European cruise with her pickleball group.

I plop down on a bench, feeling sorry for myself, and tell him I understand, and I'll text him soon, but before I hang up, he stops me.

"Thatch, wait. I just had the best idea. I'm sorry, I just had to punish a…never mind, I just wasn't thinking straight. I have exactly the answer to your problems."

"Okay…"

"Mila just moved to New York, into a huge compound, but I don't think she'll be there often. She's got so much to do, and…"

He keeps talking, but I feel lighter than I have all day. Popping up from the bench, I walk back to where I parked near the condo and get ready for him to give me an address. I won't go tonight. That would be rude. I can make it one night in a hotel. But then, even if she's not there, getting to see her at all will be…hot. My dick has never been so scared and aroused by the same person. I don't think she'll give me the time of day, but I won't be bored, and I *definitely* won't be able to get into any shit.

"So what do you think?" Teddy finally finishes his spiel. I have no clue what he said, but it doesn't matter. My best friend has come through for me, once again.

"That sounds perfect. Absolutely perfect."

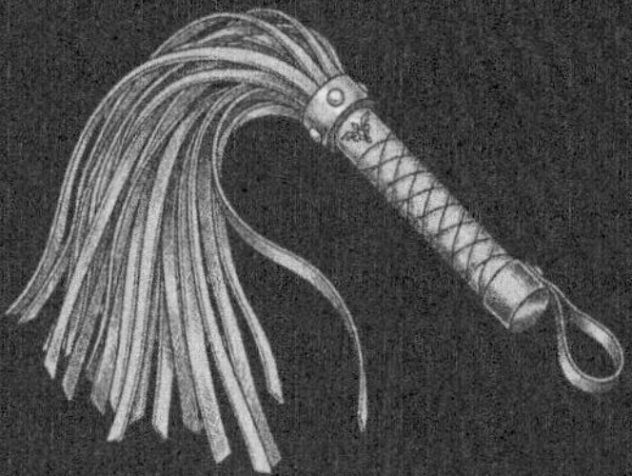

CHAPTER 5
Mila

A LAST-MINUTE MEETING REQUEST from the New York board members wasn't shocking, but I would have enjoyed a few days to get settled in first. Ivan sounded about as amused as I was when he told me, but he assured me it was a small get-to-know-you thing. Meet your new Pakhan, I suppose. Apparently, some asshole *insisted* we have the meeting this weekend before he has to fly back to Russia.

Zakhar Zadorov.

His name sounds familiar, but I can't quite put a finger on it. Of course, all of these men would know of *me* from my position at Thunder Bay. They may not have been on the same board, but as my father's second, they knew who I was.

As Pahkan, I could have easily declined. And maybe I should have, but I would have to meet everyone anyway, and a little meeting didn't sound so bad. Big mistake. I've sat in on enough of Thunder Bay's board meetings to know what is and isn't normal, and this was the latter.

Looking back, I should have made *sure* I was the one orchestrating any first meetings, so my men knew who was running the show. Instead, I agreed to a last-minute meeting and wound up on someone else's turf for my first run-in with the board.

As soon as we walked into his office, I knew there would be problems. One advantage of being a woman in this field is my ability to read people by things like decor. Call it perception, insight, intuition, whatever, but I've always been able to predict someone's intentions earlier than any of the men I've worked with. And an office filled with as much ornamentation as his shouldn't *feel* as sterile as it does. A clear indicator of the facade Zadorov is hoping to sell.

By the time I realized this was merely a fraction of the board, it was too late. Only six people sat around that conference table. Myself, Ivan, Zakhar, and three other men, who all seemed to look at Zakhar for their stance on every policy I plan to enact in New York. It was an ambush. And while I know that his henchmen will follow the strongest leader, Zadorov may very well prove to be a problem for my takeover.

To nobody's surprise, the issue of my gender was the main concern of all four men. Ivan remained stoic when they basically spat on his decision of a successor. "*Women are good for two things: pleasing their men and birthing them heirs. Not leading Bratva outfits.*" For once, I was glad Misha had to wait outside. There would have been four dead Russians and a war on our hands, not even a week into my reign.

By some miracle, I held it together with thoughts of my bed, the only thing keeping me from a mental breakdown. The only problem was that I was imagining *my* bed. The one in Thunder Bay. In the house I spent years cultivating. It wasn't until I flopped back on the bed in New York that I remembered this nightmare is now my room. Closing my eyes, I tried to imagine it's the beautifully decorated bedroom I left behind, but all I could see was fucking red.

My frustration at the loss of my safe space finally boiled over, and I left the bedroom in search of a distraction…which leads me to my current location and, quite possibly, one of the most important rooms in the compound.

It doesn't take much rummaging through the liquor cabinet to find a drinkable vodka.

Thank God Ivan stocked the good stuff. I waste no time with a glass and instead sink to the floor and turn the bottle up. After decades of drinking, it would take nearly the whole liter to have any effect on me, but the burn down my throat is therapeutic.

Fuck me, it's been a day. Actually, it's been like this every day since I moved. Misha was right, having Father around in Thunder Bay made a huge difference. I guess the men there tolerated my position at the table as long as I wasn't the one steering the ship. And by tolerated, I mean benefited at every turn from my expertise both in the field and in the boardroom. If anyone truly thought it was Father calling the shots for the last five years of his life, they were dumb as fuck.

No, as soon as he got his diagnosis ten years ago, he ramped up my training. In his later years, he was merely a figurehead signing his name to my hard work. And it was all for nothing. He was barely in the ground when I found out he left the empire to his bastard son, my brother Teddy.

I was shocked when Ivan offered me his branch, especially considering he has a son of his own, Sasha. Apparently, they both found *love* and want out of the Bratva completely, or at least as far as possible. That's the difference between us. The Bratva *is* my love. Teddy was lucky to marry someone familiar with the lifestyle. Ellie grew up with the same dangers and has the proper training to withstand this life, so my brother didn't have to deal with the guilt of putting her in harm's way. But for me…

Love is a weakness I cannot risk.

Only two people could *really* be used against me: Misha and Teddy. The former would never allow himself to be my weakness, and the latter will never know that he is.

A knock on the door startles me into sitting up straight. "Who is it?"

"Ivan."

"Oh. Come in," I say, standing and hiding my vodka.

He opens the door with a warm smile on his face and immediately reaches for my not-so-hidden liquor. "I knew you had good taste." Taking a swig, he hands it back to me.

I take a drink and smile. "How did you find me here?"

"You aren't the only one who needs a reprieve sometimes. Now, would you like to tell me what's led you to the liquor cabinet before lunch?"

I don't know how honest I want to be. It's against my nature to show any weakness, but Ivan is one of my few sources of sound advice, so I want to share my frustrations. As wonderful as he is, though, complaining about being a woman is *not* how one conducts business with a Bratva boss.

"What made you decide to hand this over to *me*? Surely, a male cousin of ours somewhere would gladly take the reins. It would definitely make everyone else happier to have a man leading the New York branch."

Ivan is still for a moment before he answers. "I know you've met my son, Sasha. But did you know I have a daughter?"

"Yes, of course. Katarina, right? Sasha talked about her a lot when he was helping train Teddy, but I'll have to admit, I didn't know about her until recently."

"You wouldn't have. She was raised as my brother Pavel's daughter. Her mother was forced to marry him, but the two of us fell in love. She died in childbirth, and Pavel always assumed Kat was his, so I kept my distance for everyone's safety. He kept her hidden from the world, locked behind these compound walls, but regardless of her gilded cage, she blossomed into one of the most intelligent and kind humans I've ever known. She faces life head-on and never backs down from a challenge." He smiles wistfully, and I hope I get to meet Kat sooner rather than later.

"Then there's Sasha's wife, Lucy. She lost the only family she knew when her mom died. She didn't have anyone and was only in her early twenties, but she never let life's darkness in. Instead, she continues to see the best in everyone and everything. I truly believe her light saved my son. I hope you have someone in your life you can turn to when the shadows of the business threaten to swallow us whole."

If he means brother from another mother and right-hand man, I have Misha. If he means a lover, someone to share both my deepest thoughts and the banal ins and outs of everyday life...

"And last, there's my wife, Blanche, who could run circles around any man I know. She certainly does me. She's cunning and strong, and I know I couldn't have accomplished so much in the past few years without her help. I studied your operations in Thunder Bay until I physically couldn't read any more. I listened to the way your father talked about you, always with respect. I saw what you did down there when you started running things. You're more capable than anyone I know to take over this Bratva. And quite frankly, I think the fact that you're a woman makes it even better. You've got this."

"Thank you." I nod at him as he leaves, straightening my clothes as soon as the door shuts behind him.

I was born for this.

I've just put the half-empty bottle of liquor back on the shelf when my phone buzzes, and I smile as my brother's silly picture pops up.

"Hello, Cuddles, everything okay?"

"Sis! Yeah, everything is *great.*"

"Good, good. Did you need something?

"Can't a guy just check in on his most favorite sister in the whole wide world? Why does it always have to be me *needing* something? How are you getting acclimated to New York?"

"Okay, well, thank you, I guess. Um, it's fine. Sorry, I don't typically talk on the phone for no reaso—"

"Oh great, I'm glad you're liking it! Actually, there is one *tiny* favor I have to ask of you."

I knew it. God, I hope the house in Thunder Bay is still intact. "What?"

"Well, since you aren't going to be at the compound much—"

"I'm actually stuck here for the next few mon—"

"Thatcher needs a place to stay, and I told him it wouldn't be a problem for him to just stay there."

"No, absolutely not. I have—"

"He won't be in your way much at all, I promise. I mean, I've seen pictures of that mansion. Even if you were there, I doubt you would even notice him."

"Teddy, I have a lot going on right now and—"

"I wouldn't ask if he had a better option. His condo building caught fire, and his only other option right now is a hotel, but he gets sad when he's cooped up in a hotel room without any friends."

"His condo *caught fire*?"

"Yeah, about that...actually, just make sure he doesn't have any candles."

"Doesn't have any candles? *Wait*, the fire in the condo was—"

"It'll be *fine*. Just tell your housekeepers to check his rooms several times a day, just to make sure—"

"Theodore, *no*. He can't stay—"

"Oh shoot. Listen, I've gotta go, but he's on his way. Can you make sure your gate guards know to let him through?"

"*Teddy*!"

"Bye, Sis!"

The blank screen of my phone mocks me as I stare, but not for long. I'm still processing the fact that Teddy fucking *hung up on me* when I get a call from the front gate.

"Hello?"

"Boss. We have a man here who insists you've invited him as a guest, but he doesn't seem like the type of person you would—"

"*Thatcher Prescott. Just tell her my name, and she'll let me through.*"

Pulling up the surveillance app, I filter to the entrance, and sure enough, Teddy's friend is hanging out the window of his SUV like the goddamn puppy he is.

"Boss? Do you want me to let him in or take care of it?"

"*Take care of it? Sir, I'm sorry, I'm not into men like that, but I'll definitely take a hot blonde if you've got one of those in that guardhouse with you.*"

"*Boss?*"

Sighing, I grab not only the bottle I put down earlier but two more as well. Something tells me I'll be double-fisting drinks for the foreseeable future.

"Let him in."

CHAPTER 6

Thatcher

NO PARTIES. OKAY, I can work with that. Except…maybe just a *little* party. First, I need to order, well, everything. It was fucking depressing to get to the hotel last night and realize that I only had my phone, keys, and the clothes on my back. The firefighters said anything left in my condo would have too much smoke damage to be used now, and the remediation company will have to see what they can restore. Luckily, I'm not a sentimental guy, but I hope they can at least fumigate some of my hockey mementos.

Even though Mila's welcome speech was short and to the point, she *did* technically give me the green light to explore the main house. Well, I guess she said "don't go outside," but I think they mean the same thing. I won't open any doors marked "secret" or anything, but I have to find out the delivery address for this place so I can order some clothes and a new laptop. She did at least tell me which direction the kitchen was in, so I head that way first, hoping to find something I can munch on for brunch.

I'd be lost almost immediately in the maze-like corridors if not for the voices drawing me to an archway at the end of the hallway. One is familiar, and I stop to observe the scene in front of me.

"You're almost there, Kirill. You have to flip the pancake just a moment sooner, before it gets too brown. The pan might be a little too hot, I think. Here, let's try a cool pan and a fresh burner on the stove. That should help."

Misha, Mila's huge, strong right-hand man, wears an apron featuring the Swedish Chef on the front while guiding another giant through making the perfect pancake. It's as domestic a scene as I've ever seen, and after observing Misha's ferociousness in the training gym when I met him at Teddy's new estate, it's nice to see a softer side of him. He was patient with the men he was training, though, so I'm not surprised to see that he doesn't even flinch when Kirill immediately burns another pancake.

They're unlikely to see me from this angle, so I'm about to knock to announce my presence when Misha turns.

"How long are you going to skulk in the doorway, Thatcher Prescott?"

"Uhh. Please just call me Thatch. And how did you know I was here? I wasn't in your line of sight at all."

Kirill laughs, and Misha rolls his eyes before pouring a perfect row of pancakes onto a griddle. He says something to Kirill in Russian, and it must have been a dismissal, because he comes to take a seat by me at the kitchen island while Misha cooks.

"If you think I couldn't hear you barging down the hallway, that's one thing. But if you think I don't know when a man is behind me with my back turned, you do not know me well enough, yet. I have a feeling that will change soon, though. Pancakes?" My stomach rumbles in the quiet kitchen, and he chuckles. "I'll make you a big stack."

It's a luxurious space, but lacks charm. This would be a kitchen I would expect in a hotel or maybe a high-end restaurant, not in a home. From what I've gathered, Mila and Misha haven't been here long at all. Before them, it was Teddy's cousin who lived here, but they've moved on to greener pastures, or something. It seems like a long, convoluted story, and Teddy wasn't even sure how they were related for a while.

"You don't seem surprised to see me. *Oh God,* thank you!" I could kiss Misha as he puts a tall plate of steaming pancakes down in front of me, then does the same for Kirill. There's chopped strawberries and some whipped cream on the counter, but I go for the classic syrup container.

"I'm usually Mila's first stop with any news or unexpected occurrences. You, Thatcher Prescott, are an unexpected occurrence."

I'm in pancake heaven, but still. "Dude, it's weird that you keep full-naming me. Thatch only, I'm begging you."

Misha's making another big batch of pancakes, and as good as these are, he can keep them coming as far as I'm concerned. "What Mila didn't have time to tell me, though, is why you're here."

"Well, uh. It's a long story. But I don't like hotels, and I didn't have anywhere to go. My, uh, teammates and...friends are all out of town or busy. So Teddy thought this place would be empty, but now you guys are here. It's pretty big, though, so I don't think I'll be in the way. I can stay in a wing out of the way, and you won't even know I'm here. In fact—"

"It's fine that you're here. I was just curious. You're right. There's plenty of space. Did someone already take your luggage and show you to a room?"

Misha's eyes are kind, and I remember how patient he was with Kirill. Maybe he's the calm to Mila's crazy. A thought strikes me, and I'm surprised it hasn't hit me before. I can't stop myself from ignoring his question and blurting it out.

"Are you and Mila together?"

Kirill chokes on his pancake, but Misha doesn't even blink. It's like he's used to people thinking this, or maybe it's true. Either way, he's unfazed.

"No."

"Oh. You just seem very—"

"Close. We are. More brother and sister. She and I have been together for a long time. But not the way you're asking."

"Ah, okay." He continues to look at me expectantly. "Oh! The luggage. I don't have any. Basically, everything I own was smoked up in a fire. I came here with the clothes on my back, my phone, and my wallet. That's it. After the cleanup and fumigation, the companies will finish their work, and we'll see what I have left. I was actually going to ask someone about that. The address for delivery so that I can order a new laptop, clothes, toiletries, etc."

Misha regards me for a moment before addressing Kirill. "He looks about Timofey's size, don't you think?"

Kirill appraises me before agreeing. "Yeah, roughly the same, I'd say. Maybe a small height difference, but not much."

Misha's on the phone in a second, summoning Timofey to the kitchen. Wherever he was must not have been far because I'm barely starting on my second plate of pancakes when he jogs into the kitchen and stands at attention, speaking to Misha in Russian.

He waves him off. "At ease, Timofey. And English for now, please. This is Thatch. He'll be here for a bit, and he lost all his belongings. You're about his size. Do you think you have anything you could loan him to wear?"

Ah, man. Now I'm a charity case? This isn't necessary. "Oh, that's okay. I can really just order stuff and be fine."

But Timofey doesn't look put out at all. "Certainly. We have duplicates of everything, and since I've been here for years, I've accumulated plenty of tactical pants and long- and short-sleeve shirts. I have unopened underthings, too, from our last quarterly warehouse order. You're welcome to all of it. And it's nice to meet you, Thatch."

He puts out a huge hand to shake, and I gratefully take it. I wasn't expecting a stranger to hand over his clothing so readily, but if it's not an imposition…

"He'll also need a laptop. You're in tech ops, right? Do you happen to know if there are any not in use at the moment?"

"I can order a laptop, no problem—"

"I'm sure we have an extra, and if not, we'll take one from a rookie and wipe it. They spend too much time watching porn anyway."

Kirill chokes on a pancake again, and Timofey gives him a helpful smack on the back. Misha turns to look at my empty plate and piles more pancakes on it.

"Can you think of anything else you might need?"

Kirill and Timofey look at me expectantly, but I really can't think of anything else I need. Except…

"I'm going to need to work out. A lot." The men share a confused glance. *Okay, so not everyone's a huge hockey fan.* "I'm a professional hockey player. Even though it's the offseason, my stamina and conditioning can't take a hit." *Misha really helped Teddy, so maybe…*"Do you think I can join you again in the training gym? Assuming you're planning similar stuff here as you did in Florida."

At this, Misha fills plates for Kirill and Timofey, then turns off his griddle. "Oh, Thatcher Prescott, of course you'll be joining us," he says with a dark smile. "And it's going to be so much worse."

Four hours later, I'm flat on my back, sucking wind and trying to remember why it's important for me to continue living. At the moment, it seems like if I could just never move from this spot, and take an eternal nap, that would be preferable. I got a taste when I visited Teddy, and he told me briefly about the horrors of his training, but *holy fuck.* I thought I was in great shape, but I was wrong.

I'm not alone on the mat, which makes me feel a tiny bit better. A few of the rookies are also struggling, and one guy who isn't new. His name is Greg, and when I told him that didn't sound very Russian, he just shrugged. We were paired for a few of the agility circuits, and it seems he's going back through training after being off for six months on paternity leave. Hearing he got leave at all shocked me, but he shrugged again and said, "Taranov Bratva cares about its employees."

Finally, Simon, a rookie who's strong but not fast, gets up first and offers me a hand. "Come on, Sunshine. Let's hit the showers."

Shit. "Uh. How did you know that's my nickname?" They all laugh as we wince and hobble toward the locker room.

"You're the talk of the group chat, man. As soon as we heard you were professional, we had to look you up. You're pretty good."

"You'll be better after you train with us, though."

"Yeah, your breakaways will be more explosive once you've been through Misha's program."

"And your hand-eye coordination and peripheral reflexes will get a lot better."

"That breakaway you couldn't put in the net against Thunder Bay last year..."

We shower and dress while the guys talk about my hockey career, how the training will help, and how they used to play when they were younger. All of them have different ideas to help me, and I can't believe I only met them earlier today. I'm not sure why they've accepted me into the fold so quickly, but it feels damn nice to have a group to hang out with during the offseason.

CHAPTER 7

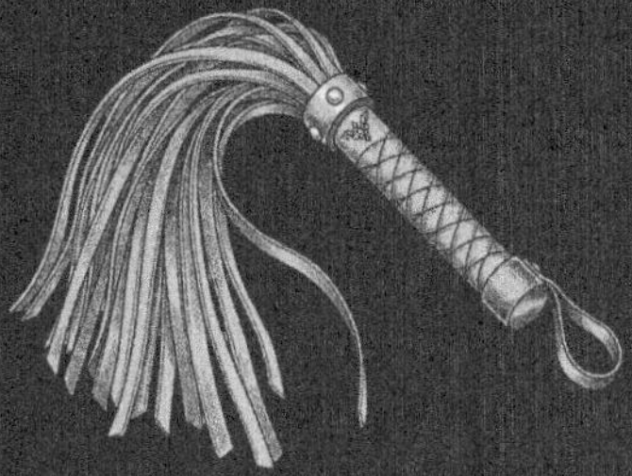

Mila

"IT'S WEEK ONE. We knew we were stepping into a challenge. This is manageable."

Glancing around the gaudy office that Ivan never got around to renovating, manageable is the *last* word I would use to describe my task. *Take over a bigger Bratva branch, they said. It'll be fun, they said.* Still, Misha has a point. It isn't like me to be flustered like this over minor inconveniences. *Although I haven't had a lifestyle change this monumental since…*

"If it would make you feel better, I can make the renovation of your main suite of rooms my priority and knock it out within a couple of weeks."

"Your priority list is already too long. Integrating the men we brought into the existing structure here without ruffling feathers, building rapport with the house staff, gathering intel on any bad apples that need to be weeded out—"

"Making breakfast for stray hockey players you collect."

I swivel my desk chair back around to see a smirk on my best friend's face. "You made Thatcher breakfast?"

"Mm-hmm. My famous pancakes. I was bonding with Kirill. I think you're right, by the way, that he's a high-potential guy who's been underutilized. Your instincts are still sharp, even in your old age."

"Mention me turning forty next year again, and see what happens. I don't know how many more scars your face can handle before the women stop finding you devilishly handsome."

"Infinite scars, moya tsaritsa. The answer is always infinite scars when it comes to looking dangerously sexy to attract women. Besides, these days, handsome doesn't even matter. Have you seen the books the women are reading? Minotaurs, snakes, *doors*—"

"Doors?"

"Doors. So I think with my height and my substantial co—"

"Okay, you win. *Please.* I don't need to hear about anything that's substantial, other than your ego. Tell me more about your fucking Brady Brunch breakfast with Thatcher."

"Not too much to say, really. The kid seems a little lost."

"I don't know if he's a kid. I mean, he's twenty-five—"

"That's fifteen years!" Misha dodges a stapler I launch at his head, barely missing yet another scar. "But I stand by it. Lost. He had a good training session with the guys. I don't think we'll have too many to cull, to be honest. The group overall has a few cliques, but they seem centered around hobbies and whether the individual is single or married with kids. Nothing prevents them all from working effectively across subgroups. I don't think we'll have to separate any units that currently operate together."

"Hmm. He trained with them?"

"I love that *that's* the first question you have after hearing the intel I've been working so hard on." My death glare, which has made grown men piss themselves, has just as little effect as ever on Misha as he laughs. "But yes, he did well. He seemed happy to bask in the camaraderie. Maybe we can keep him around, poach him from the hockey team. Not sure he can fire a gun, but we can always—"

"Eeeeeeeeee!"

A screech interrupts us, gone as quickly as it began. The office overlooks the backyard and the forest beyond, but I've had the curtains closed all day. Drawing them reveals exactly why I was afraid to let a party-crazy hockey player into my house.

The sloping lawn leading to the pool is covered in black tarps, which are sudsed up into the biggest slip and slide I've ever seen. Speakers come to life, blaring house music, and what looks like fifty men are in swim trunks, either in the pool or in line for the slide. Someone's manning the massive grill in the outdoor kitchen, and a table is being set up for beer pong.

Misha approaches and leans over my shoulder to look out before guffawing loudly in my ear.

"You *have* to be joking. This isn't funny! I told him not to go outside, and I told him no parties."

"Did you specify not to go outside *the house*? Or did you leave it open to interpretation? Maybe he thought you meant not to go outside the property."

"What kind of idiot would need that spelled out for him?"

"And did you tell him no parties, or that he can't have people over? Because it looks like it's all off-duty men of ours, so nobody would have had to come through the gates."

Pulling the curtains closed, I try to channel my annoyance into a more productive emotion, to no avail.

"Why are you encouraging him?" I finally manage to redirect my anger to Misha, who's backing out of the office slowly but still smirking.

"I'm not encouraging him."

"You *are,* and—"

"I *do*, however, find him amusing, mainly because I think he's going to annoy the fuck out of you while he's here. *And* I think you'll be better for it. Besides, you're too tense. You need to let loose. It's been too long since you've been to the club."

He *cannot* be suggesting…

"Use him for some stress relief. He followed you around every chance he got in Florida. See if he'll let you—*shit*!"

Finally, I hit my mark, and Misha leaves, nursing his temple where my stress ball connected. Sighing, I turn back to the window, the muffled sounds of frivolity growing louder as the party gets thoroughly underway. I have emails to reply to, and I've been wanting to take advantage of the huge bathtub in my suite anyway. I'll give them the few hours it should take me to finish before I confront the troublemaker.

"Nice party."

"Ah!"

I step back to avoid the splash from Thatcher falling into the pool, biting back a laugh. It wasn't my *intention* to startle him, per se, but I'm not displeased at the outcome. He hops back out with the agility Misha was so complimentary of and shakes himself off. The effect isn't unlike a golden retriever, with his blond curls and dimpled grin. *He's not a dog, Mila. He's a thorn in your side.*

"Hi, Boss."

"I'm not your boss."

"Misha said while I was here, you were, and that you'd like it if I called you Boss!"

Oh, I am so reminding Misha of this the next time we spar in the gym.

"I really would prefer it if you called me Mila." For some reason, this seems to please him even more than calling me Boss, and he stands a smidge taller, still flashing his double-dimpled smile. "Grab a towel and walk with me, please."

The sun is setting, and the party is winding down on its own, so I have nothing to gain from shutting it down. I can see some wariness from the New York crew as Thatcher and I move toward the house, but instead of showing my displeasure, I offer what I hope are respectful nods. Clearly, I'm not here to take part in the party, wearing my usual uniform of long black pants, black shirt, combat boots, and my wet hair in a braid down my back… but I can still show that I'm not *mad* at their party.

Even if I am. At least a bit.

"I'm sorry about—"

"Deliberately misinterpreting the very few rules I laid out for you while you're staying in my home?"

He manages to look regretful for a solid two seconds before one corner of his mouth turns up again.

"Yeah. That. I'm sorry about deliberately misinterpreting the very few rules you laid out for me while I'm staying in your home. *Mila.*" My name sounds forbidden on his lips, and I turn on my heel to lead him into the house before he can continue. I wish he'd put a shirt on, anything to cover more than the fucking *Speedo* he's wearing, but he seems perfectly content to waltz around almost naked. I guess he's comfortable in his own skin, given the abs, and the glutes, and the...oh, screw this.

"Apology accepted. Misha mentioned that one of the guys is loaning you some clothing. I'll give you the delivery address for anything else you might need. Not all the bedrooms are fully furnished, but this one has everything you should need, plus its own bathroom. The decor is apparently from the previous owner's very *particular* interior designer and—"

"Holy *shit*, red latex? This room is hot! Are you putting me in the sex dungeon room?" He spins in a full circle in the center of the room before turning back to me, looking pleased. "Is this because you think I'm sexy and need a super-sexy room? For all my sexiness?"

Jesus, he's drunker than I realized. And now that he mentions it, maybe this room *is* too sexy for him. And far, far too close to mine.

"On second thought, maybe you'd be better off with more space to yourself. Let's go." Weaving through the hallways I only know after studying the blueprints of this house for weeks, I take Thatcher to a wing on the other side of the house. I *think* this was once for the children and staff, and everything here is clean. Although less grand, it's *completely* free of red latex.

He takes in the largest bedroom in this wing, pulling a sheet off a chair in the corner and sneezing as a dust cloud puffs up into his face.

"I'll have it cleaned as soon as possible, of course—"

"This is perfect, my own wing! Party wing, let's go! And this room is huge. There's so much room for activities. It smells a little musty, but that's okay. I love candles, and a few burning in here for a while will make it nice and fresh."

"Can Thatcher stay with you? His condo burned down, and he has this weird thing with hotels..."

"Just don't let him have any candles, okay?"

Teddy's warning echoes through my mind like a shot, and I'm pulling Thatcher behind me once again. It's the last place I want to put him, but it's impossible to deny it's the safest for us all at this point.

"On third thought, I think you'd rather not be so far from the main rooms of the house. Do *not* burn any candles."

Finally, we arrive back closer to where we started, and he seems hesitant to make any comments in case I move him again.

"Bathroom is through there. I'll make sure everyone knows this is your room so they can bring your things. The only rule with this room is not to open the door over there." I point at the wall opposite the bathroom. "Otherwise, make yourself at home."

He's eyeing me with a clearer gaze now, and I can tell he's sobering up a bit after our trek back and forth through the house.

"Will I be seeing a lot of you while I'm here? Misha mentioned you'll be training the—"

"No, you won't."

"Oh." His sad puppy face might make a lesser woman feel guilty for being so curt, but regardless of what Misha says, an energetic shadow is the last thing I need right now.

"Or at least, I'm hoping you won't. I'll be on the property, but my to-do list is a mile long." As Thatcher continues looking at me with his freshly sober eyes, I note that although I'm dressed in my usual comfy spy wear, he's still just wearing his Speedo.

His Speedo that's currently *not* hiding much. I have to get out of here. "Anyway, that's all. Don't forget, the only rule is don't open that door."

I turn to leave as he calls out his thanks, only to remember that there are actually two rules. "Also, no candles!" Finally, I'm alone in my room, door closed, and my Thatcher problem handled. Breathing a sigh of relief, I move to unwrap my braid when I hear the unmistakable click of a door opening behind me. Turning to face the wall opposite my bed, the dimples that greet me are those of a man far too pleased with himself.

Who's opened up the fucking connecting door between our rooms when I explicitly told him not to, not even ninety seconds ago. If...no, I'm not even thinking about that. But if...I would spank his ass raw.

I'm deciding how to respond when he breaks the silence, and it becomes crystal clear that Thatcher Prescott will not be ignored while he's here. Even if I couldn't see his face, the smirk is evident in his tone.

"Hiya, roomie!"

"Good. Your explosion is excellent, as I'm sure you already know. But your energy efficiency needs work. You're giving 100 percent too much of the time, something that your coach probably appreciates for your shorter shifts. I can teach you how to move smarter, not harder, so that your 80 percent is just as lethal as your 100 percent, and—"

"Lethal?"

"I mean, whatever the hockey equivalent of lethal is. Goal-scoring, on-target, whatever you call it."

Misha's the best teacher I've ever met, and he's been taking people under his wing since the moment we arrived in the States. For all his talk about *me* catching strays, he's worse by far. His patience seems endless, and I can count on one hand how many times I've seen him lose it. In the business world or the gym, at least. In *other* aspects of his life, Misha has been known to keep people on much shorter leashes.

"Exactly like that. Now, focus on your deceleration into the next pattern, without wasting so much energy. If you shift a bit earlier, you'll be able to..."

It's clear why Thatcher has been so successful on the ice, even from just a few minutes of watching Misha train him. The agility courses that we drill our men on are meant to represent a more strenuous environment than they'll encounter in the field. One of our men compared the course to "trying to get into the *Home Alone* house," whatever the fuck that means. But if you encounter a viper, a sheer cliff, and sniper fire during a training run, it makes running into any one of the three in real life a walk in the park.

This early on, I think Teddy was still struggling with the incline climb. Then again, he's a goalie, and his build is different from Thatcher's. Where Teddy is broad, Thatcher is lithe. He's still solid muscle, not quite as tall as Teddy but taller than average. His waist is trimmer, and even though Teddy is in excellent shape *for a goalie,* Thatcher's role as a quick goal scorer is clear from his physique.

"Well?" Misha sidles up to me, sipping water from a bottle before pouring the rest over his head.

"Well, what?"

"Do you believe me now about him holding his own?"

Thatcher's taking part in a team trial now, with Kirill, Timofey, and another soldier. The course requires every ounce of all four men's strength to complete, and it's a new wrinkle in Misha's training program. Our old space wasn't big enough for such elaborate setups, and I know he's already called to tell Teddy that Thunder Bay needs an expansion as soon as possible.

"He's good. Better than Teddy this early on. But he's leaner, so I'm not *that* surprised."

Misha shrugs noncommittally. "On the agility stuff, sure. He's no slouch from a pure strength standpoint either, and he has core strength that might rival mine one day. Not that I'd ever admit that to *him*, of course. And he's a natural leader."

"Hmm." No matter how much I want to deny it, his physical prowess and ability to ingratiate himself into a team are impossible to deny. Misha's keen eye, however, has misread one key aspect of Thatcher's personality that I picked up on immediately. There's a reason I'm the boss, after all, and it's not *just* my pedigree.

He barks out instructions for the next set, and we watch as the teams merge, immediately going on defense against a fresh set of men entering the course. Then he gestures for me to explain my equivocal response.

"Everything you say about Thatcher is true," I admit. "Except for the very last bit. He might have the capacity to lead if the situation calls for it. But it's obvious what that man needs, more than anything, is someone to tell him what to do."

CHAPTER 8

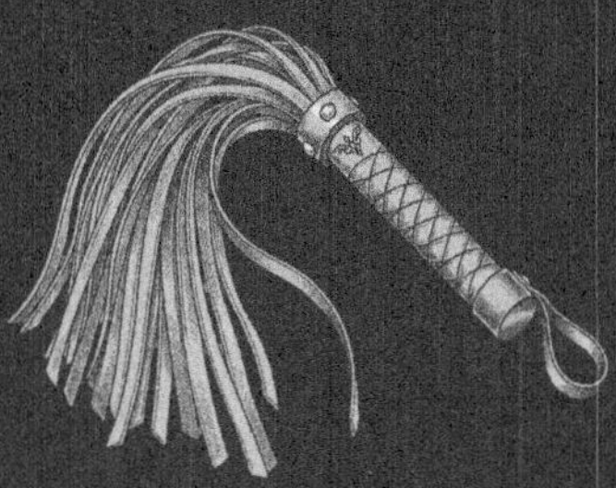

Mila

MY IRE ISN'T for Misha, but he's the messenger, and he's *this* close to being shot.

"This might be a good thing for you. If you aren't going to fuck anyone, you can let off some steam with your other favorite pastimes. Scheming and torture."

"Fuck you. This is bullshit, and you know it." I *do* love both of those things, but they take *energy*. Energy that I don't currently have.

As always, his demeanor doesn't budge an inch. He's calm, relaxed in the chair across from my desk, and ready to provide me with whatever I need. A shoulder to cry on? It's mine. A weapon or five? He'll be back in fifteen minutes with a selection for me to choose from. An ear to listen to me bitch unproductively, then try to offer a solution, even if I don't want to hear one? As annoying as his advice can be, he's usually right, and he *always* lets me get every ounce of my frustration out before trying to fix my problems.

"I do know it, moya sila."

Fucking *fuck*. As if I don't have enough shit on my plate already, one of the board members has come to me with an "amazing opportunity" from a former lawyer of Ivan's brother, Pavel. Based on the way he ran things here, my guard was up as soon as we received the meeting request. Misha handled the initial contact, and without a hint of subtlety, we were basically handed a piece of paper with a giant "screw you" written on it.

It's a joke of an offer from a syndicate that's been a thorn in this branch's side for years. The fact that Pavel's lawyer is the intermediary makes me wonder how much information he took with him when he left. Their offer is to stop fucking with swaths of our shipping in an area that borders their territory, in exchange for us allowing shared access to one of our priority shipping lanes *and* extension of protection from various maritime law enforcement agencies that we pay off handsomely.

"They want us to back off territory we already own and give *them* access to our protection. And all we get is a couple fewer bombed shipments per quarter?"

"The last one was a pretty solid hit, and it took out one of the men who'd been here a while. He was getting ready to go on paternity leave. And they're framing this as a welcome gift for you, the new Pakhan. It's not a bad strategy, if you think about it."

My hand itches with the urge to shatter my teacup against the wall, but instead I sip it, enjoying the burn on my tongue. "Hmm. So the men who lost a friend will enjoy the stability that's offered, and anyone else will see the weakness of conceding territory for what it is."

"Indeed. The timing is—"

"I know what the timing is." A warning shot, right across my bow just as I'm approaching the safety of port. Someone wants me out of here, and they have enough sway to use our rivals to do it. Anyone willing to lower themselves to do business with these brutes will stop at nothing to see me ousted. "Do we have any clues about men in the ranks who are this disgruntled over our takeover?"

Misha shrugs. "We're doing our best to ease in and find out. You know I wish I had loyalty-vision goggles just as much as you do. It takes time."

It does take time. Time that I clearly have even less of than I realized. "Who else knows we received this?"

Now he winces, and I swear. "Well, once the men in the unit that suffered the casualty found out, I think news spread quickly."

"That's what they wanted. Not the lanes or the protection. They want factions in my men. Half will think we're weak if we take the deal and cede their demands. The others will think I don't value their lives and view them as cannon fodder. Whoever here is pushing this must have paid a pretty penny for the syndicate to stick their neck out like this and bet on the fact that I wouldn't wage war."

"Will you?"

The grandmother clock in my office chimes before I answer. Finishing my tea, I message the chef to prepare an afternoon snack before answering Misha's loaded question.

"I refuse to have my hand forced. Based on everything I know about the syndicate, they're too unstable to risk provoking us much more than they have been. I have a suspicion that they got lucky with the recent strikes, if they even consider those outcomes positive. They may have preferred to continue to cause minor damage and shit themselves when they drew blood."

Of all the things I learned sitting at my father's side, haste wasn't one of them.

"We'll continue with our own agenda as planned. As you worm your way into the ranks, we'll see who advocates heavily for a conciliatory attitude with the syndicate. Ensure the widow and the child are provided for, and I'll move up the announcement of the enhanced resources we'll be offering across the board. As far as I'm concerned, business as usual. Don't send a response."

"They'll consider that a response, you know."

"They can consider it whatever they wish. Now, I think you were right earlier. Anything good in the barn for me?"

"Of all the sick things about you, each of which you know that I love, this has to be the sickest."

Clinking my champagne glass against Misha's in a toast, I drain the remainder and help myself to another scone. The chef prepared an excellent spread for my afternoon tea, inspired by a lazy summer beach day. Citrus and mint prevail, and the tiered tray wouldn't be out of place in the tea parlor of a five-star hotel in London.

"See, that's where I disagree. If you can make an argument for mercy for any of these men, by all means, I'll hear it. I see it as meting out exactly the justice that they deserve."

Although our business isn't saintly, I do pride myself that it's as above board as any illegal operation can be. My father felt the same way, as does Ivan. We're working to undo the worst of what Pavel was involved in first, with many of his underworld contacts already taken out. I'm under no illusions that we make the world a better place, but I don't traffic humans or animals, and I also offer...closure to some of our agents in law enforcement who scratch our backs as we scratch theirs.

For some crimes, the American justice system is just too soft. Too lenient. Although I hope I never set foot on Russian soil again, it's impossible to escape the fact that many of my most formative years *were* spent there. Perhaps the only way I feel more Russian than American is in my belief in justice.

The men we're watching are both child predators, and when they were sentenced to a non-life sentence, a few of our agents staged their deaths in a prison brawl and brought them to me for what they actually deserve. Sometimes these men are used to train recruits in the art of information extraction or intimidation. The bodies are useful after death to train our in-house physicians and forensics investigators, so really, we're just recycling the trash the earth has given us.

A scream tears through the glass barrier, pulling my attention away from a delectable cucumber sandwich that I'll have to ask the chef to put into regular rotation. The older man is yelling and sobbing about how unfair this is, and begging for his life. The younger man is sitting silently, watching the display with a cold, psychopathic calm. They're father and son, and they were in cahoots to prey on children using a "friendly neighborhood grandpa" shtick.

The intercom crackles as I key it to give my final reminder. "Both of you know the rules."

The *fun* part is, they have different rules. The son's instructions were that if he could stay calm and not speak to his father, I'd spare his life once his dad lost his mind. The father was told that only one of them was making it out alive. Neither is allowed to speak, although the elder man has started to crack. Every time he vocalizes, the room is *enhanced.* The sprinklers were on for hours overnight, and now it's a breezy sixty degrees.

"You've always been worthless, and now you're making this worse for us by talking. Shut the fuck up!" The son launches a diatribe at his father, who finally snaps and attacks. "He's lost it! Come get me, I win! He's totally lost it!"

Before long, he's too busy fighting for his life to waste his breath on anything else. Misha and I watch them claw at each other for a few minutes, but I've finished my tea, and the fun's mostly over anyway. As we make our way back to the house, storm clouds approach from the west. *Perfect.* A stormy afternoon will be an excellent backdrop to my office hours.

"What's on your agenda for the rest of the day?"

He chuckles. "Oh, my usual. Gym, tan, laundry, attempting to manage your boytoy who you *refuse* to toy with."

"If you wouldn't constantly mention him, I'd forget he was here, and my life would be much more peaceful."

"I don't think I *constantly—*"

"And why does he need managing? Can he not entertain himself? He can spend all day in the gym, you said he liked working out with the men."

"Don't worry about it. Like I said, I'll attempt to manage him. He's not the best listener, though, I can tell you that. It's like trying to train a puppy."

"You've never been firm enough when you train men. He probably needs a shorter leash and a good spanking, and he'd be sitting at your feet behaving."

Misha's diabolical laugh as he heads into the house makes me realize what I've said. I call after him, "I didn't mean it like that, and you know it. Just keep him out of my way!"

"Of course, moya tsaritsa. I'll certainly try. But you should think more about what I said. Three things you enjoy more than anything, and two of the three today haven't sated you. I can still see it in your eyes."

See it in my eyes. He's never more annoying than when he's right. A thunderclap tempts me with the simple pleasure of staying outside in the rain. My office work can wait a bit…Lightning strikes a bit too close for comfort as the clouds part, and although the odds of being struck are in my favor, perhaps it's not the best idea to push my luck today. Moving quickly inside, I reconsider my options.

Maybe a bath to reset, then back to the office.

"Ahh!"

The scream pierces the air as I open my bathroom door, and my gun is drawn on instinct, pointed at…*Thatcher, naked except for bubbles, holding a rubber duck?*

"What the fuck are you doing in here?" In here being in *my* bathroom, in *my bathtub,* with *my* bubble bath, and…well, he must have supplied his own rubber duck.

He sinks back down into the water, recovering quickly from being held at gunpoint and flashing an apologetic smile. "When I turned on the jets in my tub, black gunk came out. I don't think it's been used in a while—"

"Gunk?"

"*Black* gunk."

"You breached the threshold of *my* space, uninvited, because of gunk in your tub?"

"It's still there. If you go look at it, you'll feel differently. It is *nasty.*"

His cheeks are pink, either from the heat of his bath, getting caught, or something else I *refuse* to consider. His ass should be pinked too, for barging in here and violating the sanctity of my space.

"Leave. Call maintenance if you have a problem with your plumbing."

When he rises from the water this time, his smile is cockier, but I turn after a glimpse of his Adonis belt. Whatever he's cocky about isn't my business. Finally, he wraps himself in one of my towels and is gone, trailing water the entire way.

This is fine. I'll drain and rinse the tub, have myself a bath as I planned, and there won't be any evidence that Thatcher was ever here. By the time I've gathered my things, the tub is empty...of water. Perched near the drain, however, is a memento to ensure I don't forget about my guest in his absence. Upon closer inspection, I have to laugh.

The duck is wearing a hockey jersey with "Prescott 19" proudly printed across the back.

CHAPTER 9

Thatcher

"HEY, MAN, HOW'S the New York compound? I haven't visited yet. I told Mila I would come soon, though. I'm due to visit Grandma once she's back from her trip, so I thought I could swing by and check it out then."

I prop my phone on the bathroom counter so I have both hands free to shave my face. I really should shave everything, but it's such a pain in the ass.

"It's going great! I've been getting to know the guys here. They don't say much at first, but after a few shots of vodka, they open up. We've already had some fun."

"I wish the men here would lighten up some. I've tried everything, including liquor, but they haven't cracked."

"You just need the special touch. I bet I could have all of them partying it up in no time. Maybe before the season starts, I can come down and visit."

"I was going to say, you can come down if you ever get lonely at the compound since Mila isn't there much, but it sounds like you're good."

"What do you mean since Mila isn't here much? Is she going somewhere?"

"When she left, she said she would likely not be at the compound much at all with all the business she has to do. That's why I mentioned you staying there in the first place. I guess something must have changed."

Oh, something changed, alright. Thatcher Prescott moved in, and now she can't stand to be too far away. She moved me into the bedroom right beside hers. She wants me...she wants me bad.

"I gotta go. I'll text you later. Thanks for checking in."

I hang up the phone and turn the shower on. Time to get smooth, just in case.

"Late night?" Misha asks as I skulk into the gym.

I drop down onto a weight bench and prop my elbows on my thighs, rubbing my temples. I guess it looks like I'm waking up from a rager, but *this* is the opposite. *This* is the result of getting turned down *again* by Mila. After trying and failing to impress her, I pulled out the big guns this morning. I've never once had a woman turn down my breakfast. I make a killer omelet and pancakes. After years of cooking for puck bunnies, I've learned to use only egg whites and perfected a low-carb pancake.

"No. Early morning."

"Okay? And why are you moping around? You didn't *have* to get up early. You could literally stay in your room all day, and nobody would bother you."

"Yeah, that's the fucking problem," I mumble.

Misha chuckles and pulls a bench up to mine. "Wanna tell me what's really going on, loverboy?"

"What? How do you...? Why would you say that?"

Misha shrugs. "I know everything. Am I wrong?"

"No, you aren't wrong."

"So do you want to tell me what happened to have you walking into my gym like someone killed your puppy this morning?"

"I've been trying *everything* to get Mila's attention, and she won't take the bait! I thought she liked me when she moved me into the room next to hers. And then Teddy told me she didn't plan on staying at the compound much, but she's been here every day, and, you know, maybe that was because of me—" Misha bursts out laughing. "*What*?"

"Okay...first off, Mila put you in the room next to hers because she's afraid you'll *burn the whole house down*. And second, she hasn't left because she has a shit ton of work to do and only a few months to get it done. Look, don't take her attitude so personally. She's head under water right now with the transition and, actually—" He looks at me with a raised brow and smirks. "Actually, you might be good for Mila right now."

"Yeah, well. She doesn't want anything to do with me, so it doesn't matter."

"What happened this morning?"

"I got up super early—"

"Yes, you've said that already."

"To make her breakfast before the staff needed the kitchen—"

"By staff, you mean our in-house, highly rated chef, who needed the kitchen to make her breakfast. Go on."

"And she laughed in my face! Then she walked away without even *trying* it."

"I would presume she went to the kitchen to get the breakfast that the Michelin-star chef made. You know, the one you woke up super early to beat..."

A blank stare is my only response.

"I'm sorry. That was a very nice gesture. What did you make for her?"

"I made my famous pancakes and egg white omelet! I make the best low-carb pancakes. It took me years, but I perfected my recipe."

"Mm-hmm. Did you tell her that too?"

"Of course I did. Why do you think I make low carb in the first place? I learned my lesson a long time ago that women don't like carbs. I even brought her some sugar-free syrup with them. And *yes*, I told her that too!"

"Well then, you deserved for her to laugh in your face."

"Why would I deserve that?"

"Do you realize how brutally that woman trains on a daily basis? No? Would you normally eat low carb when you're at the height of training? And do you think a few egg whites are enough protein for her?"

"Well, no. But all of the other women I've ever—"

"That's your problem, Sunshine. *Mila isn't like other women.* You're doing the same vanilla, basic things that you do for little bunnies, and she's a fucking valkyrie. You've gotta spice things up."

"Spice things up? How can I spice things up? I've been giving her my best game, and nothing I say even makes her smile."

"She knows her worth, so simple flattery isn't going to cut it. Unless you can offer her something better than she would get elsewhere, she isn't going to bite. For example, accepting the breakfast you made would have only been an inconvenience to her. She had a much better option, so why would she choose yours? Was it a nice gesture? Of course! But she isn't one to care much for something just because it's sentimental."

"What do I do with that?"

"You have to offer her something she can't get anywhere else. Something exceptional."

"Are you insinuating I don't have a good dick? I'm an incredible fuck, thank you very much."

"She can throw a rock and hit a man who can fuck. But Mila is a very...dominant woman. What she needs is someone who can handle *her*. Not the other way around."

I've had some wild times over the years, but I've never been with someone I couldn't handle. She's not a tiny woman, but I'm strong enough to throw her around, and I have incredible endurance. Maybe he just means her attitude, but I think that's sexy as hell, no problem there.

"Someone who can handle her?"

Misha squeezes my shoulder as he stands and walks over to his favorite rack. "Come watch her train today. We're sparring this afternoon after meetings. I'll text you before we start."

Why the hell is everything dark? Shit! My "quick" nap apparently turned into quite the event. After taking a moment to stretch, I grab my phone. The messages and missed call from Misha confirm that I'm late for the one thing I was looking forward to today.

Fuck, fuck, fuck.

I've literally been waiting on this bat signal all day. That's why I got so sleepy in the first place. I was *waiting*! The message is from an hour ago, so maybe they're still sparring. *If I run, I might still have a chance.*

Speeding down the hall, I ignore everyone on the way to the training facility. Misha and I train every day, and I've seen most of the men there at some point, but I've never gotten the chance to see Mila. I've heard things, insane things, about her agility. The men hold her in an almost mythical esteem, and the lore of her prowess precedes her. Her schedule has been so packed that I've barely seen her since I arrived, so I'm not surprised she isn't in the gym often.

My cardiac fitness is excellent, but by the time I burst into the facility, I'm gasping for air. When Mila crosses my path, any chance of catching my breath vanishes.

The moment I see her, whatever breath I had left is gone. The stories of her athleticism don't do her justice. She's magnificent. Mila isn't a lithe woman—she's tall and strong and resplendent. But the way she moves around the sparring mat is almost otherworldly. Her movements are fluid and unpredictable, as if she's dancing, not fighting. It's beautiful, and Misha is struggling to survive. He's been kicking my ass since I got here. Misha is the strongest, most agile, in shape motherfucker I've ever met, yet here he is, getting his ass handed to him by this...this valkyrie.

Her skin is its usual porcelain color, no flushing from over-exertion. She's not even sweating, although Misha is drenched. He's as red as a beet and panting. Meanwhile, Mila is as quiet as a panther stalking her prey.

Fuck. Misha is right, she's not like all the other women I've pursued. This isn't any regular woman I'm dealing with. Mila is extraordinary, and it's going to take extraordinary measures to win her over. I can, though. One thing I know for certain is that I can handle this woman. The longer I watch, the more assured I am that I was born to handle Mila Taranova. I just have to prove it to her.

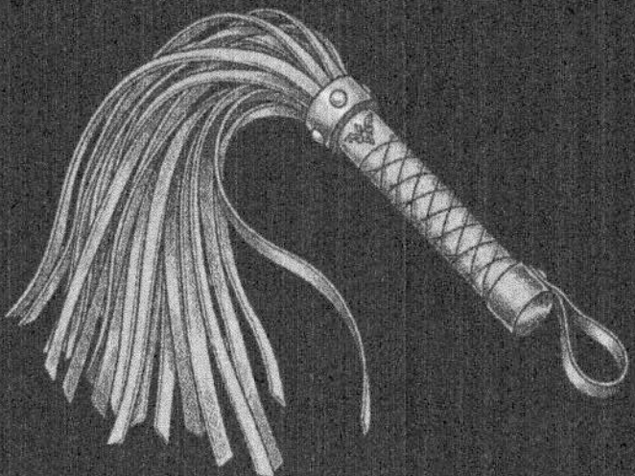

CHAPTER 10

Mila

"WE'LL PLAN TO offer a discounted rate on shipping in the northern part of the state to increase utilization of that market—"

"*That'll undercut the take from the families in the west.*"

"The household team here will be more highly trained, but a smaller crew at any given time. This will allow re-distribution of men on a rotational basis, as I have no interest in living the lifestyle that Pavel did—"

"*If you aren't willing to play the game and host receptions for investors, you aren't going to get nearly as far as you think you are with your grand plans.*"

"Finally, our budget for extravagances will be decreased incrementally—"

"*She wants us to live like paupers because that's what she's used to in her hovel in Florida.*"

"That's enough!" Barely resisting the urge to slam my hands on the mahogany conference table, I stay calm and collected, just as I was taught. Any reaction would be seen as fire in a man, but these misogynists would accuse me of being an emotional woman in a heartbeat. Never mind the fact that it's men who yell, shoot, and beat women, and suffer from a complete inability to do anything but aggressively protect their egos.

The smug bastard mumbling a rebuttal to every statement I made smirks at me as I stand calmly and lean at the head of the table. Fucking Zakhar Zadorov. After the impromptu board meeting, Ivan warned me that he would be the main opposition to my takeover in New York. While the Thunder Bay contingent hid behind legal paperwork during my ousting, Zadorov has no reason other than his own prejudices to want me out. That, and his own ambition.

He turns now to the man next to him and speaks as if I had given him the outburst he tried to provoke. *This fucking bastard…*

"I cannot believe dear Ivan thinks that a *woman* can come up here and—"

"My final point of discussion for today is the enhancement of the widow and family funding. We'll be utilizing the resources freed up from the aforementioned extravagances. Mr. Zadorov, if you don't believe in my leadership or initiatives, you are more than welcome to leave. As is any other man here who questions my ability to lead this Bratva."

He slowly stands, gathering his papers into his briefcase lazily. "Your father knew that it takes a man's control and testosterone to hold the reins of an outfit this size. That's why he went behind your back and wrote you out of everything while still allowing you to peacock around down there and act like you were training to take over."

He waits for me to give him a reaction, any reaction, to show that he's under my skin. But my breathing is calm, there's no hint of the blush of rage on my cheeks, and I revel in the tiny tells of his frustration: the squint of his eyes, the clench of his fist... Sure. *I'm* the emotional one.

As he leaves the room, without a single man following him, he calls back over his shoulder for one last parting shot to try to rile me. "You know, you could marry my son. He's around your age. I don't think he'll settle down, necessarily, but at least you could stay on as a consultant. With a man by your side, you might actually be able to get something done around here."

With that, he's gone, and the men who remain turn back to me. They see nothing but a calm, controlled visage that I've perfected over the years. *Years I spent training for situations like these as my father plotted behind my back, just like Zadorov said.*

"These changes, the financial forecasts, and the updated training programs for each of you to take back to your regions are all in the packets that you were handed upon arrival. I'll take questions and comments *after* a twenty-four-hour period to allow you time to read it thoroughly and consider the information *carefully.* Does anyone have anything I need to know right now?"

Silence.

"Great. You all know how to contact me if you need anything."

Sparring with Misha in the gym didn't help. Throwing knives until the target board split in half didn't help. And Misha's raised eyebrow before he left me alone, which managed to say "I told you that you need to get laid and you didn't listen to me, now look at you," didn't help. My last-ditch effort for tonight was a long, steamy soak in the bathtub, but not even lavender epsom salt is enough to put a dent in my rage. Braiding my wet hair and wrapping myself in a fluffy robe, I reach for a bottle before realizing it's almost empty.

Fuck, I'm drinking way too much these days.

Suddenly, every ounce of rage that I've so carefully kept dampened today, all the fire that I *tried*, really *tried,* to get rid of through all my stupid fucking healthy channels, surges to the surface. With an animalistic, guttural scream, I launch the bottle at the wall, and the euphoria that floods my veins as it shatters is exhilarating.

Destruction. Why didn't I think of that sooner?

Before I can unplug the glass lamp on my nightstand and damn it to the same fate as the bottle, the shared door I had hoped would never open again does so with a creak.

"Uh, Mila? Is everything okay?" The concern in Thatcher's voice would be touching if it wasn't accompanied by his shirtless torso coming through the cracked door. Who just barges into someone's room like that?

"I'm fine, please go."

Even facing the opposite direction, I can tell he's not going. No, the aura of his presence that seems to have infiltrated more and more of my life lately is still present in this room. I can *feel* him.

"You don't seem fine. Are you sure there's *nothing* I can do to help?"

When I turn around, this little *shit* has made his way closer and is leaning against the back of the red leather couch that sits in front of the fireplace. He has the same flirty eyes he's had for the past week, and his abs flex in a way I'm sure he thinks is appealing.

"I don't know what you think you can provide for me that I can't obtain myself, but—"

"Maybe something only *a man* could do for you? Are you sure what you need isn't a man?"

He's trying to flirt, but every painful, grating memory of today's multitude of misogynies erupts from the mental box I tried so hard to keep locked. In a flash, I'm across the room and on him, bending him over the back of the couch and leaning into his face so that we're eye to eye. With three of my fingers in his mouth, depressing his tongue, he's finally unable to try to sweet-talk me, and I know he can feel the sharp points of my stiletto nails threatening the back of his throat.

Misha always made fun of me for choosing to keep long nails in our line of work, and there have certainly been times when they made a fight harder. But the fear mixed with lust in Thatcher's eyes reminds me exactly why I like my claws. *So I can dig into any men who get too close.*

"The *last* thing I need is a fucking man." Even I can hear the venom in my voice, and he doesn't deserve to reap what other men have sown in my life, but he's a captive audience. "You've been invading my space, my *home*, as godforsaken as it is, for the past week. While I've been trying to prove to hundreds of strangers that I'm as worthy as anyone with a dick to lead their business and improve their lives, you've been trying to feed me egg whites and flexing your biceps for me. I have biceps of my own, haven't you seen them? And *still*, you push your luck. I know you've seen me put Misha on his back on the sparring mat, so what can you—"

He whimpers, and I feel what *can't* possibly be...*God.* If that's his cock hardening against me...it's fucking *substantial.* And if my degradation and manhandling are what have him so excited, maybe he and Misha are both right. Maybe he's exactly what I need. Only if he can be *good.*

"Is that what you came to offer me?" I purr, digging my nails harder into his tongue. He's drooling nicely for me, not fighting or trying to swallow, and he's smart enough to keep his hands firmly on the couch instead of attempting to touch me. Briefly, the thought that someone else might have trained him as a submissive flashes across my mind, and the jealousy I feel is unwelcome and unexpected. I brush it off and grant myself one long grind on what's *definitely* more than enough to fulfill my needs.

"Mmmprh," he gargles, eyes rolling back into his head. I have to agree with him. We might be onto something here.

"If you really want to impress me, you can kneel at my feet quietly like a good boy while I finish sending emails tonight."

He nods pathetically, eyes begging to please me. How sweet.

"I don't want to hear a peep. If you're still and quiet, you might earn the privilege of resting your head on my thigh. *Might.* And only if you're very, *very* good. Do you understand?"

He nods again, and I remove my hand from his mouth, granting him the favor of wiping his spit on my robe instead of his face. This is a one-night release, after all. It's not like I'm actually training him to keep him.

Moving to the desk that, while smaller than the one in the main office, is still tall enough for my purpose tonight, I grab a pillow off the bed and toss it underneath, in front of the chair.

"Kneel. Get comfortable and keep your eyes down. You can shift as you need to, but no noise, and don't touch me. If you need something, you may ask respectfully. Is that clear?"

He nods and scrunches himself into position under the desk, eyes down and shoulder muscles taut as he rests his hands on his thighs. I pull the desk chair forward, realizing that with nothing under my robe, his face is about ten inches away from my bare pussy. It's been too long, and the thought of how easy it would be to force his head between my legs is intoxicating.

A few things must be handled this evening, though, so I send several emails over the course of fifteen minutes. Thatcher has made it without a peep or movement from under the desk, so it's time for his reward. Rolling back my chair, I find him still kneeling, posture perfect.

"Thatcher, look at me." His pupils are blown wide with lust, and his eyes are glazed, as if he's found himself close to subspace, even if he doesn't realize that's what it's called. I have a feeling that few people ever force him to sit still and do as he's told, but maybe that's exactly what he needs. "You're doing well. Do you feel okay?"

He nods.

"Lean forward and get comfortable with your cheek resting on my thigh. I want to see if your hair is as soft as it looks while I read these last few reports."

Thatcher leans forward, widening his knees and hinging at his waist to place his right cheek on my left thigh. As we arrange ourselves, though, there's a problem. I didn't account for how broad his shoulders are. Unless I want him with his cheek on my knee...

I open my legs, but even as my robe rides up higher and higher, Thatcher focuses on settling in. My pussy is exposed now, and I'm sure he caught a glimpse of my dark curls, but he's either too blissed out to try to sneak another peek or he's still trying very hard to be good.

As I scratch my nails into his scalp for the first time, his entire body melts. His hair is just as soft as I expected, and the thick waves mixed with more defined curls are the perfect sensory play to keep me calm as I read the increasingly incendiary emails from Zadorov's secretary.

I'm so mad at the demands he *dares* to make of me in the last email, dated just after he left the meeting today, that it takes far too long to realize that Thatcher has *moved.* Instead of sitting still, he's turned his head to trail tiny, hot kisses up and down my inner thigh. His range of motion is limited by how we're sitting, but he's covering as much ground as he can. I want to be mad at him for disobeying, but I also really, *really* like his initiative. He's been a ball of energy since the moment he arrived on my doorstep, and if that energy is directed toward my pleasure...*at my command, well...*

"Thatcher," I scold, and he freezes like a child caught with a hand in the candy jar. "It's naughty of you to move, don't you think?"

He doesn't answer, instinctively knowing that there's no correct reply. *Not trying to train him...let him get you off...*The animal corner of my brain wins, and I bask in the lust filling his eyes as I spread my legs over the arms of the desk chair.

"If you want your mouth on me, I decide where it goes. Is this what you wanted?"

Nodding, he flicks his gaze between my core and my eyes.

"Do you think it was very nice of you to touch me before I told you to?"

This pulls his attention immediately, and contrition is evident in his eyes. "I'm sorry. I shouldn't have. Not without your consent."

"Hmm. You're forgiven. But since you're so eager, I have *very* high expectations for you. Starting with your words. You've been so chatty all week, wanting my attention. I promise you, you've got it now. So tell me. What do you think of my pussy?"

Reaching down, I spread myself for him, delighting in the way his gaze darkens as he notices how wet I already am. Gathering a bit of myself on a finger, I offer it to him, pulling back just before he can lick it off.

"Ah, ah, ah. Tell me what you think first. Then I'll let you taste. If you're going to be good, you need to learn to listen."

"You're beautiful," he says quietly, and he's looking at my face instead of the glistening center I'm offering him. After a long moment, with a minute shake of his head, he looks back down. "You're beautiful, and you look delicious."

One deep breath, and he's looking at me again, like he wants to see into my soul and wouldn't mind what he found.

"Please let me taste you? I promise, I'll be good."

CHAPTER 11

Thatcher

F*UCK, PUSSY HAS never tasted so incredible.* And I've tasted my fair share. I may be a notorious playboy, but I make it my point to give more than I ever take.

Mila directs me even though I think I could do well enough on my own. This is what she needs, plus every woman likes it differently. Even though I could rock her world with no guidance, knowing exactly what makes her shake will only help my cause going forward.

"Trace it with your tongue first. *Yes,* around the edges just like that. Circle my clit every third time, and every sixth pass, you can give it a long lick…*yes, just like that.* What a good listener you are."

Her cooing praise threatens to undo me. I may be dense occasionally, but I'm perceptive. I pay attention to every word, every stutter, soaking her up so that each time I have the privilege to touch her, I can please her more.

Her grip in my hair tightens as I try my hardest to heed her instructions. Counting diligently at first, I'm soon so zoned in on her gorgeous noises that our rhythm becomes second nature.

"That's it. *Fuck,* right there...Good fucking boy. Now add your fingers, slowly at first."

Moving my hand from her thigh, I add one finger, exploring until I find her sweet spot. As her tight warmth welcomes me, I slip in another. I do what I was told slowly, working them in tandem with my tongue. I want to pick up the pace so badly, but I don't. Instead, I delight in the fact that I even have the opportunity to touch her while I wait for her next command.

"Yes, just like that. That's exactly right, solnyshko. Keep going...faster now. That's exactly how I like it. Now prove you can work me up to my release."

My cock twitches at her praise, and for once, I don't care. The only thing I'm concerned about is getting this woman off. Whatever spell she's cast on me has me euphoric at the thought of being the reason she comes. If I can bring her to orgasm, I'll be happy for the rest of my life, even if I never get to touch her again.

Luckily for both of us, I know exactly how to seal the deal. It can be tempting to just go hard from the beginning, but a woman's body is delicate. Even Mila's. Now that I know what she prefers, she's mine.

She's telling me everything I need to know about when to pick up my pace, and I give her exactly what she silently asks for, paying attention to how her legs shake and her pussy tightens around my fingers. Her nails dig into my back with one hand as she pulls my hair. She's so close, but she never truly loses her control.

There's an urgency in her voice as she continues her praise, but she doesn't lose herself like all the other women I know as they reach their climax.

Finally, she explodes as she finds her release, and I make sure to lick up every last drop. I know immediately, intrinsically that I'll never get enough of her taste. I'll never get enough of this *woman*.

"That's enough, solnyshko. Sit back on your knees and look at me."

I'm robotic in my obedience, doing exactly as I'm told without a second thought. I'm floating in the clouds, and the moment I lay eyes on her, I know I must be in heaven. She may act devilish, but I've never seen anyone so angelic. She's radiant, glowing as the sheen of sweat from her orgasm sparkles under the light. And her eyes... her bright-blue eyes are crystal clear, as if inviting me into her soul.

"You did very well. Your talent is remarkable, but you also followed my directions like such a good boy. I'd like to reward you, would you enjoy that?"

When I don't respond, she takes my chin in her hand and smiles down at me. "You really are a *very* good boy. When I ask you a direct question, you may respond with 'yes, Ma'am' or 'no, Ma'am.' Now let's try that again. Would you like a reward?"

"Yes, Ma'am."

"Good boy," she purrs, running her fingers through her hair as she stands. "I'm going to let you come now, but it will be by your own hand, and you will follow my instructions. Can you do that? Can you stroke yourself for me?"

Holy. Fucking. Shit.

"Yes, Ma'am."

"Good boy." Mila tightens her bathrobe and lies back on her bed. "Now, stand up, take everything off, and come closer. I want to see the blood pumping through the veins in your cock."

Step by step, I close the gap between us, until she motions for me to stop.

She smirks as I wait silently for her next command. "Your body is a masterpiece. Every chiseled inch of you is mouthwatering, but that cock is really something else. Long and thick, curved just the way I prefer."

She chuckles as my cock twitches. "Do you like it when I talk to you like this? I can see the precum beading up from here. Would you like to touch yourself?"

"Yes, Ma'am."

"Spit in your hand and work it down. I want to see your cock glistening. It won't get you as wet as my cunt would, but it's better than nothing."

Doing as she asks, I restrain myself from saying anything, but I'm unable to stop from shaking as I imagine it's her sweet pussy that has me lubed up.

"Very good. No need to stay silent. If you need to express yourself verbally, you may. Now slowly work from root to tip, with a very light pressure in your grip."

Every stroke feels like heaven, and I throw my head back, groaning.

"Ah, ah, ah, look at me. You may speak, but your eyes stay on me. Is that understood?"

There's no problem there. I'll gladly gaze upon the goddess before me. It was her I saw when I closed my eyes anyway. *I don't think I can remember what another woman looks like right now.*

"Yes, Ma'am."

"Good boy. Now increase your speed, stopping about halfway down your shaft. Squeeze a bit tighter...Good job, just like that. Now *stop*."

Fuck, I was so close. I was close before I even touched myself. The taste of her alone had me on the verge of my release. I try not to let my posture falter, but the disappointment is hard to hide.

"Oh, my poor boy. Did you want to come? Not so fast. I want more of a show than that. You listened so well, stopping for me when you wanted to keep going. For that, you may continue. Same pace, same grip. I think you were enjoying it."

Relief floods through me as I stroke myself again. I've never been edged before, but I understand the hype. The brief ache was worth the sensation that followed. Every touch is more intense than the last, and it doesn't take long at all before I'm approaching my pinnacle.

My orgasm crests, but I keep my eyes on Mila, imagining it's her I'm spilling into. *Maybe if I continue to be good for her, she'll let me.*

I'm so lost in that fantasy, I don't notice she's gotten up from the bed until I feel her touch. Two delicate fingers run up my lower abdomen, sending chills through my body.

"That was quite the show, solnyshko, but I didn't give you permission to come."

She's so close, just an inch away. I'm only taller than her by a couple of inches, so her eyes are almost level with mine. She leans in closer, and my lips part involuntarily, closing my eyes. I want so badly to kiss her right now. After tasting how sweet she is between her legs, I can only imagine…

Something fills my mouth, but it's not her tongue. It's her fingers. And it's not her I'm tasting, it's…

"Do you like the way you taste?" My eyes pop open to see a devious smirk. "Coming without permission is not how good boys behave. But I'll let you make it up to me."

She scoops up more of my cum from my stomach, then brings her fingers back to my mouth. "I want to see you clean up the mess you made. Lick up every last drop for me, and you'll be my good boy again."

I stare into her gaze and suck her finger completely into my mouth, relishing the lust that fills her eyes as I twirl my tongue around in a show of getting it squeaky clean.

"Good fucking boy. Now get on your knees and clean it off my floor."

I drop to my knees before her and look up one last time before performing my task. I've never felt the peace I do at this moment as I follow this woman's every command.

"Yes, Ma'am."

CHAPTER 12

Mila

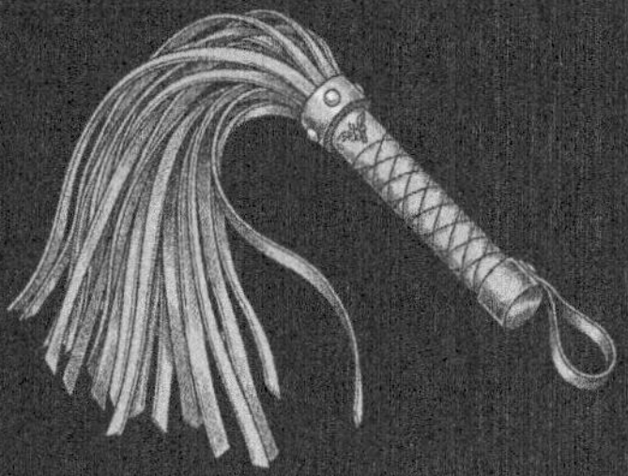

U*GH.* WHY AM I so damn *hot*? Did someone light the fireplace in my bedroom after I went to sleep last night? I don't even remember coming to bed. I was so mad about the afternoon meeting that I wore myself out any way possible and then…

Oh.

Oh shit.

A sleepy groan from behind me might as well be a foghorn with how it rattles my skull and forces me fully awake. The source of the ungodly heat tightens his arm around my middle, and I remember everything with startling clarity.

Thatcher offering himself up for my pleasure. Coming from the efforts of someone else for the first time in recent memory…Praising, chastising, soothing, degrading. It's been too long since I felt the heady intoxication of being in control of someone so completely, and I had almost forgotten the height of sensation to be found when I'm so focused on leading someone to mutual pleasure. My brain was quieter last night than it's been in…I don't know when.

Except *fuck.* Despite Misha thinking a good fuck would simplify my life, and we *didn't even fuck,* I feel...like I need coffee. The blackout curtains hide any hint of how late I've slept, but when I wrench myself from Thatcher's hold and check my phone, it's only five in the morning. My internal clock remains undefeated.

He rolls over immediately and burrows into the comforter, clearly not a morning person. I don't know how I fell asleep with him in my bed last night, considering that usually my alarm bells ring if there's anyone at all in the room where I'm sleeping. I can't think of a time I've ever shared a bed overnight with someone, and in shared spaces, I always slept with one eye open.

I'm so groggy now, though, that I must have slept *hard* last night. Maybe the release of months of pent-up tension was enough for me to pass out, or perhaps I just instinctively know Thatcher isn't a threat to me. That has to be it.

Silently, I pull on my morning uniform of all-black sweats and sneak out, closing the door quietly behind me. I'm too tired to try to dig Thatcher out from my bed. I'm sure he'll wake up, see that I'm gone, and take the hint. The walk to the kitchen reminds me that I need to get my coffee bar set up in my bedroom sooner rather than later because it's impossible to try to be anything less than a gremlin before my first cup. Luckily, I don't run into anyone in the house. I have a persona to maintain, and cranky coffee-deficient Mila isn't someone the men need to see.

It's no surprise at all to turn the corner and see Misha already in the kitchen, nursing what's likely his second cup of the morning and staring out an east-facing window, waiting for the sunrise. Although it used to annoy me that he invariably rose at least half an hour before I did, once he started to supply my coffee, I conceded the morning crown to him. Sure enough, on the counter sits a steaming mug of coffee in the perfect color.

I join him at the window, quietly sipping and watching the inky sky transform to navy, then gray, and finally a pale, pinky blue as a new day dawns. I'm not sure how many sunrises we've seen together. At this point, we're probably approaching ten thousand. If he hadn't started this tradition, my sunrise count would have stopped decades ago. I've never asked if he was an early riser before me. Just like I haven't asked if he ever wishes he hadn't pledged himself to my cause. He could have a family by now, if not for the weight of our shared past. These are just two questions, out of many, on the list of things I'll never ask.

Finally, both cups are empty, and golden rays are sneaking toward the kitchen when the dreaded raised eyebrow turns my way. I feel confident that I'm relatively intact and covered by my hoodie and sweatpants. Misha's only hints of what transpired are my face and my eyes, which means I'm screwed. The man has always been able to read me like a book.

"So—"

"Nope! No 'so.'"

With a sigh that I know is him coming to terms with my attitude this morning, he flops down into a chair at the breakfast table and spreads his long legs out, crossing his arms to assume his defensive position.

"Alright. How?"

"Not even a how." I curl up on the bench on the other side of the table, thinking that maybe Thatcher has the right idea. Being cozy in bed with him would be much better than facing the Spanish Inquisition. *Shit.* Being cozy in bed *alone*, I mean. Not with *him.*

"That bad?"

Ugh. As much as I don't want to, we have to have this conversation. There are no secrets from Misha.

"It wasn't bad. Not at all. It's just not a good idea. I know you think it is, but there's just too much going on. Plus, it's not like he's a stranger I'll never see again. He gets hurt, he's still around. He's Teddy's best friend."

"Hmm. Well, I stand by my initial assessment. I think it's a good thing. I don't think anybody needs to get hurt with your usual rules up front. If he catches feelings, that's on him. But he's a grown man, even though I know I call him a kid to rile you up. He can make big boy decisions and take responsibility for his own emotions."

"I don't know how you've gotten to be such an emotional expert. You're as chronically single as I am."

"Hmm," he replies, but this time, he doesn't continue.

"Well," I say, sitting back up and feeling my coffee start to kick in. "*My* gut says that it's easier and less messy to stop this before it truly starts. This is not a thing. I'm not allowing this to be a thing. So you and *your* pet hockey player can have as much fun as you want training and cooking and having movie night, or whatever the fuck else you have planned—"

"A lot of these guys have never seen the classics. If they can't get my *Mean Girls* references, I don't know how you expect me to—"

"And have a great time! I'm not questioning your methods. You know damn well I can't do this without you, and I don't care how you do it. Now, can I shower in your room? I, uh…" I ignore his smirk. "I don't want to use mine right now."

"You can, but it's the soap you hate," he calls after me, but I'm already hustling out of the kitchen, disinterested in continuing this conversation for a moment longer.

"I'll deal."

And I will. With the soap, with Thatcher, with Zadorov. *I'll deal.*

If you had asked me a few months ago whether one of the things I most look forward to is my weekly calls with my little brother, I would have laughed in your face. But here I am, tea steeping, excitedly awaiting my chance to catch up with Teddy. As always, my phone rings at exactly six o'clock. *At least my long-lost brother is punctual.*

Smiling, I answer the call. "Hello, Cuddles. How's life in Thunder Bay? Still enjoying my home?"

"Ha. Ha. Are you going to ask that every time we talk? Even though *your* new home is apparently significantly larger than this one?"

"You haven't been here yet, you don't understand." The thought of how long it'll take to eradicate the red latex sends a shiver down my spine.

"Oh no, I've heard." Teddy laughs. "Misha told me it's a nightmare. I think it's a bit garish even for Thatcher. He would never admit that of course, but—actually, how is everything going with him?"

Fuck. Words. Any words.

"Mila?"

Say any words at all, Mila. Anything. It can't be worse than this silence.

"Are you there—"

"I don't know what Thatcher has to do with our weekly call. He's certainly not important enough to waste our time on. This is for business, remember?" I'm harsher than I intended, and Teddy notices immediately.

"So he's driving you crazy, then. I'm really sorry about the intrusion, you know. If I had known you were going to be at the compound so much, I wouldn't have told him to—"

"Theodore, snap back to it!" I chirp, "Bratva business call! I don't have all night. Tell me what's been going on in Thunder Bay."

"Alright. Um, well, nothing actually. It's been eerily quiet lately. For the Santoris, too. Or at least that's what Nikki told me. I think the union between our families has everyone spooked."

As chaotic as his and Ellie's relationship began, I have to admit that marrying into the Santori family was probably the best thing Teddy could have done for himself. The first few years after a takeover are the most vulnerable time for a new Pakhan, but with the Santori Mafia as his ally, nobody would dare mess with him. Of course, he had no idea what he was doing when they met. It wasn't until tragedy struck and her family blamed Teddy that we all realized the two lovebirds were together. It was an oversight on my part, not paying attention to his dating life, but Ellie was a Mafia princess and knew how to cover her tracks well enough.

"That's good," I sigh. "I honestly don't know what I would do if storms were brewing down there right now. I barely have any fucking time to deal with all the bullshit going on up here."

"Oh? Anything I should be concerned about?"

"No. Nothing you'll ever have to worry about, my dearest brother. Just some misogynistic assholes who can't deal with a woman being Pakhan. Same shit I was going through before you came along, except this time there aren't any long-lost brothers to appease the board. Ivan named me his successor. The only solution would be to kill me or to marry me off. I'm sure they're plotting for the former in private, but they aren't bashful at all about pushing marriage on me."

Teddy laughs so hard he snorts at the mention of marriage.

"Thanks a lot, Cuddles. Glad you're so concerned for me."

"I'm sorry, I really am. I just can't imagine you married. To anyone."

"Me either, little brother, me either."

"Those guys don't realize who they're dealing with, Sis. You'll let me know if I can do anything to help, won't you?"

"Of course. But don't worry about me. It'll all work out. If there's really nothing going on there, we're good for the week. Give my best to Ellie."

"Will do. Talk to you next week."

Sipping my tea, I consider the unsettling news that everything's quiet in Thunder Bay. I suppose there's no reason to look a gift horse in the mouth. If Teddy and the Santoris have my former stomping grounds under control, great. Our call was so short, though, that I have another half hour to relax before my nightly walk through the bunks. Usually, it would be impossible to avoid perseverating on all the issues plaguing me here in New York, but all I can think about is last night with Thatcher. Just the thought of his mouth on me sends sparks of arousal straight to my core.

If I were a weaker woman, I'd go to him now. Push him further to see if he's really as good a boy as he seems. But I can't. I shouldn't have let him touch me in the first place. I know Teddy wouldn't care, but it's just too messy. I can never give him anything more than fun, and if he became attached…I don't want to break his heart.

Last night was a wonderful reprieve from my recent stressors, but I'll simply have to cope with them on my own until I can get to a club. I'll only have to resist for a few more weeks. How hard could it be?

CHAPTER 13

Thatcher

SIX, SEVEN...EIGHT. FUCK. Dropping the heavy weight to the floor of the gym, I ignore the black spots clouding my vision. I didn't *plan* to wake up at three in the morning and immediately lift heavier than I ever have for eight fucking reps, but here I am. Since I woke up alone in Mila's bed after the most intense experience of my life, it's been clear that she thinks it was a mistake. If she was avoiding me before, she's a ghost now.

I know she's still on the compound somewhere, but other than hearing the faint rustle through our shared wall as she comes to bed late, then gets up early, she might as well be a figment of my imagination. *Except my imagination has never been robust enough to call into existence a siren like Mila…*

The door opens, and light floods the space, pulling me out of my melancholy thoughts and scaring the shit out of me.

"Ahh!" I wish my screech of alarm wasn't so high-pitched, but it's only Misha. If my presence surprises him, he doesn't show it.

"Good morning, Sunshine. I think you're the first one to ever beat me to the gym. Couldn't sleep?"

"Uh, no." Misha lifts the weight I was struggling with like it's nothing and re-racks it for me before striding to the stair climber and starting his warm-up. *Which is jogging up the stairs while continuing to chat with me like it's nothing.*

"So you decided to take your frustrations out on the weights? Did it help?"

"Also no." I accept that he'll be on the stairs for a while, so I start at a leisurely pace on the machine beside him. Fuck, I forgot how much I hate this machine. My quads and glutes are in amazing shape, thanks to so much time on the ice, but something about the never-ending climbing…I hate it.

"Do you want to start by telling me that something happened between you and Mila and now she's closed off and ignoring you, or do you want to beat around the bush some more?"

"Uhh. How do you—wait! Did she say something about me?"

"Not necessarily, but then again, she didn't have to. We communicate almost exclusively via telepathy."

"Okay, well then, what did she *think* about me?"

That makes Misha laugh, and he finally stops his jog to move on to his actual workout. *Thank God.* "She's a complex woman. More than anyone will ever understand. And she has an absolute fuck ton of shit on her plate right now. Steaming shit that's taking up almost all of her mental and emotional energy."

"I don't want to *add* to her stress. But I feel…I like her a lot. I feel safe with her around, and I'd like to help with her stress! I don't think she sees me that way, though. I think I'm just another item on her long list of annoyances. Which is true for basically everyone in my life, so I really shouldn't be surprised." I can't keep the bitterness out of my tone as I grumble the last part, but

Misha still hears me. A bear paw on my shoulder turns me to face him. *Jesus, he's tall.*

"You aren't annoying. I'm not sure exactly why you think that about yourself. But I guarantee Mila probably feels a lot of things about you that confuse her, and annoying likely isn't one of them. Well, maybe a little bit. Annoyed by how you make her feel."

We lift in silence for a few minutes, the quiet of the morning only interrupted by our grunts and the weights thudding to the floor. Finally, I can't take it anymore.

"I know what you told me about my usual tricks not working on her, but I feel like I'm past that. I feel like she saw what I had to offer and isn't interested. Even though you say she's just complex, what do I do with that? If it were you, what would you do now?"

With a loaded look, he hands me a kettlebell as if it weighs five pounds, only for me to realize, as I fall to the ground with it, that it's seventy-five. He barely smirks before giving me what I can tell is his most serious advice on the matter.

"I think you're going to have to talk to her. She appreciates honesty, and having the balls to lay your cards on the table would be a positive thing. I can't promise how she'll react, though. It might seem like I have her figured out, but she still surprises me sometimes. The worst thing that could happen is she rejects you, which sucks, but it's still better than never knowing what could have been. Shoot your shot."

With that, he's out of the gym, and I'm left alone, drenched in sweat but with an inkling of a plan.

Rummaging behind the garish bar, I finally find something worth drinking. Although it seems the previous tenants left behind seemingly endless top-shelf vodka, I've always preferred whiskey. Well, if I had a choice of any drink in the world, I'd pick a frozen margarita. Or frozen anything. But since everyone in this house seems determined to prove their manliness with straight liquor, I vastly prefer whiskey.

Just as I'm pouring myself three fingers of Kentucky's finest, the reason for my drinking finds me.

"How'd you get in here?"

She's not just being nosy. This bar is a small room, hidden in a false panel in the hallway just outside of our bedrooms. Based on some of the furniture and hardware protruding from the walls, I'm guessing that it was used for some kinky shit and not just as a lounge. When Misha told me I might find some whiskey in here, I asked him if there was also a dungeon hidden behind a panel somewhere, but he wouldn't tell me anything.

"Heard from a friend that what I needed might be in here. Sorry, I didn't think about the fact that you might not want me looting your property." And I am sorry. I would never want her to feel like I'm skulking about in her home…

"It's fine," she says, taking a seat on a barstool across from me. "As long as there's enough left in there to pour me a glass. I can't believe you even found that bottle. I looked but must have missed it."

Finding one more rocks glass behind the bar, I oblige her. "I didn't know you were a whiskey drinker. Don't you prefer vodka like a true Russian?"

She snorts, toasting me with her glass before taking a long swig. "I'm not as picky as everyone thinks I am." She considers the brown liquor for a moment before continuing. "Misha prefers a Miami vice."

Both of us laugh before succumbing to the silence once again. I can't help but break it. "I started drinking much too young. I don't even know if I was out of middle school. Not that I've ever gotten out of hand. It's just funny to think about the first time I got drunk on Johnny Walker. I was probably twelve years old."

"Where were your parents?"

Ugh. I led her into that line of questioning, but it still stings. "Uh, probably France. Or the Caribbean. There's no telling. They left me to my own devices, and I never really faced many consequences."

"You don't say!" Her smile softens her words as we laugh again.

"Yes, laugh at my expense. Poor little rich boy who craves attention and love because he never got either as a child."

"Well, at least you're self-aware. They must have at least cared about you enough to think of putting you in therapy."

"I asked for it for Christmas one year," I say quietly with a small smile, and we're quiet for a while after that until Mila is brave enough to break the silence.

"You seem sad."

"I suppose I am a bit sad. I had a very sexy, very fulfilling night with a terrifying, beautiful woman, and she hasn't given me the time of day since. And, other than training, I'm dealing with the melancholy that always sets in during the postseason. At least playing hockey, I'm useful and have a purpose. There are only so many hours during the day I can spend in the gym. Otherwise…" I give her what I hope is a handsome, mischievous smirk. "Otherwise, I'm liable to get in all sorts of trouble."

Mila looks at me for so long that I break away from her gaze, picking at the wood grain of the bar. Finally, she stands, stretching, and cracks her neck with a satisfying pop.

"I'm very busy, you know. Tons to do around here. Dealing with fucking misogynist assholes who are pissed they're old with wrinkly dicks, and take it out on me."

I know you're busy. It's okay. I'll find something to do. I always have.

She stretches, her shirt riding up to show a sliver of the skin that I know is softer than you'd ever expect from such a lethal woman.

"That's okay. I'll—"

"I could really use some help. But it won't be an easy job, Thatcher. I expect you to work just as hard as I do."

Her smirk raises my spirits more than anything ever could, and I pop off the bar top to follow her around like a puppy again, this time with her blessing.

"Anything you say, Boss."

CHAPTER 14

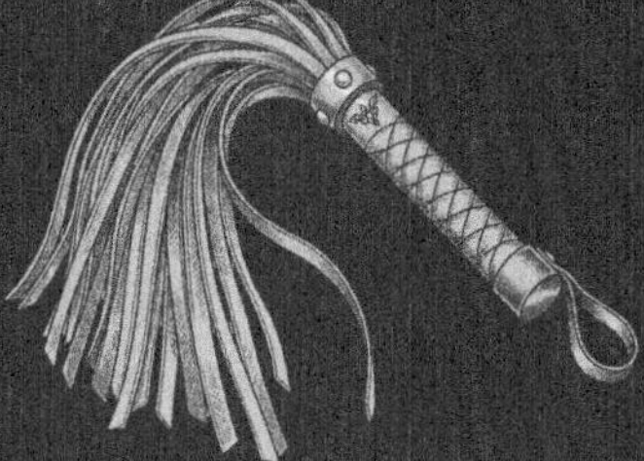

Mila

F*UCK DEALING.* I scowl at the baby birds chirping along the path to the training gym. It's not their fault that they get to sit in their trees, eating worms and…whatever the fuck birds do for fun. But listening to them living their best lives as I deal with an egotistical, misogynistic thorn in my side who's determined to tear my destiny from my hands is too much to bear. Someone will have to bear the brunt of my frustration, and since I've resolved *not* to break my brother's best friend into a million tiny pieces, the sparring mat is the only thing that'll suffice.

Luckily for the drywall, I learned my lesson long ago about kicking in doors when frustrated. Instead, I count three sets of breaths, pulling all of my anger deeper and into its box, to be unleashed at the perfect time onto whoever is brave enough to step onto the mat with me. Misha will rise to the challenge, regardless, but the two of us have fought so many times that it's more of a choreographed dance than a true bout.

Men immediately stand to attention when I enter, a ripple traveling the length of the gym like a line of dominoes I've kicked over in my rage. They fall back into their workouts soon enough with a wave of my hand to put them at ease, but my presence comes with a certain level of tension, as it should. I'm their boss. I'm *the* boss. The day any man feels truly at ease in my company is the day I've lost my touch.

"Hiya, Boss."

"You look like a bear with a sore head, moya tsaritsa."

Of course, the two men who couldn't give less of a fuck about my Pakhan status appear at my side as if magnetized. Misha is as unbothered as ever, giving no clue as to whether he's been running sessions or taking part. Thatcher, on the other hand, is dripping. The white T-shirt he's wearing does little more than serve as a sweat receptacle.

He realizes this at the same time as I do, and peels the offensive garment from his shoulders just to toss it onto the floor with a wet thump.

"The laundry hamper is *right there*, Prescott. Jesus—"

"It looks like he's got his own washboard for doing the laundry—"

"Don't disrespect the boss like that, man!"

The mostly friendly jibes directed at Thatcher bode well for his reconnaissance mission, and even Kirill tempered his defense of my honor with a playful shoulder nudge.

"It's alright. It wasn't my intention to interrupt any of your training. I just wanted to see if you had even groups on the mats or if you needed an extra body."

Any tittering that had continued in the wake of Thatcher's strip show ceases, and you'd think I just revealed that Grandfather Frost isn't real based on the depth of the silence.

"I've just finished with Dima, so I can—"

"Want to take a crack at me?" Thatcher interrupts Misha, and I swear I hear a brief "ooo" before silence falls again at my sharp gaze. If he looked any less earnest, I might admonish him for toeing the line of disrespect in front of the men. As it is, only his playful wink, hidden from the group, belies the flirtiness I *know* he can't help.

There's no reason to waste time thinking about a decision I've already made, even if I end up regretting putting myself in this position. It's just two bodies struggling for dominance, writhing for any upper hand, *any* moment of weakness in the other to gain the upper hand. Nothing sexual about it. I've sparred with Misha thousands of times, not to mention hundreds of other men, and never felt any lust except for blood.

The mat is still warm from the last set of men as I strip to my sports bra and bike shorts. The long braid that's my everyday staple won't serve me well here, so I take it down and quickly rebraid it into a pull-proof style while Misha attempts to get the rest of the men back into their workouts. He's sending most of them out on a long run to end the session, which is probably for the best.

"You know I would never pull your hair, right?" Thatcher's soft voice doesn't surprise me, since I'm always hyperaware of him these days, but his sincerity makes me pause. He's chosen to remain shirtless for our bout, and I can't blame him. His lack of shirt will give me one less grip point, and if I'm sliding off his sweat-soaked torso…

"Mila? Hello?"

Fuck. Thatcher and Misha are both in front of me now, and I zoned out for long enough, *thinking about sliding up and down the former's torso like a surfboard*, that I drew their attention. "Yep. I'm ready. Let's see what Misha's been teaching you."

I'm gifted a full smile at that, and the rest of the room fades away as I focus on the radius of our mat, and nothing else. He's never looked more like a golden retriever than at this moment, golden hair pulled back with a headband and eyes locked onto mine as he tilts his head to receive last-minute advice from Misha. This is the only place I let my guard down and don't waste any energy on monitoring my periphery. In the gym, with Misha close by, all that matters is myself, my opponent, and the mat.

"I like being the center of your attention like this."

"Just like this?" *Shit, don't flirt with him, Mila. What the hell?*

"Touché. Not *just* like this." His grin is infectious enough to *almost* make me forget to be surly, but I rein it back just in time.

"Hmm. We'll see how long that lasts. You might feel differently once the pain kicks in."

"I agree." He laughs. "But it might not be in the way you think."

Misha's snort reminds me we're not alone, and Thatcher moves into position, stretching his hands above his head in the process. His abs flex, and the material of his gym shorts pulls taut, outlining the appendage that's seared into my brain, regardless of how hard I've been trying to forget it.

"What has Misha taught you?"

His head tilts again as he settles into a loose stance, ready for anything I have to throw at him. I'm not making the effort, though. If he wants anything from me, he can come and try to take it. My defense is my best offense, using my reflexes and decisiveness against men who are almost always bigger than me. I could spend a lifetime in the gym, and I have, but the reality of the world is that fighting a man's natural testosterone is an uphill battle. The idea of exogenously boosting my own levels has tempted me in the past, but until it's necessary for my health… *why the fuck am I thinking about menopause when Thatcher's first jab is coming at my face?*

It's predictable, and I waste no time telling him so.

"I know for a fact," I say as he stumbles, my parry throwing him off balance just a touch, "that he taught you not to telegraph your next moves before you make them."

"He *did,* and I'm *not*—fuck!"

His back hits the mat, and he groans briefly before kipping himself up and pouting.

"You are. Tell him, moya sila."

Thatcher leans in for advice from Misha, which is better than anything I could give. I'm an expert at destroying and belittling, not rebuilding. I can tell someone what they're doing wrong all day long, but when it comes to teaching and helping them understand how to improve…Well, there's a reason Misha does all the training.

By the time he re-enters the mat, he's a golden retriever again instead of a mopey basset hound, and it's remarkable how quickly he's managed to regain his swagger. That's a useful quality, and one that no doubt serves him well as a professional athlete. It's also annoying, considering that I've struggled to rebound from failures big and small for my entire life. Misha calls it "eldest daughter syndrome," when I'm being particularly moody.

"So you're telling me my hips don't lie?" His serviceable belly dance attempt ends with him on his back again, and my forearm against his windpipe.

"You're focusing so much on who you think you see across the mat from you that you forget yourself." Something about his stupid dance has pissed me off, and I feel the reason I came in here today bubble back to the surface. Whether it's him treating Misha's time and energy flippantly or something else, I snap. "Do you understand?"

I'm not compressing his windpipe, exactly, but he must wise up just in time to realize I do *not* want an answer to that question. He shakes his head, regarding me as the threat that I am. *Good.*

"I'm not sure what you're seeing when you look at me. I'm a woman, and that's a fact. You're bigger and stronger than me, although I'm undoubtedly closer to you in every metric of strength and agility than any woman you've ever met. I'm your hostess, since you live in my house, and I'm your best friend's sister. Anything else you see when you look at me is yours alone, and I can't control that. But you're joking on a training mat while we practice, and if it's because you think for a second I couldn't kill you right now with my bare hands and no blood spilled, you're a damn fool."

He's turning purple, and I finally release the pressure I was holding to allow him to breathe deeply again. As I sit back and move to stand, the rock-hard cock underneath me shocks me into complete stillness. Time freezes, and I vaguely note Misha making an excuse and clearing out with the few men who had still been in the gym.

Alright, how do I regain control of this situation? Apologize for being an asshole...eh, he kind of deserved it. Maybe I can still salvage this lesson and give him some pointers, even if teaching isn't my forté.

"Um, sorry. I've had a rough day, and I didn't mean to take it out on you." Okay, I guess I *am* apologizing. *What the hell...*

"You can."

"Sorry?"

Thatcher turns back around, having collected himself and tucked things securely away, based on my glance. He doesn't look too put out about anything, although he isn't as bubbly as he was either. "You can take things out on me. Besides, you were right. I wasn't taking this seriously enough, and I know better than to goof off in a gym where people could get hurt. But truly, when you're having a bad day, you can take it out on me. I can handle it."

The heavy thwomp of the air-conditioning unit kicking on saves me from having absolutely fucking no response to that. The decision I made not to pursue...whatever this is, or could be...I can't even remember why it would be a bad idea. *Teddy, distraction, danger, to-do list...*

Okay, the reasons are valid. Compartmentalization it is, then.

"Still, you didn't deserve that. I do have a lot of pent-up energy today, though, so if you're not too tired..."

For half a second, his eyebrows threaten to wag suggestively, and I can *see* the restraint it takes him to keep his face neutral. *Good boy.*

"I can try to teach you how to fight more spontaneously. Or rather, how to make it seem spontaneous while also being calculated to stay well ahead of your opponent. I'm not as patient as Misha, and I've never taken pedagogy courses like he has. But I can try to teach you some things. Maybe even some of the tricks I use to get him on his back."

Thatcher lights up again at the suggestion, and my laugh escapes before I can stop it this time.

"I will do literally *anything* necessary to learn that skill. I'll probably only ever get one shot at it, so please have a camera ready when I try, but I promise you've never had as eager a student as I am."

He repositions his headband, and my hand twitches with the urge to run my fingers through his thick hair again, even as wet with sweat as it is. Clearly, I'm just going to have to deal with my unprofessional, horny subconscious desires when it comes to this man. As long as I resist, I can avoid anybody getting hurt.

"I'll try my best. Lesson One: Your Hips *Have* to Lie."

CHAPTER 15

Mila

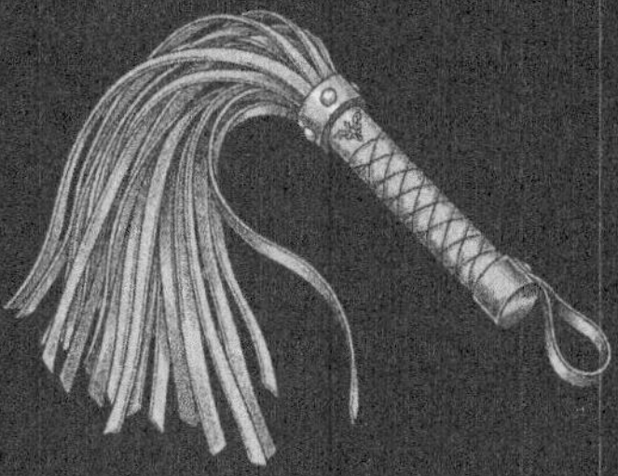

"HERE YOU ARE, Madam." A server arrives with my afternoon tea tray, including my favorite guilty pleasure accoutrements of petit fours.

"Thank you, you may leave it on my desk."

Tea is exactly what I need on a lazy Sunday. The past week has been filled with just as many strenuous meetings and tasks, but somehow it all seems manageable now. Thatcher's help in winning over Ivan's men is an enormous weight off my shoulders. I have Misha of course, and plenty of my own men from Thunder Bay, but they're looked at as an extension of myself.

Our lonely hockey player really does have a talent for making friends. Not a single person on the compound doesn't smile when they see him. And how could they not, when he lights up every room he walks into? I've come across plenty of pretty boys like him, born with a silver spoon in their mouth, never having to work for anything. They all possess a certain charm, but it's skin deep. This is different. Thatcher genuinely cares about the people he interacts with, and it shows.

It's almost endearing to watch. *Almost*. And luckily for me, it's precisely the skill set I need to help break the ice with the men here.

When he told me that he becomes reckless without a purpose, I knew exactly what to do. Luckily for him, one of *my* skills is placing people in roles they're best suited for. Of course, in the Bratva, it often has more to do with combat proficiency than with personality. All I asked of him was to help me build rapport with the New York team. Simply drop a compliment here and there to help them trust me. Well, that, and I also asked him to keep an ear out for anyone plotting against me.

It's been an immense relief to hear his reports that there aren't any whispers of mutiny. At least I can rest easier knowing that the minute Ivan officially leaves, his men won't try to kill me in my sleep. Of course, I still have all the misogynistic assholes breathing down my neck, fighting over whose son would make the best husband. The men who would rather watch it all burn down than see a woman seated on the New York throne. That threat alone makes it so much more important to have my men's loyalty.

I always wait five minutes for my tea to steep before pouring a cup, but I'm restless today. For someone who's been wishing for an off day, I don't know how to relax. Three minutes will have to do. It's a berry blend today, so I skip cream and opt for one cube of brown sugar.

Confirming it's at least drinkable, if weak, I grab my cup and make my way down the hall. I gave almost everyone the day off, so it's particularly calm around here. A quiet house is usually my preference, but with everything going on, the peace only magnifies the commotion in my mind. Alcohol helps dim it, but I've been drinking way too much lately. The next best thing is sex. *Nope, not ready to go there yet.* Which leaves option three, training.

I shoot Misha a text to meet me in the sparring room in an hour and continue my walk around the house. Of course, I've barely taken ten steps when I catch sight of a blond stud outside, skimming the pool.

Fuck, he's pretty.

But he shouldn't be cleaning the goddamn pool. We pay people to do that.

I'm about to open the door and yell for him to stop, but I decide to take in the view for a moment longer. He's sporting a pair of gray sweatpants that ride low on his hips, showing off his impressive Adonis belt. His golden skin glistens in the sunlight as beads of sweat drip down his eight-pack. I've trained with a *lot* of very fit men, and I've seen and felt plenty of muscular physiques, but none of them have had this effect on me. They were just bodies, just flesh. They didn't pique my interest sexually, much less give me fucking butterflies like a goddamn schoolgirl.

You've got to get a grip, Mila.

Finally looking my fill, I open the sliding door and call out to him several times. He never looks up.

I'm halfway to the pool when I realize how stupid I look with my heels and my tea walking through the yard to catcall a boy fifteen years my junior. And of course, he takes the exact moment I'm about to turn around to finally acknowledge me.

"Hey, what are you doing out here? Do you need something?" He wipes his hand across his brow, and I'm close enough to see the beads of sweat fall, sending currents of arousal straight to my core.

"No. Well, yes, actually. What in the *world* are you doing cleaning the pool?"

"Some of the guys were out here cleaning it and were erm… kinda grumbling about it and—"

Oh, that's right. I assigned some of the groundkeeping chores to ten men who finished the physical assessment in last place. "Who was complaining? I'll—"

"*It doesn't matter who it was*, remember? *We're* trying to win them over, and if I rat them out and they stop trusting *me*, *we* don't stand a chance."

We...

As if we're a team running this Bratva together. Anyone else, aside from Misha, who said that would get kicked off the property before they could finish their sentence. I alone hold the power here, and any man who might insinuate otherwise could only be a threat...except Thatcher. When he says "we," it doesn't feel threatening at all. It feels like true camaraderie. Similar to Misha but very different at the same time.

"Okay, you're right. Go on."

"Well, some of the guys were complaining, uh, about you. So I, um...I told them that you sent me out here to clean the pool instead. That you saw how much hard work they were putting in and wanted them to have a day to relax and—"

"Thank you. I appreciate that more than you know."

He flashes his goofy little smile and winks. "Anytime, ba—"

"That's enough." I roll my eyes, but can't help returning his smile. "You know you don't have to finish this, right? I'll get our pool guy to do it when he comes next week."

"It's fine. I don't mind at all."

"If you're sure..."

"I'm sure." He looks at me with a lazy smile, then hangs his head. "It's not like I have anything else to do."

"Very well."

When I turn to leave, a hand catches mine. "Will I see you later?"

I stand frozen for a moment. Part of me wants to slap the shit out of him for touching me without permission. It's not something I'm used to. All the men know not to lay a finger on me unless prompted, but he wouldn't know any better. The other half of me wants to lay him down on one of the pool chairs and ride that insane cock I've been dreaming about for a week. Instead, I just look over my shoulder and smile.

"Yes, you'll see me later."

As I make my way back inside, the thought crosses my mind that maybe this could work. Thatcher is a loyal friend, or Teddy wouldn't be so fond of him, and Misha seems to like him as well. He's been extremely helpful to me this week. Then there's the fact that he submits so beautifully. And *fuck,* is he gorgeous. Maybe it wouldn't be the worst thing to let him alleviate some of my sexual frustration after all.

If he's *actually* up to the task.

CHAPTER 16

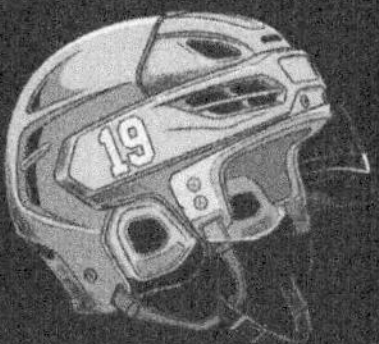

Thatcher

AFTER FINISHING THE pool, I dove into planning. I've been setting up parties all my life, but I've never arranged a romantic evening. With women coming out of the woodwork, *wooing* a potential partner has never been necessary. There hasn't been anyone worth it until now, but it seems I finally have my work cut out for me with Mila. Work I will *gladly* do, by any means necessary.

It's quiet since the majority of the men are off today, making it the perfect time for a romantic evening with the boss. I know she wouldn't let her guard down with too many eyes on her. It's going to be hard to get her to let loose with even the bare bones crew around. Luckily, Misha agreed to help me keep anyone away from the pool area.

The groundskeeper maintains the estate, so the baseline ambiance is already nice. A few LED lights placed around the pool to set the mood are all I added. The real work was figuring out exactly how to convince her to give me a real chance.

That is, if I can ever summon the guts to approach her. *She said she would see you later...stop being a pussy and go see if she wants to have dinner.* I've been standing outside her study for entirely too long, lifting and lowering my hand like an idiot, when the door flies open.

"Thatcher? Are you going to stand out there all evening?"

I'm at a loss for words as I take Mila in. She's always beautiful, but I've never seen her dressed so casually. Black leggings and a black cotton shirt replace her normal tactical attire, and she looks so domestic. So *normal.* Except Mila is anything *but* normal, and the juxtaposition blows my mind.

"Um. No, Ma'am. I, um—"

She crosses her arms, sighing. "Is there something you need, or are you haunting my door for the sole purpose of tormenting me?"

Summoning all of my bravery, I state my case. "I came to collect on your promise of seeing me later."

"Thatche—"

"Eh, no takesies backsies! Besides, it's just dinner. You have to eat, I have to eat, so we might as well do it together."

"Fine." She doesn't sound enthusiastic and rolls her eyes when I try to offer her my arm. But she isn't scowling as we make our way through the labyrinthine halls of the mansion. At least, until she realizes we've taken a turn she didn't expect.

"This isn't the way to the dining room."

Instinctively, I move to place my hand on her back, but stop when she stiffens and instead reach around to open the door that leads outside to the pool.

"No, but it *is* the way to our dinner."

She raises a brow at me but doesn't protest, taking the lead to the buffet of food set up under the pool gazebo. I follow, trying and failing not to ogle her incredible ass. Her years of training have had quite the effect on her physique, and I'm only a man after all.

"What is all this? Is something wrong with the dining room?"

"No, I...I just thought it would be nice to have a change of scenery, and today's weather is perfect for an evening picnic."

Mila examines the smorgasbord I had the chef prepare. "You didn't make this, did you?"

"Oh, no, I—"

"Very well. I suppose this is fine." Her plate is loaded quickly, and I'll have to thank the chef for being so confident in choosing Mila's favorites.

By the time I've made my selections and joined her at the table, she's already dug in, and I can't help but stare. I've never been around women who eat anything more than a few pieces of lettuce, so it's refreshing to see her eat to fuel herself.

"Why are you looking at me like that?" She catches me staring and glances down to see if she's dropped food onto her shirt before wiping her mouth with her napkin. "Is something on my face?"

I smile and shake my head, finally taking a bite from my own plate but barely tasting it. "You're astounding."

And she is. She rolls her eyes as she continues, and I follow each bite from her plate to her mouth. Despite her harsh exterior, she's graceful, her etiquette as flawless as any old-money New Yorker I've known. It's just another reminder of the mystery behind this woman. My hunger grows, and it's not for anything the chef prepared.

Like magic, she finishes just as one of her favorite songs begins to play. *I have to remember to thank Misha for the remote for the stereo and for telling me a few of her favorites.* Rarely does a genuine smile cross her face, but when it does...wow.

Standing, I reach for her, hoping that despite my massive, crushing vulnerability at this moment, she'll accept. "Shall we?"

"Shall we *what*?"

"Dance of course," I say, hand still extended.

"This isn't a song to dance to."

"Any song is a song to dance to if you try hard enough."

She sighs as she begrudgingly takes my hand. "Fine, I'll dance. One song. Then I'm going back to my office to work. And keep your hands to yourself."

If one dance is all I have, I'm going to make it the most amazing one she's ever had. Knowing Mila, it might be the only one she's ever had.

"How are we supposed to dance together if I can't touch you?"

She grabs my hands, placing one on her shoulder and one on her upper back. "Light touches only. And *don't* move them."

"Yes, Ma'am. But just so you know, you can touch me anywhere." I wink.

The song really *isn't* one to dance to; she was right about that. It's upbeat enough not to be romantic, but not so energetic that you can party it out, leaving only the middle awkward fun moves. Surprisingly, Mila follows as I sway us back and forth, catching on to the rhythm quickly.

I get a single chuckle from her when I start doing the disco. "You're a very silly man, Thatcher Prescott."

"Of course, life's not worth living if you never have any fun!"

"Life isn't just about fun. Say that to the people who have had to fight tooth and nail to be here today."

I place my hands back where she gave me permission to touch her, holding her a bit tighter than before. "What kind of life are they fighting for if they don't intend to enjoy it?"

"It's not always about serving yourself. Sometimes you have to fight so that others can live."

"And what do you think they would do if they didn't have to fight? What would they do for fun if they could?" I ask, rubbing my thumb up and down with such a light brush, I'm almost unsure if I'm dreaming of the warmth of her skin.

"I don't know. Everything I do has a purpose, including my leisure. My time is all calculated. I can't recall a time I've done something nonsensical."

"Do it now! Jump in the pool."

"Oh, I don't think so. I have my clothes on and—"

"So? I'll do it too, with our clothes on and everything. It's nonsensical. You shouldn't have zero memories of doing something *just because*. Please? Jump in with me."

She looks between the water and me several times before letting out a defeated, "Okay, let's do it."

"Hell, yeah! Alright, um. Take my hand?" She reluctantly does as I ask and follows my lead to the deep end of the pool. "Alright on three. One. Two."

I swear she yelps when I pull her close to me and jump one count early. Keeping her in my arms, I swim up to the surface, reveling in the feel of her body against mine.

The second her head pops out of the water, she's cursing me between coughs. "You...motherfucking...You said on *three*. I wasn't *ready,* you asshole. Water. In my nose. Wait, where are you taking me?"

I can't help but laugh as I pull her over to the shallow waters. "If you're going to kill me, I'd like for it to be on my own two feet."

I stop when I can stand with my shoulders above water and turn to face her, and *fuck,* I wasn't prepared for the vision before me. The sun has finally set, but the lights surrounding the pool reflect off her glistening skin, brighter than any star. Her long black hair has fallen free from her braid, framing her face perfectly as the water drips down her cheeks to her chest. She's still wrapped in my arms, and I'm careful not to let my touch linger anywhere unwelcome even though I want to so badly.

"I'm not going to kill you," she whispers, and her warm breath against my skin sends chills through my body.

"What are you going to do to me, then?" I ask, leaning forward so that our lips are only a hair's width apart.

Respecting her desire not to be touched, I don't dare go any further…I *do* dare to hope that she'll bridge the gap between us and kiss me. Instead, she pulls back and searches my eyes.

"What is it?"

"You want to be my good boy?"

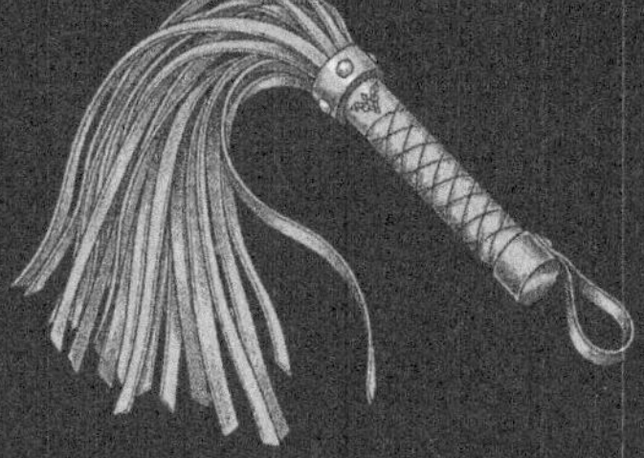

CHAPTER 17
Mila

"YOU WANT TO be my good boy?"

"Yes, Ma'am."

"You don't even know what that means."

"If it means I get to please you, that's enough for me. Ma'am."

The combination of the heated water of the pool and the fact that I'm fully clothed, yet still able to feel every taut muscle of the man begging to fuck me is enough to make me snap. I'm way too horny to have the discussion that's mandatory before we really play, but we're to the point that I'm torturing us both. *And I'm not the one who's tortured when I fuck.*

It's late enough at night that we should have relative privacy throughout the house. "Carry me to my bedroom. Quickly." Luckily, we don't have far to go, and in no time, he's placing me beside the bed and reaching for my waist. I step back out of his radius and allow my appreciative gaze to rake down his soaking wet body, softening the blow of disallowing his touch. *He'll have to get used to that.*

"Strip. And I have one rule for tonight. *Don't touch me.* Not with your hands, at least. I'll tell you exactly where I want your mouth, but your hands stay off me. You can put them behind your back if it helps, or behind your head, but so help me, if you touch me, I will *chop them off.* Got it?"

He peels off his soaked clothes, then clasps his hands behind his back, eyes raking up and down my body as I remove my own wet attire. "Yes, Ma'am."

Fuck. He looks so delicious, heavy cock bobbing against his stomach, leaning to the side under its own weight. I can't help myself. Dropping to my knees in front of him, I revel in the widening of his eyes and the strain evident in his biceps as he prevents himself from touching me.

"You really have been so good for me, Thatcher. You handled the tasks I set for you well, and you always follow my instructions to the letter."

He whimpers as I trail one sharp nail up his thigh, every muscle in his body seemingly clenched against any movement that he knows will get him in trouble. From his thick base to his tip, tracing around his flushed head and enjoying the sticky drop of cum that beads up under the pad of my finger.

"Do you like it when I touch you? You have such a pretty cock."

"Yes, Ma'am. Thank you, Ma'am." His teeth are ground together, every cell in his body tense against the pleasure that I'm offering. I press a wet, open-mouthed kiss to his weeping tip, tracing him with my tongue in one languid motion before releasing him with a pop. His knees are shaking now, and I think I'll have to put him on his back soon, or he'll fall over.

"What if I told you that I wanted to use you? If I told you to lie back on the bed and let me play with you for hours, would you?"

"Yes, Ma'am."

"What if I ignored your cock for the rest of the night, and instead, I sat on your face for hours, barely letting you breathe, only concerned with my own release? Would you lie there and take it?"

"Yes, Ma'am."

"How sweet. I think for both of our sakes, you deserve a quick reward. I'm dying to taste you, and I want you to focus on nothing else but my mouth. Can you do that?"

I don't give him a chance to answer, taking him as far into my throat in one go as I can. Few men have ever had the honor of me sucking their cock, but *feeling* a man melt into putty as soon as I start working him with my mouth is intoxicating. I want to taste Thatcher's desire for me, and given how much tension has been simmering between us, I don't think it will take long.

Digging my nails into his thighs and enjoying his hiss of pain, I set a merciless pace. Deep strokes with vibration from my wordless praise, followed by kittenish lollipop licks to his tip, have him groaning in a way I *know* means he must be close. With a deep breath, I push forward and moan as I meet his gaze for the first time.

That's all it takes for him to explode into my mouth with a tortured sound that's music to my ears. I swallow everything he gives me, happy to have taken the edge off and pushed him further into the soft space I want him in. He sways, but doesn't move his hands an inch to try to catch himself. Standing, I can't take it any longer, pulling him harshly by his hair into a searing kiss.

I swallow his gasp and let him taste himself, asserting the dominance that's already clearly mine. If Thatcher ever fancied himself a Dom in the bedroom, it's obvious he was denying his true calling. Finally coming up for air, he's so dazed that I only have seconds before he topples over.

"Lie back on the bed, legs together, hands clasped behind your head."

Climbing on top and settling on his shins, I admire the vision before me. His golden curls have started to dry haphazardly from the pool water, but his brow is re-dampened with a sheen of sweat from enduring his pleasure. The perfect cock that was just as delicious as I expected is still half hard, and I don't doubt that his refractory period will be short. He *is* quite young, after all.

"You did so well," I coo, although it seems he's barely registering my words. "I'm proud of you for giving me what I wanted so quickly. Now, do you remember how I taught you to lick my pussy?"

"Yes, Ma'am."

"Do you think you can do it upside down?"

He's just as talented as I remember, and I've gotten off twice while riding his face as I edged him. His legs are shaking, so I know it's time to take what I want before it's too late and I have to wait again.

When I flip back around, my clit throbs at the sight of his arms still stalwartly placed behind his head. Straddling his red, abused cock, I slowly start to grind back and forth. He can barely keep his eyes open, so lost in the pleasure of not making a single decision and existing only for my pleasure.

"You've been so good tonight. My *very* good boy. You're just my personal toy, aren't you? You don't have to think or do anything at all except take what I give you. If I left you here hard, alone, and told you not to touch yourself, what would you say?"

His abs contract beautifully as I drag my claws down, leaving red scratch marks in their wake. There's barely any air in his lungs as he replies.

"Yes, Ma'am."

Placing my hands on his shins and lifting my hips to give him a view of my messy core, no doubt glistening from the wetness I've been grinding and spreading on his cock, I soak in the adoration and heat in his eyes.

"Is this what you want?"

"Mmmm…"

"Now, Thatcher. That's not an answer. If you want something, you have to tell me. In detail. This is the only time tonight I want you to say more than "yes, Ma'am." If you want it badly enough, tell me, and I might just give it to you."

He licks his lips and briefly flicks his gaze to mine before dropping back to my core, where I'm slowly circling my clit and teasing my entrance, ensuring he can see everything.

"Please," he whispers in the sweetest little voice. "Please, *please* let me feel your pussy around my cock. Ma'am, I…I think I'll die without it. You felt so nice grinding on me. Hot and wet, and I just want you to use me. Please."

Leaning forward, I give him one more languid kiss, suckling on his lower lip and relishing the twitch of his cock against my core. Pulling back to look at him, I can't help but lavish praise while I rise to line us up for what we've both been craving.

"You're so pretty, solnyshko, and you're my good boy, telling me what you want. I think I'll give it to you."

Any plans I had to sink all the way onto him are immediately dashed, and I hiss, feeling the sweet stretch of my first thick cock in far too long. With a few slow strokes, I'm finally seated flush against his hips, and *goddamn. This cock is every bit as excellent as I knew it would be from the first moment I felt it against my thigh.*

Leaning back, I give myself a few moments to luxuriate in the stretch, swiveling my hips and grinding for my own pleasure. A whine from the head of the bed reminds me of the man attached to the cock, and I catch his eyes locked on where we're connected.

"Do you see what a nice stretch your beautiful cock is giving me? You've spread me nice and wide, haven't you? Such a good boy, letting me use your cock like this. You're bigger than any of my dildos, so I think you might have to replace them. I bet you'd do that for me, wouldn't you? Stay right here, naked and ready to be hard for me at a moment's notice so I could use you any time I wanted."

"Yes, Ma'am."

I think I've broken him. I've made him so pussy drunk that he'd agree to anything. Instead of the tension he's been holding all night, he's finally relaxed beneath me, limp except for the *very* hard dick I'm riding faster now. Moving into a squat, I thank the stair climber for my quad stamina and move one hand to my clit.

"You're allowed to come because you've been such a good boy. But I'm not going to wait on you. If you miss your chance, you'll have to wait until next time. Tell me when you're close."

His whine is barely audible, but I manage to make out that he's close, which is fortunate, because so am I. When the first monumental spasm of my orgasm pulls me under, I pop up and off him, reveling in the force of his own release as it shoots onto his abdomen. I fall to his chest, unable, even with all my strength, to stay upright while riding this wave of pleasure.

His soft gaze, once we've both caught our breath, is enough for me to *almost* wish he had his arms around me, holding me tighter to his muscled chest. Almost.

Instead, I breathe in his scent: chlorine, sweat, *Thatcher*...and his hands stay firmly behind his head.

CHAPTER 18
Thatcher

HAVE I DIED and gone to heaven? This is so much better than I ever expected heaven to be. Not that I thought I would go, because of, well, plenty of reasons, but even if I did, my dreams pale in comparison. I'm lying on a cloud, perfectly relaxed, as someone, an angel if I had to guess, scratches my scalp. Once every few passes, her thumbs trail down to trace my eyebrows, and if my muscles loosen any more, I'm afraid I'll sink straight through this cloud and fall out of the sky.

A chuckle wakes me up slightly, and I feel…flesh? *Lying on top of me?*

"Welcome back, solnyshko."

The angel's voice is sinful as she purrs against my chest, and I realize she's lying naked on top of me. When my dick twitches, excited at this development, it meets resistance, and the angel groans as she sits up, grinding against my length sandwiched between us. I can't help how pathetic my voice is as I beg, rasping out the only word that comes to mind at the moment.

"*More.*"

"I don't think so. You're still floating, and—"

"*Please. Please, more...*"

"Alright, just one more. Only because you're so fucking *cute* coming out of subspace. Not because this is how it'll be all the time. And you *will* be punished for interrupting me. Even if I haven't explicitly told you, I know that you know better."

My vision is hazy, and as the angel sits back into a squat and begins to ride me...*fuck.* She's so wet, *impossibly* wet, and suddenly a dam of memories bursts into my mind. *Mila, Mila, Mila...I made Mila come, and now she's using it as lube to ride me for round two.* I'm not in heaven; this is real life. But if I come again right now, I might die.

"You can do it. You've been so good. I know you want to come again. And I can tell you're close, Thatcher. Come for me."

My strangled groan perfectly encapsulates the pleasure and pain of how she's using me, but I'm powerless against her command. When I feel her squeezing around me, tight as a vise, I lose myself just as she rises off me, forcing my orgasm with her hand. I *think* I whisper her name, but before I can hear her reply, everything turns black.

When I wake up, the room is dark apart from candles flickering on the nightstand closest to me. It smells like...*home?*

"I hope you don't mind. It's one I confiscated from your things when you moved in. Figured you'd like to smell it when you woke up. Drink this. I know your mouth is dry."

The bottle of water she hands me is tinted pink, but I down it in one go without caring what it is. She's right. My mouth is dry, and I feel like I got hit by a truck, then dragged through a swamp. When I woke up the first time, I felt *so good,* and now I feel like shit. What the hell happened? Before I can gather the strength to actually ask, Mila speaks, but not to answer my question.

"Want to take a bath?"

Thirty minutes later, I'm lying back against her in the tub with one hand resolutely in my lap while the other receives the best hand massage of its life. Mila must have taken classes to be able to work every single muscle in my hand, freeing all the stress I didn't even know I was carrying. She's worked her way down both sides of my neck, releasing knots in my traps that I would never let our team trainer touch. But she's noodle-ized me, and I'm as relaxed as I've ever been, so I let her work her magic.

This tender, post-fuck Mila is hard to reconcile with her usual exterior, and my thoughts feel like they're still slogging through a haze. She saves me from having to say anything, pulling my head back to rest against her chest. I clasp my hands tightly together, resisting the all-consuming urge to touch.

"I shouldn't have listened to you. You were too in between, and it made your come-down harder than it had to be."

"My come-down?"

"Mm-hmm. We had a really intense experience, and it was totally new for you. From the beginning, we should have discussed more ahead of time, so that didn't help. But the second round, even if you thought you wanted it, wasn't what you needed at that moment."

"I did want it, though. I was totally consenting, if that's what you mean." I'm so confused. Does she think she took advantage of me? She's quiet for a moment before she explains.

"It's not that you weren't, solnyshko..."

There's that word again. I'm still afraid to ask her what it means. Maybe Misha will tell me.

"It's that you weren't in the space to make that decision for yourself. That's my job, as your...well. In this situation, it was my job to decide for you. I chose wrong, and as a result, you're having a less enjoyable aftercare experience. You should be feeling hazy and gooey but still relaxed. I think if we had stopped, you would have gotten that. And for that, I *am* sorry."

We're quiet until the water grows cold, lost in our own thoughts. I feel better after hydrating, and if I eat something, I think I'll be back to normal.

"If I go get some snacks, will you stay and eat with me?"

I can't help but laugh, and she deflates a bit, thinking I'm laughing *at* her. *Who made her so defensive?*

"You don't have to—"

"I'd appreciate a snack, it's not that. I laughed because that's the second time that you've managed to respond out loud to a need I only expressed in my head. Earlier, with the water. And just now, when I was thinking about how hungry I was."

"Alright. Let's get out, and I'll go find something for us to snack on."

By the time I'm dry and wrapped in a towel, she's back, dressed in loose pajamas, *black of course,* with her braid re-done and flawless once again down her back. She's carrying a tray laden with cheese, fruit, crackers, and jam, and a pack on her shoulder bulges with more water bottles. I'd usually jump up to help a woman carry things, but Mila doesn't need my help. If anything, she's stronger than I am. I hope someday she'll *let* me help, *want* my help...but I'm getting ahead of myself.

Pulling a paper plate out of her bag, she adds a sampling of everything and hands it to me, along with another bottle of electrolytes. I drop my towel and sit on the bed, enjoying her appreciative gaze over my figure, including my half-hard cock. I can't help it. I'm always sporting a semi these days when she's around.

"This isn't the normal order of things when I take someone to bed, I hope you know."

Munching on my snack, I raise an eyebrow to prompt her to continue. She sits in the velvet chair and sighs, toying with her braid.

"I don't like to categorize myself, but if you had to put me into a sexual box, I suppose I would mostly fit what people would refer to as a Domme. I'm a woman who prefers the dominant role during sex, requiring and expecting submission and rule following from my partners. My special interests include restraints, degradation, edging, and impact play, although on the sadism spectrum, I'd say I'm on the low-to-moderate end of things. I'm not a lifestyle dominant, either, if you start googling and run into that. I have no interest in controlling what you wear or eat. My interest is strictly sexual and within the confines of intimate situations."

Impact play... "You want to shpank me? Like across your lap?" Even with a mouth full of food, the question escapes before I can stop it. She doesn't look displeased by my poor manners, only happy to see me eating.

"Don't forget to drink that water." She nods toward the electrolyte bottle that I had, indeed, forgotten. "My hand isn't my preferred implement, but that's likely where we would start until you were ready to move on to other things."

"Like if I'm bad? Or you'd hit me just because?"

"It's never *just because.* There's a reason for every one of my decisions. That's why it's frustrating for me that I let you influence me earlier. My control is paramount, but we're getting ahead of ourselves. I don't want to dive into this any more right now. It's too soon after our encounter for either of us to have clear heads. What I'd like to know is if anything sounded interesting to yo—"

"Yes." Her glare tells me she doesn't appreciate the interruption, but if this is my chance to let her know I am fully interested in exploring anything she's offering, I'm taking it. "I'm sorry for interrupting, but yes. I feel so light and floaty with you, when you take control. Even if I wasn't restrained today, not touching you made everything feel ten times more intense. And I'm willing to try the spanking—"

"Impact play."

"Yes, impact play. I've liked everything you've done so far. Clearly, I thrive when I'm not in charge." With a wink, I go back to eating and watch as she rises to rummage around in her nightstand.

"Fill this out for me. You can google anything you don't know, and you can read my preferences on the back. Once you do, we can compare notes, so to speak, and decide where to go from there."

Cane, flogger, whip...

"We'll chat about it before we...*do* anything else, to make sure we're on the same page—"

Ruined orgasm, milking, sensory deprivation...

"Which, as I said before, I should have taken care of already."

Degradation, stress positions, exhibition...

"But once you fill this out and we talk, I think we'll each have a clearer idea of what we want moving forward." Her phone alarm blares, and she curses before apologizing. "I have to take this. Are you okay? I can check on you..." Her eyes flick to the door that joins our rooms, a hint that's clear but not unkind.

"I'm okay," I say honestly, gathering my snacks and water and moving to my room, still naked. "I have some research to do, but I'm okay."

She nods and takes her call as I close the door behind me, missing her presence immediately but feeling more awake now that I'm fed and hydrated. *And now that I have homework.*

Opening my phone, I ignore all the texts and calls from my party friends and past hookups. I don't have any from Teddy that I haven't already responded to, and my teammates can wait until tomorrow. With safe search off, I start with a phrase on the page I've never heard of.

Queening throne.

The images that flood my screen have my dick hard again in no time, and I huff a laugh. I have absolutely no idea what I've signed myself up for. *And I can't fucking wait.*

CHAPTER 19

Mila

"AND WHAT WILL you say if you want to stop?"

"Red, Ma'am."

"If you need to slow down?"

"Yellow, Ma'am."

"And if I ask to check in and you're enjoying everything with no concerns or complaints?"

"Green, Ma'am."

He looks so *earnest*. I hope he knows what he's in for.

"Very well. Let's begin."

"Do we really need to have a formal meeting in your office? I thought we already talked about things you liked and things I wanted to try."

Thatcher's earnest confusion softens me a bit, and I remember Misha's warning.

"This isn't a stranger at the club, moya tsaritsa. This is Teddy's best friend. He'll be in our lives forever, at every family gathering and birthday party for the children. Don't forget that he's used to being the user in his relationships, not the used."

"I wanted us to have a chance to go over the document you filled out for me, and to make sure you didn't have any questions about mine." The list of activities I sent him was abbreviated from the boilerplate version I usually send my submissive partners, but I figured it's better to start small with Thatcher since he doesn't have any experience in the kink world. "It would have been awkward to have you fill out a sex questionnaire, then fuck you without us talking about it, don't you think?"

My smile reassures him, tension leaving his shoulders as he relaxes. "It was a shorter list than I was expecting."

"I only included my favorites. Do you have any questions? I have a few for you, but I want you to go first."

He pulls a piece of paper from his pocket and clears his throat. *Cute.* "This might be the only time I've ever been excited about homework." He laughs, and I want to *eat him alive.* "First, regarding the tying me up...the shibari, the list called it? I googled it, and some of the designs were intense."

"Mm-hmm." I give him my most encouraging look. He needs to learn now that he has to ask if he wants to know.

"What, uh...What do you like about it, and what do you think I would like about it? Is it about pain? I saw that further down the list. And would it cause any injuries that would affect me playing hockey?"

He's got a pen in his hand now, ready to take notes, and I make a mental note to reward him for being such a good student. For the first time, it's endearing to have an inexperienced submissive, and I'm proud he came prepared.

"Those are all very good questions. I'd like to answer the latter two before the former. In no way will I *ever* injure you. If that happened, it would be a fluke, some element of our scene beyond my direct control. For example, if I have you suspended from the ceiling and a structural beam of this mansion fails, then I suppose you could sustain an injury. But so would the architect who signed off on the blueprints."

He relaxes a bit more, and I hate that he thought I wanted to hurt him. *Well, I do.* But only so he can come harder than he ever has, and to relieve the tension between my shoulders. I'd never *injure* him.

"So no. Certainly no injuries. I've never had a submissive with anything more than a rope burn, and that was per their request. This leads into pain, as you said, further down the list. You may be sore from being in one position for too long, but that should fade within a day or two and not be any worse than what you might experience after a strenuous yoga class. I'll never push your muscles past their ability to stretch, and I'll check in often to make sure your circulation is never impaired."

This is the part that's harder to explain, and I hope I don't lose him.

"As far as the pain, I do enjoy inflicting it, I won't deny that. Unless we uncover that you're a closeted masochist, though, the pain that I give you will be overwhelmed by more pleasure, always, and driven by what we learn that you like. It might not be *immediate* pleasure, or the pleasure that you would choose, but you'll always find the balance will ultimately tip in your favor. Does that make sense?"

Thatcher's doing an excellent job of listening, even as his cock hardens down his thigh. If he's interested so far…

"It does make sense. I guess I didn't realize how much thought you'd be giving to my pleasure, to be honest. Sorry, I don't mean to make you sound thoughtless…"

With a sigh, I come around my desk to sit in the chair beside him instead of facing him down like his boss…even though I will be, in a way, soon.

"You don't have to be sorry for telling me how you feel or what you think. That's a big part of the first two questions you asked me, about what we would each gain from this arrangement."

I have his absolute attention now, beautiful eyes locked on mine as I try to explain why I am the way I am, *without* actually explaining.

"As to what I like about bondage in particular, as you may have gleaned from spending time with me, I prefer to be in control of as much of my life as possible. This is magnified during sexual encounters for me, where I prefer complete control. Bondage ensures that I know exactly how you can and can't move, and knowing that lets me relax and enjoy myself in a way that's very hard in my everyday life. I've told people before that it's like playing chess, but with the bonus of controlling all the pieces. For me, that relieves a great deal of anxiety and allows me to connect with someone in a way that feels safe and on my terms. Shibari is a more aesthetic, intricate type of bondage that I enjoy but don't always take the time to do. Sometimes you'll be very simply bound."

"Why do you—"

Ugh, he was being so good. He doesn't need that answer. As far as I'm concerned, Misha and I can take it to our graves.

I interrupt his interruption and raise a censurious brow so he doesn't try again.

"And the infliction of pain I like is because I like it. As simple as that. Regarding what you get out of it, with the bondage…I really think it might be something that centers you. I'm in charge, and you can just float for a while and not have to think about a single thing except enduring what I give you. It's an intense connection, and I hope you'll enjoy it just as I do. The trust you'd have in me to give you more pain and pleasure than you think you can handle, only for you to realize you can take more than you thought you could."

He's quiet as we compare notes on the remaining items on the short list, and I'm impressed by his willingness to try new things. I tell him as much and ask him if he has any questions. Apparently, enough time has passed for him to regain his usual confidence because he leans into my space, stopping an inch from my lips to give his answer.

"Just one, Boss. When do we start?"

We stayed in my office a while longer that day, having a lighter-hearted conversation about my favorite flogger and how soft the jute rope I prefer is. He asked if I had any rules for him outside the bedroom, but I demurred. If he was disappointed that I just asked him to continue bonding with the men, he quickly covered it and asked if I'd punish him during a scene. *Those* rules were easy to describe, and he turned beet red at the mention of maintenance spanking. I don't plan to start too heavy with the degradation, though. Too many variables could spell disaster during a first session.

The tension was thick by the time I left for my evening meeting, and with the merger ramping up seemingly every day, it wasn't until today that I had time to give Thatcher the attention he deserves. *And to get what I deserve, too.*

Now, lost in my thoughts as I enter the peaceful zone of tying someone up at my mercy, I enjoy the needy, panting boy waiting for me.

"Are any of your muscles straining in any way? Anything pulling, pinching, or uncomfortable, including where the ropes touch your skin?"

"No…Ma'am," he pants, and I can't help my low chuckle. He's in for such a long evening. By the time I'm done with him, he'll either be running for the hills or begging for a full course of what I'm offering. Tonight's just an appetizer.

"I would enjoy this position if I were you, solnyshko. This is the only time you'll ever be this comfortable with me. But I need to know you truly enjoy being immobilized, so we'll start here."

He really is getting off easy tonight. Well, not *getting off* easy. Seated on the plush bench at the end of the bed, his ankles are spread wide and securely attached to the solid legs at either corner. His arms are in a position I'm quite proud of, wide but comfortable, with elbows slightly bent and no tension in his shoulders. The combination of my chest harness and his wrists pulled taut to the bed posts means that, if he weren't tied up, he could be mistaken for simply manspreading and relaxing against the end of my bed.

As it is, he can't move a muscle. Not even his hips, banded and rigged to the bedframe as well. *It wouldn't do to have him able to thrust.* We decided no gag and no blindfold tonight, to ensure I can read his gaze and sense discomfort before he can even verbalize it. If he's a bad boy who speaks without being spoken to, he'll be punished, and he knows it, but I need to know how he reacts before I take away his voice.

"You're beautiful, solnyshko. Have I told you today?"

"No, Ma'am." He moans as I drag my nails through his thick hair, scratching his scalp and forcing my breasts into his face. I can only imagine how much he'd love to draw one of my nipples into his mouth, but he's still.

"You are. Sculpted as if from marble, my handsome boy." I scratch down his chest, perfectly framed by the harness I tied around his pecs, and trace each ab on my way down. Ignoring his cock, I tease his inner thighs with soft touches, relishing the carousel of emotions that flash through his eyes as he tries to thrust into my touch but *can't move a muscle.*

This first experience for him will never come again, and I know immediately, instinctively that I'll never forget it. A moment of panic, anger, *lust* as he struggles briefly against my restraints then stops, recognizing futility when he feels it. His cock, hard for ages at this point, flexes, the only part of him currently able to rebel against my command to be still.

I can't help but continue, tracing a single line in a circle around his weeping length, barely grazing his balls as I move underneath. It's mesmerizing to watch his abs flex as he fights the urge to move but tries to relax like my good boy. Even as a sheen of sweat forms across his forehead and chest, he hasn't tried to thrust again.

"You're being *very* good for me, keeping your hips still while I inspect you. I particularly appreciate you for making sure this cock was ready and waiting for me. You're keeping it nice and hard, which is useful because I'll certainly be needing it. *Later.*"

He whimpers, and I laugh again before moving to my nightstand to grab lube and the masturbator that's likely to be his archenemy by the end of the night. Edging is my priority for this evening, to push him into discomfort in only one way, leaving my flogger in its case for now. It's why I have him in such a relaxed position. Nothing should ache except his balls.

Pulling the custom stool I had delivered between his legs, I sit and continue to tease as his hot gaze rakes over me. I can only imagine how much he'd like to touch me. Dolling myself up has been one of my favorite parts of play for as long as I can remember, and the strappy latex lingerie I'm wearing should contribute to Thatcher's torture nicely. Finally touching the tip of his cock, I swipe the precum beading there and lick it off my finger obscenely. His eyes roll, then close, and I take the opportunity to make my move.

Lubing up my hand, I stop wasting time, gripping his cock firmly and giving him quick strokes. A twist at his head has his eyes popping open and every muscle in his body tensing as he tries to move.

"You poor thing. Did I scare you? Why?"

"Yes, Ma'am. I wasn't expecting…" He groans intelligibly as I continue working him like getting him off is my only mission in life. "I, ugh. I thought you would keep teasing, for a while, with the, uh…edging."

My dark laugh sparks fear in his eyes, and I sense that he only now understands *at all* what he's in for.

"There are many ways to edge a man, and it isn't all light teasing. No, I want to warm you up, then keep you on fire. *I want you to burn for hours.*"

CHAPTER 20

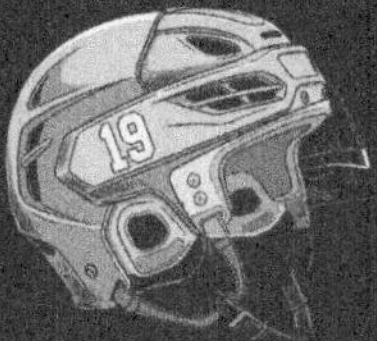

Thatcher

I WANT YOU TO *burn for hours.*

Hours. Hours of *this?* How…how can she possibly expect me not to come? I whimper, and she reminds me of what we discussed, but doesn't slow her pace or ease her pressure.

"You know exactly what I expect of you, if you're going to be a good boy like you promised. What are you going to tell me if you get close?"

"I'll say 'gonna come,' Ma'am."

"That's right. And I know you aren't about to when we've just gotten started, are you? There's no way you blow for all your women this fast, do you?"

"No…Ma'am."

"Good. That would be pathetic. But then again, I bet none of them worked you over like this, did they? They probably didn't know what a filthy little fucktoy you truly are."

A graze of her sharp fingernail under my head shocks me and pushes me too close to the edge. "Gonna come!"

She stops immediately, every pleasurable sensation gone, and leaves me shaking, abs tight, fighting not to come. When I relax, if I expected a moment's reprieve, I was wrong.

"Thank you for being a good boy for me and telling me before you came," she purrs, picking up at the same intensity she left off with. I'm already closer to coming than my previous start point, and as the reality of my situation sinks in, she notices. "You can tell now, can't you, solnyshko? It felt almost *impossible* not to come just now, didn't it? But truly, that was as *easy* as you'll have it all night."

No, no, no...

"Yes, and I'll be punishing you for speaking out of turn. Even if I don't have any plans to spank you tonight, I always remember to dole out my punishments at some point."

Shit, I didn't even realize I said that out loud. Closing my eyes, I pray that will somehow help me focus on *anything* except how good her hand feels on me. Hockey stats, saggy old man balls..."Fuck, gonna come!"

My eyes pop open as Mila squeezes just beneath my head, pushing me back from the edge. "You were close. Watch yourself. If you come before I tell you to, and you ruin my playtime tonight, that'll make you a very bad boy. And you can't begin to imagine what I do to bad boys."

Of course I was fucking close. Just as I got into a rhythm of imagining the old guys at the gym while thinking about stats from my first year of junior hockey, Mila fucking deep-throated me out of nowhere.

"I want your eyes on me. If I didn't want you to see what I'm doing, I'd blindfold you. But I got all dressed up for you, and you're going to watch."

Fuck me, watching is so much worse. She's the hottest thing I've ever seen, black braid sleek as always, long down her back and making her look like the warrior princess she is. Her eyeliner is thicker today, long lashes framing her bright-blue eyes that haven't left mine as she continues to tease me with her mouth.

"Do you wish this was my pussy?"

Yes? No? I don't know... "Gonna come!"

We continue for so long that she's allowed me to close my eyes, and my head has long since fallen back on the bed. I don't think I could lift my neck, even if she ordered me to. My stamina has waned, and it feels like it only takes five strokes of her hand or her mouth now to force me to croak out my warning. I haven't stopped shaking for the last three rounds, and my thoughts are few and far between. She shows no signs of stopping, though, and I know whenever she allows my release, it'll be cataclysmic.

"Gonna come!"

"Good boy," she soothes, scratching my scalp and leaving my dick alone for a moment. "You're shaking, solnyshko. Does anything cramp or hurt? What color are you?"

I shake my head. "Green, Ma'am."

When she touches me again, it's not her hand or her mouth, it's something else. Something soft and..."Gonna come!"

"I'm disappointed in you, Thatcher. Have you never felt a masturbator before?"

Forcing my head up, I can barely see what she's holding through the sweat dripping into my eyes, stinging and adding to the cacophony of sensations I'm struggling to endure. I barely shake my head, unable to answer, but she demands I vocalize.

"What's your color?"

What *is* my color? I feel fine, physically. Covered in sweat, sure. Muscles sore from tensing them, although I've mostly lost that ability during the last few rounds, with the uncontrollable shaking taking over. Mentally, I'm not sure how much more I can take, but I want to be good for her. I can do this.

"Green, Ma'am."

"Very well. If you've never experienced one of these, I suppose it can be overwhelming."

She slowly teases me with the toy again, just the tip of my dick in and out of something tight and wet. I squint to see what she's holding, and all I can make out is a tube with a hole in it...

"I had this custom made, and you're the first one to ever experience it."

Fuck, her pace is maddening, barely teasing me, then going all the way to the hilt with no rhyme or reason to her rhythm. When she follows a pattern, I can at least brace myself.

"*This* goes by many names. Masturbator, pocket pussy, stroker...it's modeled after me. *That* was quite the experience, if you can imagine."

With every scrap of energy left in my body, I try to see what she's talking about. I've definitely never used anything like this, and it's modeled on *her*...oh. *Oh.* The tube is flesh colored, and the opening looks like...

"Gonna come!" My whine is anguished and pathetic to my own ears, and I tense every muscle to stay away from my climax. That's the closest I've been, and I almost couldn't hold back once I decided what my dick was inside.

"*Good boy,"* Mila coos, rubbing my shaking thighs and soothing me. "You figured it out quickly, such a smart boy. It's a custom mold of my vagina, made just for me to torture my favorite toys with. Do you like it?"

"Yes, *ungh.* Yes, Ma'am." I barely had a minute's reprieve before she started on me again with fast, deep, relentless strokes.

"Do you think it feels as good as the real thing? I'm assuming it's not as hot and wet as I am—"

"Gonna come!"

Her dark laugh is a warning shot down my spine, and she grazes my balls with her sharp fingernails before continuing almost immediately with lighter teasing strokes. "So it *is* just as good, then? You don't even need my real pussy anymore?"

"No, Ma'am! It's not…*ugh,* it's not as warm or wet, but it feels like you. Gonna come!"

My breaks are shorter and shorter, and I'm barely lasting for a few touches of her hand, mouth, or toy before I'm forced to warn her of my impending release.

"You've done so well for me tonight. *Such* a good boy. I think I'll reward you. It's almost time for you to come. Where would you like to? In the toy or all over me?"

Oh fuck. Just pick one. I can barely even think of my own name right now, let alone make a decision with three amazing options…shit. "Uhh, in the toy. *Please.* Please, please let me come, Ma'am. I can't take any more."

"Hmm. I think you can take *much* more. And you will for me soon. But very well. You have permission to come."

Hearing those sweet words is all I need, and I'm off, soaring into space and imploding in on myself like a dying star. I've never felt anything like this. A release of tension I've held in my body for hours, followed by blinding pleasure and warm static in my brain. If I thought I was floating before, it's nothing compared to this.

"Solnyshko, it's okay. You did so well for me. I'm very, very proud of you." Mila's voice sounds far away, but I try to swim toward her through my gooey consciousness. When I finally make it to her, my arms and legs have been freed, but I'm still sitting in my chair.

"Thatcher, look at me. Can you see me?" She sounds concerned, and I don't understand why, until it hits me all at once. Shaking like a leaf, I do as she says and raise my head to look into her beautiful blue eyes. She looks ready to do anything I need, and I swear her gaze is full...I try to speak but burst into tears instead, sobs wracking my body as I try to figure out what I'm feeling. All I can do is nod.

"Okay, good. Can I touch you?"

Of course you can touch me, I try to say. Please, always touch me. Instead, I just nod again.

"Alright. We're going to walk to the bathroom. Does that sound good? I've already drawn us a bath, and the jets are on." Once I give one more weak nod, she puts one of my arms around her shoulders and helps me stand. A smaller woman wouldn't be able to help me like this, but not my Mila. She's plenty strong enough to help me when I need it.

Our bath is quiet, and she murmurs soothing nonsense as she rubs each of my sore muscles, feeds me, and towels me off after the water's cooled. I let her lead me to a bed with no resistance, finally feeling relaxed enough that I have no doubt I'm about to pass out into a deep sleep. Between all the pleasure she gave me tonight and all the ways she pushed me, I've felt what seems like every emotion in the book.

But as she turns out the light and slides into bed with me, I wonder if there might just be a few more waiting inside me, less deeply buried than ever before.

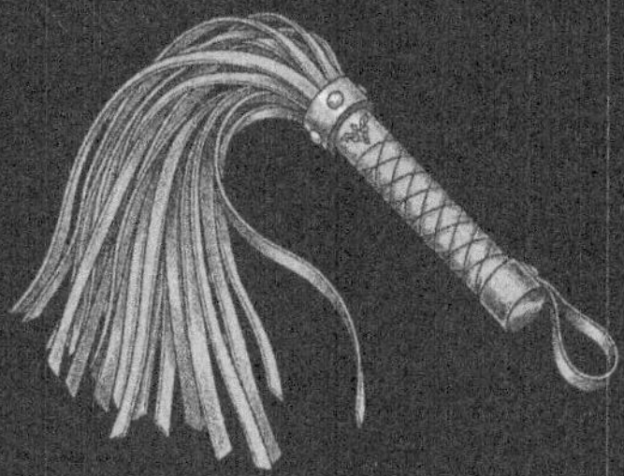

CHAPTER 21

Mila

MY ALARM WAKES me from my sleep, where I was dreaming about...*Damnit, why am I still in a cocoon?* I shimmy to get loose, but I can't move. All my wiggling does is make my entrapment tighter, and is that something sticking in my...My eyes shoot open. I've let a man sleep in my bed *again*. His dick twitches, and I'm preparing to quite literally kick this motherfucker out of my bed, but instead of grinding it against me, he adjusts so that it won't poke me anymore.

My good fucking boy.

For the first time in my life, I'm not mortified at the thought of waking up with someone. It's actually...nice. A glance at the clock tells me I have another fifteen minutes before I need to get up for the morning, so I hit my snooze and melt into Thatcher's warm body. Heaven knows that after everything I put him through last night, he deserves this.

Closing my eyes, I replay everything that transpired between us last night. The way he obeyed, how blissful he was when I finally allowed his release, and even how vulnerable he was during his drop. For his first time, he did outstanding. It's not an uncommon occurrence to see a man under as much pressure as he is to enjoy being dominated, but this was different. I've been in the lifestyle long enough to tell the difference between someone who likes to play here and there and someone who *needs* it. He's the latter. After we talked through his experience a bit during our bath, I became more convinced than ever that Thatcher Prescott was born to be a submissive—*even if he doesn't realize it yet.*

My blaring alarm pulls me from my recollection, and I pry myself from the warm arms that surround me. I wouldn't normally allow someone to touch me like this, but when Thatcher fell asleep during our approved cuddle time, I didn't want to move him. My little sunshine lets out a whimper, and I can't fight the smile on my face as I place a pillow in his arms. I *almost* wish it were me, still cocooned in bed, feeling that glorious cock already ready for another round.

I guess we're having a cold shower today since I have to go out and run a fucking Bratva, and I'm currently jealous of a goddamn pillow. Jesus, fuck.

Luckily, my cold shower does the trick, and I'm back to myself. As always, I run through my schedule in my head while I wait for my morning tea to arrive. My days here have been pretty mundane. All I've had time for is a never-ending stream of meetings and "team building" activities, as Misha calls them. The idea that my day could conclude with stress relief that involves more than liquor and a warm bath is sublime.

My moment of joy dissolves as Thatcher flings the door open, ruining my peace. "Good morning! How was your shower? I brought your tea as instructed but thought you might want to eat breakfast in your room this morning since you slept in a bit—"

"Please tell me you didn't make me breakfast again." I don't want to be a bitch about it, but I'm not eating his subpar, low-calorie shit when we employ a world-class chef who monitors my macros.

He laughs as he sets the tray on the side table. "No, don't worry, I learned my lesson the first time. This is from the kitchen. I just asked the chef to plate your breakfast. I even requested extras in case you want seconds."

Oh, thank God.

"Thank you, that's very kind."

I prepare my meal, doctoring my morning tea and cutting up the meat and potatoes on the plate. I don't know what I expected Thatcher to do. Perhaps leave, or at least eat his breakfast with me, but when I glance up, he's sitting across from me *staring*.

"What are you doing?"

He fiddles with his thumbs, an annoying nervous tic we will have to work out soon if we are to continue our arrangement. "I don't actually know what to do. On top of this dynamic being different from anything I've ever experienced, I, um, don't typically wake up next to the same woman more than once."

I snort a laugh, rolling my eyes. "Alright, playboy, calm down."

"Well, do you?"

"Do I wake up next to someone? Never. I tend to prefer sleeping alone."

"Yeah, you said as much when you kicked me out the other night." He sighs. "So why did you tell me I could stay last night?"

I take a moment to think as I chew. Why *did* I let him stay? I don't even normally have my playthings in the same house with me, much less let them sleep in my bed. My liaisons are typically at a club or hotel, with strict time parameters.

"You were a very good boy for me last night, and good boys get rewarded. Don't get used to it, though. Like I said, I prefer to sleep alone."

I warn myself, just as much as him. Because as nice as it was to wake up in someone's arms, feeling, dare I say, cherished, I don't need to get used to it either. Sex is transactional, nothing more. Developing feelings for my sub is strictly off the table. Allowing myself to care for someone, or even love them, is only a weakness. One I can *not* afford.

"That's fine with me. Last night was incredible. I've never experienced anything like it, so I'll be here for you in any capacity you'll have me."

"That's good to hear. I enjoyed it as well, and since we both had fun, I think it's worthwhile to explore more together. Actually, now is a great time to discuss anything you *didn't* like last night. A huge part of this dynamic is communication and trust. Before and after every scene, I'll always check in to make sure we're on the same page. If there's ever anything you're uncomfortable with, make sure to let me know. It's a completely separate conversation from anything we discuss during aftercare, so that neither of us is still affected by the scene."

Thatcher's gaze darkens at the mention of last night. "No, Ma'am. There wasn't anything I didn't like about last night. In fact, I look forward to exploring more."

"Very good—" Misha's signature knock on my door interrupts me. "Come in."

"Morning, moya tsaritsa." He nods a greeting to Thatcher, then winks at me. "Good night as well then, I see."

"*What* do you want?" I hiss, but he doesn't answer.

Getting the memo that he's not welcome for this discussion, Thatcher stands and straightens his shirt. "I'll, um…I'll just see myself out."

I don't miss the loaded look between the two men, and I know they'll be talking about our night later. Oh well. Misha knows about my proclivities just as I know about his, so the more advice he gives my boy toys, the better off I am.

The door is barely shut before Misha flops down where Thatcher was just sitting. "How was your night?"

"I believe you had something *you* needed to tell *me*?"

"Oh yes. Mr. Zadorov wanted to inform you that his son will be joining him later this month. Apparently, the boy is looking forward to, and I quote, 'finally laying eyes on his future missus.'"

I gag at the thought of doing anything with that asshole's son. "Never going to happen. I should kill them both just for the image in my mind. What else did you need?"

"That was it." He leans back, kicking his feet up on the table. "But I think *you* have lots to tell me."

"I should've known you just wanted to gossip. It was…great actually. He exceeded my expectations on all fronts and—"

"And you let him sleep with you? How many times does that make recently?"

"You're an asshole. *Yes,* he slept with me. So what? Sue me."

"I'm just messing with you, and you know it. I think it's good for you to have someone—"

The insinuation that Thatcher is my *someone* puts me on the defensive, and I sit up, giving Misha a glare that would bring lesser men to tears. "I do *not* have someone. It was a very long night, and he was a very good boy. That is *all*—"

He ignores me, like always, never intimidated by anything I do or say. "As I was saying…I think it's good for you to have someone right now. You've been stressed to the max with this transition, with no time off or outlet for your frustrations. Trust me, I know *exactly* how you're feeling. I hate the sentimental shit as much as you, but if I had a hot little toy living with me right now, I would be a much happier man."

"I guess you're right," I sigh, relaxing back into my chair.

"The timeline works out. He'll be starting his season around the time your schedule frees up enough for you to get to a club. I think it's good for both of you." He pauses and takes my hand. "Plus, he's Teddy's best friend, so he's already a target for our enemies. Your connection with him isn't putting him in any more danger than he would be in already."

I didn't even realize my subconscious was so concerned about Thatcher's safety, but he's right. That's one of the reasons I never have 24/7 arrangements in the first place. The more time someone spends with me, the more of a target they become. If anyone is putting Thatcher at risk, it's Teddy, not me. So why not take advantage of the perfect boy sleeping in the room next to mine? There's a built-in deadline for the relationship, and Misha's right, I could use the stress relief.

"Okay, moya sila. You have a point. Even a broken clock is right twice a day."

Misha grins. "Of course I do. One day, you'll learn that I'm always right. So how was he?"

Flashes of our night play through my head. I could spend half the day talking about it, but I don't have the time. Good thing Misha knows exactly what I mean when I say…

"He was a very good boy."

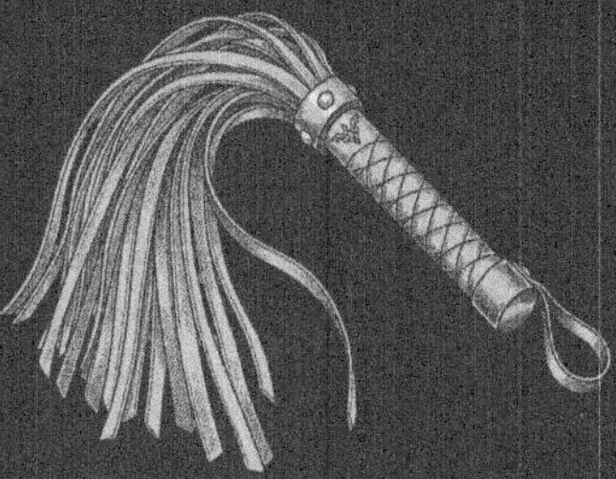

CHAPTER 22

Mila

"I'M NOT A huge fan of surprises, as I'm sure you've guessed, and I *promise* we could be doing more…stimulating activities right now."

Thatcher finally pauses from leading me excitedly down a corridor of the house I haven't spent much time in, and the heat in his eyes thrills me that I've succeeded in distracting him from his surprise plan. It's short-lived, though, and whatever he's planned must be *very* special to him, since it hasn't taken more than a passing glance lately to have him naked and on his knees for me.

"I know you aren't a fan of surprises, so I'm going to tell you what's behind that door before we go in, *but!*"

My glare speeds up his explanation of what's behind the door, although based on the raucous cheers, it's becoming clearer by the second. "You planned a party."

"Yes. No. Well, it's not really a party. The purpose isn't to party. It's game night. Uh, for the guys. And some of them who have wives and kids brought them as well. The vibes should be super chill, except for the number of people here. But the ballroom is huge, and—"

"Ballroom?"

"Yeah, you didn't see it on the plans?"

"No. And I feel pretty damn certain that a room labeled 'ballroom' would have caught my eye."

"Well, it wasn't labeled as a ballroom on the plans Ivan gave you. I think it said 'music room,' since that's what it was mainly being used for whenever that set of blueprints was drawn up. You had to notice how big the dimensions were, though, right? Most of the big country houses built around the same time as this one had ballrooms, even if they functioned in different roles throughout the years. My parents' Hamptons house has one, though I caused quite a bit of structural damage by turning it into an ice-skating rink one summer. The cooling units failed during a heat wave, and since it was on the third floor, everything below it flooded..."

"I'm both impressed by your knowledge of architecture and terrified that I now have to worry about you destroying property with fire *and* ice." He has the decency to look sheepish for a moment. "I suppose when I was reviewing the plans, I had, and still have, more pressing concerns than how big my ballroom is. Or the fact that I have a ballroom. Or a music room. Or an ice rink."

Thatcher's eyes sparkle, and I can see why he's never gotten into too much trouble, regardless of how much damage he's caused. It's highly unlikely that I'll fare much better disciplining him than his parents, teachers, or coaches ever did.

"No! No ice rinks on the third floor." Another huge cheer brings us back to the matter at hand, which is apparently hundreds of people here for...game night. "So tell me about game night."

He's excited enough about game night to forget to be sad about the ice rink, launching into what must be a practiced elevator pitch for getting me through those doors.

"Long story short, as I got to know these guys during my penetration into their ranks."

"Nowhere near a good enough reason to say penetration, and you know it."

"It became clear they needed a chance to get to know each other in a lower-stakes environment," he continues with a wink. "The gym is fine, but it's a lot of masculine ego, trying to lift heavier or run faster than each other. Movie night in the bunk wing is fun, but they fight over the movie, and inevitably, someone just wants to watch R-rated shit, and it devolves from there. Same problems with going out to the range."

"So you brought in some women and children, and what I'm assuming is a variety of games, to encourage healthy competition and deeper camaraderie."

"You fight harder for the man at your side if you've met his little girl."

That sounds like something my father would say, and Thatcher shrugs at my raised eyebrow. "One of the older guys told me that. I don't remember who."

My eyes roll so far back into my head that I can see my brainstem. "Yes, yes, Misha is very wise. So why were you so nervous to tell me what's going on in there? It didn't have to be a big secret."

"Well, you're not the most extroverted person around, you know. And honestly, it's been so hard to keep you off my co—"

"There you are! We've been waiting on you to cut the cake, and the kids are getting antsy as fuck in here." Misha saves Thatcher's life with his interruption, and we're shuffled into abject chaos that lasts ten seconds before I'm perceived. The respectful quiet rolls throughout the crowd like a wave, and once the far corners of

"So you're not a secret Bratva heir, used to all this scheming and plotting behind the scenes?"

"Nope, that was your brother, if you'll recall. Although I think he's been mostly useless in all the intrigue, at least the way Ellie tells it. He's taken to all the guns and violence much better than I ever will, though. Don't try to put a gun in my hand. Just let me work on getting people to like you."

"And wheedling out the ones who don't?"

"Always wheedling out the ones who don't." We clink our punch glasses together just as Misha pokes his head into our alcove.

"Moya tsaritsa, you won't want to miss this."

Thatcher's groan as his ball rolls uselessly across the felt of the pool table is pathetic and adorable, and he drops his head to the edge of the table in frustration. "I swear I've played before. I was not *this* bad. Are you sure the punch wasn't doctored?"

"One-hundred percent virgin punch, Sunshine," Misha jokes, goosing Thatcher as he heads for the exit. "Too many kids around tonight. No alcohol at all. Your lack of prowess with a stick and balls is all your own."

"Hey, you can ask Mila about my—"

"Absolutely not. None of that." No matter how many times I tell myself not to encourage him, I can't help but laugh. "Are you heading out, moya sila?"

"Well, as you can see, we've closed it down tonight." He gestures widely to the empty ballroom, and it's clear we were playing in our own little bubble and missed everyone else leaving. "I'll see you two kids in the morning. Daddy's tired."

Thatcher chuckles, but I don't dignify Misha with a response. Now that he's gone, the quiet of the room is magnified, and I can appreciate the man across from me who is *so fucking bad* at pool.

"Your hand-eye coordination is too good for you to be so bad at this," I tease, joining him at the far end of the table. He has a few options for his next move, but it's obvious his attention lies elsewhere.

"So you *do* think I have good hand-eye coordination?"

If I continue to roll my eyes at my current rate, they're going to get stuck. "Don't fish for compliments. I told you just the other day on the mat that you were improving."

"I can't help it. Nothing is as intoxicating as your praise. Every morsel I get, I savor."

Lining up my shot, I move things into position to give him a fighting chance of sinking at least *one* ball before we call it a night. "Do you find that I praise you too infrequently? Are you starving for morsels?"

"Not starving so much as fiending for an illicit substance. I've had enough, sure. But I want more, always."

His wrist is warm under my grasp as I stop his next shot. "Let me try to teach you *something*, at least, before we go to bed."

"We?"

"*I*. Before *I* go to bed. Now, pay attention. Your main problem is your stroke mechanics."

The effort it takes Thatcher to reel in whatever smart-ass comment he wants so badly to make is evident. When a twitch at the corner of his mouth threatens to undo all his hard work in composing himself, I take pity on him and continue.

"Don't think too hard about it. Show me your stance." He tenses again as I move behind him to adjust his hips. "Settle your weight slightly more forward. There you go. Now think of your arm like a pendulum. Don't think too much about the ball, just stay fluid as you lead the cue."

This time, his shot is true, and his whoop of joy is contagious. "I'm done. I'm quitting while I'm ahead. There's no way I'll be able to replicate that for an entire game, so I'm going out on top."

"That's fair," I concede as we finally leave the ballroom and head toward our bedrooms. "Still, watching you fail at something was a treat. You've improved so quickly in the training gym, you're an absolute menace in the pool—"

"I don't know about *menace*—"

"You gave someone a concussion!"

"Hey, *he* ran into *me.* It's not my fault that his skull was no match for mine. If your goal is to be truly impressed by my athletic prowess, what I really need is an ice rink. But since you don't want me to put one in—"

"Flood! *Flood* was the word you used to describe the aftermath of that venture at your parents' house."

"Yeah, well," he sighs as we approach our destination. "One day, maybe we can test how good you are on the ice, and see if I can impress you."

Thatcher looks as relaxed as I've ever seen him, as if tonight's success was a vindication, proof that he's *useful* and not just lazing about my house all day.

"I'll take you up on a skate one day. I might surprise you, lest you forget that I *did* grow up in Russia after all. But I wanted to thank you. For tonight. It's obvious you have a finger on the pulse of the men, especially the ones you pointed out that Misha pulled to take care of. It's made my life a lot easier to know that task is taken care of."

The shift in his posture as my praise lands is subtle, but he can't hide the blush that creeps up his neck and settles on his cheeks. I'm far fonder of that blush than I have any right to be, and the insidious pleasure of just how well he's been slotting into my life lately sinks its claws a little further into my spine. There's no time to analyze *that* feeling any more tonight, but I have plenty of time to indulge in pleasure of another kind. As Thatcher opens his mouth, presumably to say good night, I nod toward my door.

"I don't have an ice rink for you. But if you want to impress me…I could use a demonstration of another of your special talents."

His answering smile is blinding, every bit my solnyskho, and he practically jogs through the door as I open it.

"Yes, Ma'am."

CHAPTER 23

Thatcher

"YOU KNOW, I really haven't told anyone anything. About anyone or anything that goes on here, or in Thunder Bay, or anywhere...you know Teddy is my best friend, and other than that you're up there these days, big guy. My parents and I aren't close, and I don't have any siblings or cousins or anything. The team group chat has been full of pictures of beaches and babies, and I haven't contributed except to just like what the other guys send—"

"Thatcher." Misha stops abruptly in front of the massive structure that's the cause of my rambling. I can't think of a single reason he'd want to off me, but if this is the structure I'm thinking of... the guys call it "the barn," and it's apparently where all the torture happens. Or at least a lot of the torture and "target elimination."

None of the men talk about missions in detail when I'm around, and I'm not a part of any of the more specialized training they undertake. We've all bonded over blood, sweat, and tears in the gym, and I'd considered more than a few of them my friends, but I don't have the security clearance to know the ins and outs of the operation. Which is fine. I haven't heard any of the truly gory details from Teddy about what he does off the ice these days, and I don't need to know about Mila's and Misha's day jobs either.

"I'm sorry. Whatever it is, I didn't mean to. Please don't kill me—"

"Kill you? Is that why you're blabbering away a mile a minute? You think I brought you out here to kill you?"

His confusion *seems* genuine, and I'd like to think Misha is a good guy who would shoot straight with me at this point and not toy with me. "Uh, yeah. I thought this building must be the barn. Since it's out here away from the house, and I've never seen it before."

A heavy moment passes as he closes his eyes, pinches the bridge of his nose, and mutters to himself in Russian. It doesn't *seem* like he's going to kill me. But then why...

"If I were going to kill you, Thatcher Prescott...I would never just walk you out here...never mind. No, I'm not going to kill you. It's good to know that you're so loyal, though. We never doubted you."

"So this isn't the barn?"

"This isn't the barn. I guess technically it's a different kind of barn, but you have no need to know where the barn is or to access it, so don't worry about that. You'll likely never see it, regardless of how long you spend here. I'm actually only delivering you. I'm not staying. Although I can't wait to tell everyone that you almost pissed yourself thinking I was going to *kill* you, *Gospodi*!"

Still cursing, I assume, under his breath, he points at a steel door in the side of the structure and then stalks off toward the house, leaving me among the trees and without any more of a clue while I'm here. At least I'm not being killed. The door creaks open, and the cold, clean, *unmistakable* feeling of fresh ice hits me all at once as I step inside.

It's a full-size rink, lined and ready for play. The logo at center ice is one I don't recognize: two back-to-back "B"s...maybe that's a Bratva thing. A small section of bleachers and two benches make it fancier than some beer league arenas already. I can't imagine what this is doing out here.

"Surprise."

"Aaheep!" My high-pitched squeal is involuntary, and echoes through the building as Mila laughs. She's got her hands full, with a big Santa Claus-esque bag slung over one shoulder and two hockey sticks in her other hand.

"I didn't mean to scare you. I assumed you heard me coming."

"I was preoccupied trying to figure out what the hell this rink is doing in the middle of the woods behind your house. Especially when you told me I couldn't put in a rink...Wait. Did you do this for me?" *Does she feel something as remotely as monumental for me as what I think I feel for her?*

She gestures to one of the benches and plops her bag down before pulling out skates, pucks, helmets, and drill cones. "I can't say that I did, although that would have been quite the gesture. The timing just happened to work out. This building and the ice infrastructure were already here because Ivan's children used to skate when they were younger. Once they left the property, the ice was drained, but it was well maintained. It took a little plumbing work to have everything ready to go, but the refrigeration system was in good shape. Teddy suggested bringing the rink back online as another way for the men to bond and train."

"Wow. I had no idea this was back here or that you were working on it." *That's how easy it is for her to keep secrets from me…damn.*

"Well, like I said. Surprise! I was hoping you'd be willing to help me christen the ice. Nobody's been on it yet since completion."

She thrusts a pair of skates into my hands and rolls her eyes when I raise my eyebrows at her choice of words. "Are these *my* skates?"

"I had someone send them from New York. You left them in the Phantoms locker room at the end of the season. So what do you say? Want to run some drills?"

Two hours later, Mila shows no signs of slowing down. She wouldn't brag about being a strong skater without being able to back it up. That's just not who she is. But watching her speed around the ice with wild abandon, shrieking like a child whenever I beat her in a one-on-one skills challenge or feinted at the last moment to lead her straight into the boards…this is the most free I've ever seen her. For the first time, I'm able to imagine a tiny Mila, unburdened by the prospect of a legacy, just zooming around and having fun.

"Okay, I'm man enough to admit I need a break. There's no *way* your quads aren't on fire, too. Please? Just a short one."

She tosses me an electrolyte bottle and sits down heavily beside me on the bench. "My quads are fine, thanks. My stairmaster routine makes Misha's look like a walk in the park. You know my stamina isn't a problem. But we can take a rest if you need one to perform."

Her cheeky wink does nothing to quell the desire already burning at her tease, and she's damn right. I know exactly how strong her quads are. She can ride me for *hours* without complaining, and since I never have my hands for leverage, she has to do almost all the work most of the time. It was an adjustment at first, and the urge to let her relax and pillow princess for a while still pops up now and then. But she gets what she wants, and if what she wants is me on my back, well…

"You're an exceptional skater. I know this isn't news to you, since you're a professional and the captain of your team. But it's a bitch trying to keep up with you on the ice."

I *do* know that, but hearing it from her is better than any compliment any coach has ever given me. Impressing people has never been the only reason I skate, but it would be a lie to deny that a good portion of my self-worth has always been tied up in my on-ice success. A lifetime of having to find unique avenues of gaining love and affection will do that to you. The love and affection I've won may have come with challenges, like people who are only interested in you for fame, money, or your connections, but it's been enough to get me by. Until now.

"Thank you. We don't *have* to compete, you know. We could work together. Maybe try some ice dancing? I'd let you lead."

"You don't *let* me do anything, Thatcher Prescott," she huffs, but I can see the amusement she's hiding. "We can, however, try some duo drills next, if you'd like. I wouldn't mind you critiquing my edge work, too. It's always been my weakness, even when I was younger."

"Did Misha skate with you? In Russia?"

As always, the mention of her birth country darkens her mood, just a hair. It's a calculated risk to see if I can learn anything new about her today, and one I've learned the hard way isn't always worth it. Now, I'm apparently lucky enough to piggyback off her childlike joy, and she indulges me.

"He absolutely did *not.*" She cackles, blue eyes shining at the memory. "He was always athletic, but something about being on ice never *clicked* for him at all. Did he not seem grumpy bringing you out here? Weren't you surprised he didn't come inside?"

"I figured he knew you wanted to get me alone." Her exasperation fuels me, as always, and I delight in watching her fight another laugh. "I also suspected for a decent portion of the walk that he was bringing me out here to kill me."

"What? Why?" Now her gaze is suspicious, though no less beautiful. "What have you done?"

"Nothing, really! I just thought this was the barn all the guys talk about."

"You shouldn't even know the barn exists." She sighs, standing from the bench to stretch and lean against the boards. "It isn't your burden to bear."

Her tone is quiet and final, but I can't help trying to wheedle my way into her heart a tiny bit more.

"I'd still like to share it." My voice is barely more than a whisper, and for a while, the low hum of the refrigeration system is our only companion. She hops back down onto the ice, tired of talking for now.

That's okay.

I'll be right here when she's ready for more.

CHAPTER 24

Thatcher

THE PAST MONTH has been nothing but bliss. Well, I don't know if bliss is the right word—maybe more like kinky torture sex leading to the most explosive orgasms I've ever had in my life. Who would've thought I'd end up enjoying being dominated? I've heard of BDSM, but it always seemed like too much effort to learn more. As a rich, attractive athlete, sex has been thrown at me. It's always been so *easy.* Maybe that's why it was starting to lose its appeal.

Teddy lost interest in the puck bunnies early on, but he could never convince me that it wasn't one of the best perks of being a hockey player. Seeing him fall in love with Ellie changed things for me, though. I suppose I've finally grown up, but I would take coming home every day to the same woman who loves me unconditionally to a different girl every night. I crave a connection like theirs. Something *real.*

That's why I've taken a move right out of Teddy's playbook and planned a picnic date for Mila and me. It's cheesy as fuck, but there isn't a whole lot you can do when you're trapped on the estate grounds, and I've exhausted all my other options. I have to give it to whoever was here before, there are a ton of activities to bide your time, just nothing perfect for impressing your Bratva boss dominatrix lover. Something tells me that after a long day of training, she won't want to get in a fencing piste and spar. Especially not when her training involves *real* weapons.

We've enjoyed many chess matches and strolls through the library, and I think we both took each other by surprise with our knowledge of classic arts. Mila has always been full of surprises, though. It was obvious that she was special the first time we met. She barely said a word to me, barely looked in my direction, but she didn't have to. From the moment we locked eyes, I belonged to her.

The food the chef prepared is spread out on our blanket. Teddy told me to have several options, so I have pretty much everything I've ever seen her enjoy. It may be overkill, but I'll be leaving soon for preseason, and I want every precious moment I have with her to be special. I'm not sure what she has in mind for when I leave, but I hope we can continue to see each other.

"Did you bring the whole kitchen?"

Her teasing voice draws my attention, and a smiling Mila greets me in a black sports bra and biker shorts with her matching black hair braided down her back.

"I wanted you to have anything your heart desired." I stand and offer her a hand, as if she needs any help sitting on the pillow. She's more agile than I could ever dream of, even as a professional athlete. "I think I'm going to go for the chicken potpie. Teddy's grandma sent me the recipe, but I doubt this is as good. Something about an added ingredient of love or some shit."

Mila laughs and scoops some onto her plate. "I'll have to try it. I haven't had the pleasure of experiencing Muriel's, but I'm sure hers is leagues better indeed."

"You should invite her over soon if she's back in town. She's… well, she feels more like family than my own parents ever have."

"Maybe. This is delicious, by the way. Kurnik is one of my favorite dishes, but this is much creamier. I'm going to have this added to the rotation. Thank you."

"Don't thank me, thank Grandma Dubs. This is my favorite of her dishes, but honestly, everything she makes is incredible. Teddy's favorite is her roast."

"He's lucky he has such a large frame or..." She pats her belly for emphasis, causing me to almost choke as I chuckle around my fork, but at least it makes her laugh.

"Did he get his size from your father? His grandma is a tiny little thing, and his mom wasn't much taller."

"Oh, Father was a giant. He was the largest man I've ever known. That's where I get my height as well. Or so I've heard. I never actually knew my mother."

"I'm so sorry. You and your dad were close, though, right?"

Mila looks down at her plate and pushes her scraps around. "We were close enough. I didn't move in with him until I was fourteen. I lived with…extended family before then. He thought it would be safer for me in Russia, but…but I ultimately ended up in Thunder Bay."

"My parents pretty much pawned me off as well. They were older when they had me and had reached the point in life when they just wanted to retire and travel the world. Which they did… without me. I was left to the team of nannies to raise in their stead."

Mila raises a brow at me and hums. "Interesting."

"What's interesting?"

"Nothing…" she purrs, with a smug look on her face.

"*Tell me*!"

"Okay, okay." She chuckles. "It just makes more sense now why you enjoy our dynamic so much."

"What do you mean? How does that make more sense?"

"Well, you kinda have both mommy and daddy issues. You never had a loving, authoritative figure in your life, so it makes sense that your trauma presents itself in a way that would allow you to indulge in having one who pleases you. What I do to you is intense, sure, but at its core, I'm taking care of you. I'm pushing you in all the ways I *know* you'll enjoy, whether you think you will or not."

I sit in silence for a moment, letting her words resonate. At first, the thought of our sex having *anything* to do with my parents seems absurd, but the more I think about it, she might be on to something. "I guess that makes sense. I'll have to bring that up to my therapist next time I go. How should I word it? 'Hi, Dr. Fixme, I've been letting a woman tie me up, but I always have the *best* orgasms. Do you think that's because my mommy never spanked me as a child?'"

Mila spits out her water. "Jesus, Thatcher," she says, half coughing, half laughing. "Best orgasms you've ever had? Is that right?"

"No comparison." I wink. "Actually, that's something I wanted to talk to you about. I'll be leaving soon, and I know you have a shit ton on your plate right now, but, well…I don't want this to end. I was hoping we could continue to see each other."

"How would that work?" she asks, rolling her eyes. "Look, if it's the sex you want, I can find you another Domme in the city—"

"No!" I take her hand and squeeze even though I'm playing with fire. "Mila, I don't want someone else. I want you. Please. Let's just try? I can come here every chance I get, and I'm sure you'll have business in the city. You can just stop by my place. Or if you never want to do that, I can just come here every time."

Mila brings our hands to my lips and sticks out a finger. Locking eyes, I suck it into my mouth, swirling my tongue around it in the process.

"You're such a good boy for me..." She removes her hand and pulls my face to hers, kissing my brow. "We can try. I don't have much time to give, but I'll do what I can. I suppose if I'm going into the city anyway, it might as well be to meet you. You're so well-trained, after all."

"I'll make it worth your time, I promise."

And I will. I'll do whatever it takes, be at her beck and call. I'd live in her skin if she'd let me. I would absolutely move into the compound permanently. With her by my side, everything else can go fuck off. Even hockey. Because if I had to choose...Well, I don't need hockey. But I don't think I would survive without Mila.

CHAPTER 25

Mila

ZAKHAR ZADOROV IS officially number one on my list of people I want to kill, followed closely by his son, Oleg. Although with every passing moment, the boy is gaining on his father. I had completely forgotten about Misha's message several weeks back, having been caught up in work and… Thatcher. So I was blindsided when Zakhar walked into my office this morning with a younger, but somehow even more hideous, version of himself.

My schedule had been cleared for Zakhar and me to discuss the current import-export contracts between our families. Hours, he demanded. All for him to drop off his derpy protégé and leave, claiming a family emergency. He's not fooling anyone with that bullshit, but he's going to have a real emergency if his son doesn't stop trying to *fucking touch me*.

"No, I don't think involving the government would be the best plan of action," I snap, pulling my arm away from his grip *again*.

God, he's such a moron. As annoying as his father is, he's at least somewhat intelligent. The Zadorov Bratva may not be as successful as ours, but they're big enough in Russia. Otherwise,

I wouldn't be entertaining them at all. I'm starting to wonder if Zakhar is more interested in getting a foot in the Taranov door, or if he just wants to ensure his own empire continues. As it stands, the Zadorov Bratva is toast the minute they lower him into the ground. Unless he can produce another heir, that is. I'm certainly no stranger to random brothers popping up out of the woodwork.

Maybe it's best that Teddy took over after all because I'm going to lose my mind by the end of this tour.

"Oh, I love fencing. There's no need for so many pistes, though. Three is a bit excessive, don't you think? The staff and soldiers certainly don't need to use it, and as long as we have one, maybe two in case we have guests, I think that's fine. We can use the extra space for something more...luxurious? Perhaps a spa. A spa would be fantastic. Yes, I think one piste is enough and a spa."

I've had to listen to this man drone on about the changes he would make to the estate for what seems like an eternity, and we're only halfway finished. He's been critical about everything except the garish decor I still haven't gotten around to changing.

"Don't you think so, sweetheart?"

"I am *not* your fucking sweetheart," I hiss. "You may address me as Ms. Taranova or Mila, and if you ever insinuate our relationship is anything but professional again, you will be begging for your life at my feet."

He startles at my words, but he's lucky it's only that. His shock turns to anger, and he steps closer, crowding me in an attempt at intimidation. If he only knew how much restraint it's taking not to pull the knife from the inside of my sleeve and slice his neck, he would be running away as fast as his lazy, pampered ass could take him.

"My father isn't going to be pleased with your behavior today. Here I thought he had picked out a lovely Russian girl for me to marry, but—"

He pauses when I blurt out a laugh, but I can't help it. "You really think I'm going to marry *you*? Oleg, you're quite possibly the dumbest man I've ever met, and I'm more than certain your father feels the same way. But please do tell Zakhar that if he actually thought I would go through with this arrangement, he's as dense as you are."

Oleg turns as red as a tomato as his anger rises. "You're just a cold, ugly bitch, aren't you?"

A small part of me wishes he would try something, just so I would have an excuse to get rid of him. I raise a brow, smirking just to taunt him further...until a very familiar voice fills the air.

"Whoa, man! That's no way to talk to a lady." Thatcher walks up beside me and holds a hand out to Oleg. "You must be new. If I weren't leaving today, I'd give you a lesson on how to be a gentleman. You know, really make the girls go wild. Misha will help you, though. Just tell him Thatcher Prescott sent you," he finishes with a wink.

Fuck, not your name, solnyshko.

To my relief, Oleg doesn't do anything drastic and accepts his handshake. "Oleg. I was just leaving. Perhaps I'll see you again sometime, though. You seem...interesting."

"Hell yeah, bro! Tell Mila to let me know next time you're in town, and we'll party it up."

Oleg studies him for a moment as I weigh the probability of this putting Thatcher in danger versus the cost of starting a war with the Zadorovs. I'm leaning toward killing the guy right here and now to err on the side of safety, but my fear is gone when he gives the dopiest smile I've seen yet. If this oaf didn't have the IQ of a banana peel, I might need to be more careful, but there's no way he suspects anything between Thatcher and me. I'm just being paranoid.

Oleg says his goodbyes, and we watch as he *finally* leaves.

"Who was that asshole?" Thatcher asks when he's finally out of sight.

"Just a member of one of the Russian families I've been working with. Nothing for you to worry about." I turn and look at my handsome boy, tucking a loose strand of blond hair behind his ear. "What did you need?"

"Oh, I wanted to say goodbye before I left to go back to the city. Practice starts bright and early in the morning, and I need to get back to my condo to grab my new key before the office closes for the day."

Fuck, I forgot about him leaving. I've been so busy and…I think I didn't want to admit it was happening. "Ah yes, be very careful going home, then?"

"I'll be careful. Mila…" He stares into my eyes with an intensity such that I swear he must be looking for my soul, but he's searching for something he'll never find.

"Yes?"

"I'll…I'm going to miss you. I meant what I said the other day about us making things work. I'll do whatever it takes. You said you would try. Did you mean that?"

I pull the string of curly hair that keeps falling in his eyes. "Of course I will. You're welcome here anytime, and I'll always let you know if I'm coming into the city."

"You're welcome to stay with me anytime too. Our preseason games won't start for a while, so my weekends will be lighter for the next few weeks, if you want to come visit. I know it's not as safe as the compound, but I'm in the penthouse, and I'll add whatever security measures you need."

He's so pretty, shining in the summer sun like a star. I run both hands through his golden hair and pull his brow to mine. "I'll see what I can do, solnyshko."

He's so close I can feel his breath on my skin, and I can't stop myself from tasting him one last time before he leaves. I bridge the gap between us and bring my lips to his. He melts into our kiss, and I have to fight the urge to do the same. His arms wrap around me, deepening our embrace, and for once, I don't care. It's warm and safe and…nice. It's nice to have a beautiful man hold me in such a tender way. I could lose myself in him so easily. But I won't.

Pulling away, I break the kiss. "Drive safe, pretty boy. Text me when you get there."

He gives me one last peck on my cheek and walks away, leaving me alone for the first time today. My chest stings as I struggle to breathe. *What the fuck kind of reaction is this?* I'm not a sociopath. I feel *some* emotion. But I've never felt this.

It's been so nice having a live-in toy…that's it. I've had mind-blowing sex on tap for the past month, and this is just a visceral reaction to the fear of that going away. *But it doesn't have to go away.* At least not entirely.

We both said we would try to make things work. The compound is obviously an option, but I haven't been to the city in months. His condo is as safe as any could be. It was adorable of him to offer to do it himself. Still, after the fiasco with Teddy's condo being broken into earlier this year, I went ahead and had top-of-the-line security measures installed.

This doesn't have anything to do with wanting to see how Thatcher lives. I'm just due for a change of scenery. I think all the men here would agree that everything goes a *lot* more smoothly when I'm able to let out my stress properly. Plus, it's perfectly fine to have a favorite toy. With my mind made up, I pull out my phone and shoot a message to Misha.

ME: Clear my schedule for the next few weekends.

CHAPTER 26

Thatcher

THE LOCKER ROOM is already buzzing by the time I make my way inside. Today's practice felt incredible, and if it wasn't for Coach threatening my balls, I don't know when I would've gone home. The start of every season feels this way, as if something inside me locks into place the moment my skates touch the ice. This year is no exception. I was afraid it wouldn't be the same without Teddy, but there's another person in my heart now, and she's only an hour's drive away.

Bubba skates to his seat beside me and slaps my shoulder, pulling me from my memories of this summer. "You were killing it out there today, Sunshine. Did you spend the whole offseason on the ice?"

No, more like training with Russian ninjas. Misha's torture paid off, though. I'm usually winded after the offseason break, but I feel incredible today. I could've gone for hours. Don't get me wrong, I'm typically one step ahead of everyone, and I work my ass off to be able to too…there's a reason I'm the captain. But this year, I was skating circles around our best defenseman. Nobody could keep up with me, and with the new power behind my shots, our goalie didn't stand a chance.

"Just some agility work here and there. If you didn't spend all summer bumming around in Jamaica, you'd be good too."

"Well, keep it up. If you play like this all season, we might actually have a shot of making it past the first round of playoffs next year."

Toodles rolls in on the other side of me and flops into his seat. "Yeah, if Coach can find another goalie. I think you've scared Gusgus away from hockey for good. I don't even think Cuddles could've stopped your shots today."

"I guess we'll see when we play Thunder Bay this year."

For once, the thought of losing Teddy, or Cuddles as the team calls him, doesn't make me so sad. The second half of last season was rough after he left. It's taken some time, but I'm finally happy for him after what he found in Thunder Bay. *Love.* Maybe *that's* why I'm not upset anymore. Maybe I've found that too.

"Are you telling us you actually worked out this summer and didn't party 24/7 the whole break like you always do?" Milton asks, plopping down on his seat on the other side of me.

This was a very different summer indeed. The thought of Mila brings a smile to my face, and the boys immediately clock in on it. "Whoa, what's got you lighting up like that? Is Thatcher Prescott in *love*?"

A collection of oohs and aahs fills the room as everyone's attention homes in on me.

"Damn, did you finally decide to keep one of your puck bunnies?" Bubba says, hopping around on his skates like a rabbit, and before long, there's a tango line of half-naked assholes following him.

"You're lucky we need you, or I would hope you fall and break a leg." I laugh. "And no, I didn't fall in love with any puck bunnies."

There, not a lie. That'll get them off my back.

Wrong. Milton clocks onto it right away. "He said that he didn't fall in love with any 'puck bunnies.' Our sunshine is so totally gone!"

"Practiced over the summer, fell in love...Oh, you *have* to tell us about your break."

It feels fucking *good* to have the guys interested in what I did even though I can't really tell them. One, they would never believe me in the first place, and two, I'm pretty sure Mila would kill me.

"Oh, same ole, same ole...nothing—"

A choir of insults and begging interrupts my lie.

"Bullshit."

"You're such a fucking liar."

"Pleassseeee."

"Tell us! Tell us! Tell us!"

Maybe it wouldn't be so bad to be punished by Mila after all...

"Okay, okay, I'll tell you." I pause while the entire team surrounds me like it's story time in elementary school.

"So after everyone left practice for the summer, I got a call that my condo had caught fire and was completely uninhabitable." *I leave out the part about how my parents were so pissed about the fire that they forbade me from staying at any of their other properties, including the Hamptons, where I typically stay for the offseason.* "I was in a hotel for a night, but then a...friend connected me with some family that has a place Upstate. Turns out it was a Mafia compound. I spent the summer training with their best soldiers and ended up in a...relationship...with their very kinky lady boss."

The team sits quietly, side-eyeing each other before Milton speaks up. "So…you spent the summer on mushrooms? Different from your typical high, but I respect it."

Oh well, I didn't think they would believe it in the first place. I can figure out something else to get some Mila punishment.

"Whatever, man. At least I didn't have to spend my break hotter than Satan's asshole surrounded by screaming kids in a theme park."

Milton smiles. "It wasn't as bad as I thought it would be. Hot as hell. But the kids had a blast, and we brought the nanny so the wife and I were able to get some alone time too."

"Well, since you were so concerned with Jamaica, I'll have you know I spent most of the time working on cardio. And if I'm lucky, I'll see the results of all my hard work in nine months or so," Bubba says with a wink. "Hopefully, I'll be needing all of your kiddo tips and tricks soon, Milton."

Kids. The thought of having them one day has crossed my mind, but I've never felt particularly compelled either way. I couldn't be a worse parent than my own. Hell, just hiring a nanny to take care of them 90 percent of the time instead of 100 would be better.

Mila crosses my mind again, as she does so often. *I wonder if she wants children.* If she did want them, I would absolutely oblige her, but something tells me she's not dying to be a mother, and I'm fine with that. She always pulls off me just in time, and it wouldn't be like her to take risks, so she's probably on birth control. *We should probably have that conversation at some point.* She's actually the only woman I've ever fucked without a condom. I've been so wrapped up in her intensity that my usual no-exceptions policy went out the window immediately.

The thought of screaming kids does the trick. Wow, if that's what just a thought does, I definitely don't think I'm leaning toward fatherhood. I can be Teddy and Ellie's kids' funcle. *If I ended up with Mila, I would be their actual uncle.*

The boys drone on about how everyone's break went, but all I can think about is my own. It was by far the best summer of my life and ten times better than any of their holidays. Mila changed me in such a way that I know I'll never be the same.

My phone buzzes with a text notification, and I pull it out of my bag to find a message from the goddess herself, as if I summoned her.

> **MILA:** Are you still free this weekend? I was thinking of coming into the city.

I've barely read the message when I send back a resounding yes.

This is the first time I can remember not staying to lock up, but I have shit to do today. I need to make sure my condo is up to par for a queen. The decor should be fine. I have good taste. It's the...other things I need to take care of. I shoot Misha a text requesting a list of sex toys and equipment, then grab my things.

"Alright, Co-captain. Closing up is on you today," I say, patting Bubba on the shoulder.

It's all I can do not to skip out of the room whistling love songs, but what can I say? I'm smitten.

"See, I told you he was in love," Milton yells out as I make my way to the door. "You'd better introduce us soon!"

"Maybe one day. Trust me, you guys aren't ready for her."

CHAPTER 27

Mila

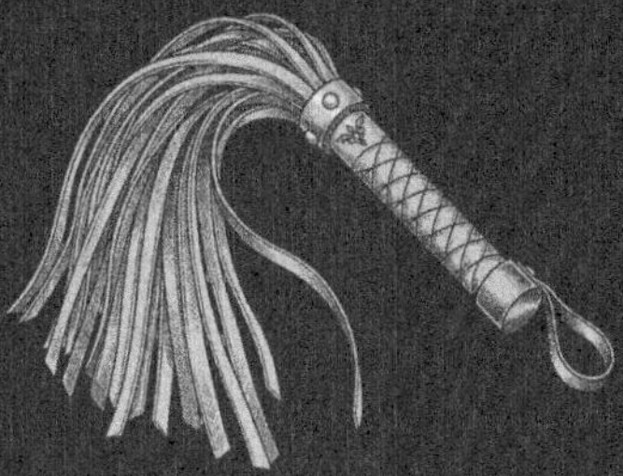

IF YOU TOLD past Mila that present Mila would be clearing her weekends and traveling even a mile for dick, she would've laughed in your face. *Or more likely, shot you.* My past partners were on *my* schedule and came to me in whatever club I was near at the time. They had to fly, whether it was across the country or an ocean, if they wanted the privilege of my presence.

And now, look at me.

Coming into the city on the weekend earlier than planned to surprise Thatcher after practice and release some of the frustration that's been steadily building since he left. The fucking Zadorovs are turning into an even bigger pain in the ass than I thought, and I refuse to drag Ivan away from his retirement any more often than I have to. Besides, I'm the boss, and I need to figure this shit out on my own.

Based on his tracker, Thatcher should be here any minute, and I have everything set up just the way I like it. After we discussed the potential to explore more, even after he moved out, I was pleased with his willingness to keep trying new things. Today should open new levels of play if he enjoys himself.

As soon as he makes it to the elevator, I move myself into position, perched on the kitchen counter with one leg crossed over the other. The stiletto of my heel is thin, and I imagine I paint quite a picture.

This is my favorite playsuit, covering every inch of my skin up to my neck. It's custom, high-quality latex that shows off every dip and curve of my body as intended. The thigh-high boots and wrist-length gloves are similarly tight, and the overall effect is as if Catwoman were a Domme. A slim leather mask completes my look. *That, and the flogger in my hand.*

"Okay, there's plenty of time to get everything. I'll shower super quick, run to the hardware store—ah!"

He screams as his phone flies out of his hand and across the room, coming to rest near where I'm perched. Once he realizes it's me, a wide grin splits his face, and he locks the door before bounding into the kitchen.

"Hey! I had no idea by this weekend you meant *now*. The place is nice and clean, but I didn't have time to get all the things Misha said you'd wa—"

My gloved finger silences his excited monologue, and once he stops speaking, he finally seems to take in what I'm wearing. I can't help but smirk as his pupils dilate, eyes roaming down to my hips but keeping his head perfectly still under my finger.

"Go shower. Put all your dirty clothes and hockey things where they go, and trim everything nice and neat for me, just how I like it. Make sure *everything* is very clean for my inspection. Then wait for me like I taught you."

"Yes, Ma'am," he replies, like the good boy he is, and heads toward the bathroom. His penthouse is nice, and I had no problems with security since he added me to his visitors list just as he promised. The renovation after the fire must have been seamless because there's no evidence at all that flames, smoke, or water ever touched the place.

In the limited time we had together, Thatcher was a quick learner, even if my basic expectations and preferences for how he presents for our scenes are simple. Hairless balls, a short-cut pubic area, and no hair anywhere near his asshole. How he achieves this is up to him, although I did tell him a quick, professional wax was likely the easiest route.

Once the shower stops, I give him a few minutes, then enter the bedroom to find him just as I asked. Tossing my gloves aside for now, I take him in. He's beautiful, kneeling for me with his palms up on his thighs, eyes down.

"Hello, solnyshko. Have any of your preferences or limits changed since we last spoke about them?"

"No, Ma'am."

"Are you here to please me as I see fit and be my good little toy today?" His abs clench at the first hint of degradation. *We're going to have so much fun.*

"Yes, Ma'am."

"Very well. Rise onto your knees and lace your fingers behind your head." He does as I ask immediately, keeping his eyes down as I trail my bare fingers across his pecs, down his abs, and past his bobbing cock to play with the soft hair on his thighs. He's trimmed everything almost bare, and if that's his preference, I have no objection. I spend a few long minutes tracing his Adonis belt before I use the stiletto tip of my nail to collect the bead of precum at his tip.

"Open." He does as I command immediately, swirling his tongue around my fingertip and tasting himself. "Very good. Now, on your elbows. Knees as wide as they can go."

This position is one I wasn't sure he would enjoy right away, since ass up isn't something most men ever experience or think about. Having a hole bared to be looked at, touched, and *played with* is often a female-only consideration. For him to allow me to see how his cock bobs beneath him, heavy balls at my mercy, and prostate begging to be stimulated…it's heady to have him submit like this.

Trailing my nails up and down the backs of his thighs, I use my knees to spread his just a little more. "Tsk, tsk, Thatcher. You're probably more flexible than I am. I've seen you do your hockey stretches. Spread wider for me…*there you go.*"

Pushing my hips flush with his, I reach forward and underneath him to tease his nipples before trailing down once more. Ignoring his cock, I instead palm his balls, forcing a whine from him as I roll them gently in my hand.

"I believe you're aware of my expectations for your silence during your inspections, aren't you, toy?"

"Yes, Ma'am."

"Hmm…I'm not convinced, given the fact that you whined like a desperate slut when I barely touched you. Be quiet for me so I don't have to punish you for breaking my focus." My thumb is teasing his perineum now, and he's quiet, but his glutes are clenched with the effort to stay still. It's the only one of my fingers not to have my standard sharp nails, instead plain and polish free. When Misha saw me for the first time after my most recent appointment, he doubled over laughing and had to walk away to recover.

"This is a very well-manicured taint. You followed my directions well. Did you get waxed?"

"Yes, Ma'am."

"Do you like being hairless?"

"Yes, Ma'am."

"I like it, too. Would you enjoy it if I waxed you from now on?" It's not something I've ever done for a submissive, but I wax my own legs, so I'm sure I could learn.

"Yes, Ma'am."

"I'll work on that. In the meantime, continue to manage this on your own. But you've done very well." A harsh intake of breath is his only response to my thumb pressing down hard on his asshole, somewhere he's never been touched. He's open to it, but that will be a longer road if we choose to take it.

"Now, while you're in this position, we have something to discuss, and I'm sure you know what it is. I counted three candles today as I was inspecting your home, and I believe I made it *very* clear that you weren't allowed to have candles anymore. Do you agree?"

"Yes, Ma'am."

"And are you aware of what your punishment is?"

"Yes, Ma'am."

"Very well. You'll receive ten strikes with my bare hand for disobeying me. Count them silently and say thank you when I'm finished, and tell me how your behavior is going to improve moving forward."

"Yes, Ma'am."

I give him two strikes with ample recovery time, using the same pressure as during our test run, then move quickly into more forceful territory. By my tenth spank, both of his cheeks are a lovely shade of pink.

"Thank you, Ma'am. I'll get rid of all my candles. I'm sorry I didn't follow through with our agreement." He sounds contrite enough, although I doubt this will be the only opportunity I have to punish Thatcher over the course of our arrangement.

"You're forgiven, solnyshko. Now, I think it's high time for you to meet my flogger."

CHAPTER 28

Thatcher

"LOOK AT HOW desperate you are for me, solnyshko. You want me so badly, don't you?"

"Yes, Ma'am."

And *fuck,* I do. Every atom of my world has narrowed to Mila. I'm strung up by my wrists to a hook she must have had installed in the ceiling, and even though she's probably only had me here for ten minutes, I'm as relaxed as I've ever been. Her flogger feels nothing like I expected, less pain and more pure, heavy sensation. The rhythmic thudding of her pattern has become more pronounced than the beat of my own heart, and I swear I can feel every impact sending more blood flowing to my cock.

Everything's faded away except her. The excitement of getting back onto the ice, the subtle black cloud of melancholy that's lived here alone with me since I left the compound…gone. Nothing but warmth on my back and thighs, scratches on my abs from her nails, and an ache that I'm not sure I'll be able to take for much longer in my balls. A long exhale is the only way I can think of to try to relax back into the blows, forcing myself to ignore my need for release.

"You're making too much noise. Don't make me second-guess your reward. You've been so good this evening. Control yourself."

Fuck. I didn't mean to whine. I just…it's all too much. The rhythm of the flogger finally stops again, and the vision who's been haunting my dreams circles to face me.

"One day, I'll get you nice and pink on both sides. Would you like that? You might find out you like a little pain on your cock." She punctuates her statement with a slap to my weeping erection, and I barely rein in my whimper as the pain travels up my spine and melds with the warmth still spreading from the flogger.

"Yes, Ma'am," I grit out, barely able to keep my eyes open to enjoy her curves, poured into her bodysuit and taunting me as I dangle here.

"Good boy," she purrs. "You've taken my hand and my flogger tonight without a single complaint. Did you enjoy them?"

"Yes, Ma'am."

"Would you like to fuck me now? Do you think you've earned it?"

"Yes. Please, Ma'am. I've been so good. I *need* to fuck you. Please. *Please.*"

"Mmm, you beg so prettily for me, sweet boy. Alright. I think you've earned it. I have a special treat planned for you."

She backs away, but doesn't move to release me, and I'm not sure how she plans to make this position work for us. *Not my problem. Mila is in charge and will take care of everything.* I float back toward reality when I notice that she's slowly unzipping her outfit, starting at the neck and revealing more and more of the body that couldn't be more beautiful if it was carved from marble.

Muscle, her rounded shoulders wide and framing her perfect breasts…her abs that aren't defined but solid, the dark curls I'd stay buried in if she'd let me. She was bare underneath, and when she removes her boots and pulls her legs free, she's gloriously exposed.

My dick, still so excited at any morsel of attention from her, twitches when she presses her abdomen flush to mine, my length straining toward her breasts between us.

"You don't even care if you get to fuck me, do you? I mean, sure, you want to. You enjoy it. But if I never let you fuck me again, you'd be right here, begging me to flog you and give this pathetic little cock any attention at all. Wouldn't you?"

It's impossible to focus as she trails her nails through the sheen of sweat I'm covered in, but I knew the answer to her question before she even asked it.

"Yes, Ma'am."

"Mmm, that's my *good fucking boy.* I believe you. And I've been craving something I haven't had for years. I'm going to lower your chain from the ceiling, just enough for you to be on your knees. Let me know when you're comfy."

My hands are still above my head, but she relaxes the tension as promised until I'm comfy on my knees. My shoulders are less taut, but I'm still completely at her mercy. After she ensures I'm right where she wants me, I'm forced back onto my heels with the force of a kiss that takes me by surprise.

Even though I'm more used to keeping my hands to myself than when we started, my palms itch to touch her. To feel her smooth skin, grip her hips as she rides me…

"You've been so good. Now prove you've got the stamina I deserve and fuck me from behind."

Black spots cloud my vision as the goddess I've worshipped turns and drops to her hands and knees, backing up toward my thighs. *Oh fuck.* She drops her cheek to the floor and reaches back, spreading her lips to help me find my way inside. I take too long, apparently, mouth watering at the sight of her wetness, because she wiggles her hips and admonishes me.

"Thatcher! Don't make me wait. You'll have to watch me make myself come if you don't—"

I surge forward, afraid to wait another second and risk my chance to be in this perfect fucking cunt. Every time, every *goddamn* time, regardless of how far into space I've floated, it feels like coming home.

"Yes, that's so good. You're so good for me, solnyshko. So deep for me like this."

She's working her own clit, and I hope this angle is doing as much for her as it is for me because I'm not going to make it. Even without being able to grip her hips and drive into her, this is the first time I've ever seen her ass bounce back on me, and I'm about to embarrass myself. No amount of distraction will pull me back from the edge.

"Ma'am, I—"

I can't help the anguished wail that escapes me as she scoots away, ruining what was going to be an explosive orgasm. She stops just beyond the reach of my dick, and I swear a tooth cracks as I clamp down and try not to come.

"You're not getting off that easily. Do you really think I deserve to be fucked for five strokes?"

"No, Ma'am, but I—"

"I don't care. Do whatever you need to do, but do *not* come until I give you permission. I plan to enjoy your cock for a while yet."

The following minutes, or hours, pass in a similar daze...Mila teasing and giving me more or less time in her perfect warmth before denying me, whether I was on the edge or not. She doesn't deny herself at all, coming three times at least, based on the telltale vise grip of her release, testing the bounds of my self-control.

Technically, if I played this right, I could come before she even knew it was happening. If I kept an unbothered rhythm and didn't show my intention...

"Don't even fucking think about it. Toys don't get to decide when they come, and they don't fucking trick their way into orgasms. Be better. Do you understand?"

"Yes, Ma'am. I'm sorry."

She's even worse now, more torturous, displaying herself for me as lewdly as possible to ensure I'm overstimulated. The ache deep in my core feels almost unbearable, but I continue, pounding her relentlessly every time she backs up and allows me to.

Finally, she's had enough, and her permission transforms her from my damnation to my salvation as she spasms around me one last time.

"Come for me. Come for me now, Thatcher."

Thank fuck for that. With a roar, I push myself as deep inside her as I can, the familiar endorphin rush wrapping around me like a warm blanket as the entirety of the evening breaks like water from a dam. Within a few breaths, Mila's lips are on mine again, a languid, appreciative kiss that I want to taste every day for eternity.

"Very few people have ever had that privilege. I hope you know how lucky you are. Now, let me get you down, and we can take a bath."

Hissing as the lukewarm water hits my sensitive skin, I try to relax. The drop I now know to expect isn't the same this time. I feel drowsy but more aware of my surroundings. Mila seems to sense that I'm not feeling chatty, though, and gathers my snacks and electrolyte water before joining me quietly in the bath.

"I won't sit behind you today, since you're sensitive," she explains, facing me and scooting as close as she can to feed me a cracker with meat and cheese. "But I do have a cream that will help once we get out. If you feel like it. Otherwise, we can just sleep."

"I'll take your hands on me any chance I can get." She laughs, but I don't, and when she notices the serious look on my face, she simply hums and feeds me a grape. "How do you have a cream for after you beat the shit out of someone? Do you search like flogger cream online? Is there a dominatrix essentials shop?"

She laughs again, a full, throaty thing that makes her throw her head back, and it does more to soothe me after our session than a million baths or snacks ever could.

"There actually are a number of really excellent sites these days, although when I was starting this journey, the internet wasn't quite so readily available or advanced. Most of my knowledge and product references come from people who taught me, almost always at clubs or workshops. It was mostly word of mouth then, a friend of a friend would send you somewhere, or—"

"Clubs? In real life? I thought those were just in books and movies."

Based on her raised brow, I'll be getting spanked again for interrupting, but I don't even care. Maybe I'm a bit of a brat. And she just glossed over the word clubs as if it was common knowledge.

"Yes, clubs. As I said, mostly word of mouth. The ones that are worth going to have high standards for membership, and it's often a cost barrier for people just looking for a thrill. Of course, having money doesn't mean someone can play well with others or have a moral code. That's what background checks and stringent recommendation requirements are for."

She's fully captured my interest now, and even when we get out of the bath, I keep asking questions. It's distracting me from the soreness from the flogger, even as her gentle hands applying the cream threatens to put me to sleep.

"So there isn't necessarily one that offers everything?"

"No, it really just depends. Some are much more geared toward people who want to share or find swaps. Others are more so for things that can't be as easily organized without the help of the club management like orgies, hunter/prey parties, gloryholes, reverse gloryholes, and dark rooms. Things like that."

"Dark rooms?" I groan as she rubs into my instep, having finished her bruise cream application and treating me to a full-body massage.

"Basically an orgy in the dark. You can't see anything, so everyone operates on feeling alone to grope, penetrate, etc. Ideally, you leave never having seen who you sucked or fucked."

"Are those the clubs you prefer?"

"You know me well enough to know the dark room is a huge no from me. The places I enjoy certainly feature things like that from time to time, but I tend to enjoy bondage demonstrations, themed rooms for private play, exhibition areas, and places where submissives or pets can just exist as themselves."

"What do you mean?" I've flipped over, and after a hard week of practice, her strong hands on my quads are therapeutic and heavenly.

"One club in London is just a fine dining establishment with multiple Michelin stars. People can bring their submissives and have them eat nude and on the floor, or nude in their lap. Masters can leash their pets and bring their dog bowls to eat out of while enjoying good conversation, food, and wine. There's no intercourse allowed at all."

"Hmm...ugh, that feels good. You're a saint."

"Not sure I've ever heard that one before." She laughs. "Demon, certainly. Succubus, a time or two."

By the time she pulls a blanket over both of us, I'm almost asleep, but intrigued.

"What would you do with me in a club?"

She thinks for a long moment before answering. "It would depend on what you were comfortable with, solnyshko. I could string you up with more intricate patterns than before and use you as a mannequin for a Shibari workshop. I could edge you to within an inch of your life and let everyone watch you struggle and sob for me."

"Hmm..." She's playing with my hair, and I'm drifting fast.

"Or I could leash you and display you but not let anyone touch you. Just parade you around like my little toy, because you are. *Mine.*"

I try to reply, but I'm already halfway into dreamland, and I'm not sure if I heard her right, anyway. But if I did, that'd be alright with me.

She can do anything she wants to me if I'm hers.

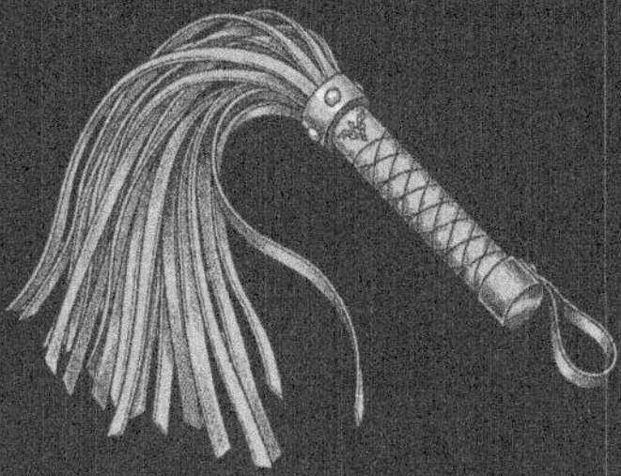

CHAPTER 29
Mila

IT'S ALMOST UNFATHOMABLE to me that Thatcher's never been to a sex club before. I know many high rollers who value the discretion that the clubs provide, but I assumed he wouldn't care about privacy. Professional athletes can be annoyingly flashy, always happy to show off how many women they have hanging on their arms.

If he wasn't so fucking adorable, I would have slapped the blush off his face when I asked about going to a sex club, and he thought we were going to see strippers. And by blush, I mean he actually blushed at the thought that I would take him to look at naked women. He turned completely maroon when I corrected him, and I couldn't help but laugh. I informed him that there will in fact be women *and men* in varying degrees of undress. But that they won't be dancing, they'll be fucking.

He's been equal parts excited and nervous about it, and it's amusing to watch him flip between the two. It makes me think back to my first time going to a sex club. I was only seventeen and entirely too young to be there, but Misha convinced me to get a fake ID and sneak in with him. I really have Misha to thank for my ability to enjoy sex at all. After the…incident, I vowed celibacy, but he swore I needed to see something first. There was a special exhibition that night by a popular dominatrix, stage name Miss X. He found a flyer for one of the older soldiers in the bunkers and, after a quick Google search, determined that the Domme lifestyle was well-suited for me. And he wasn't wrong.

I was in awe of the young dominatrix the whole time. One performance was all it took to convince me, and the two of us started sneaking in more frequently. It didn't take long for Misha to buy into the kink life as well. We're basically the same person, so it was no surprise to me how much he enjoyed being a Dom. We were years away from being old enough to become members, so to help our ruse, we joined as a married couple. We had a fake marriage certificate and everything. Being a Bratva heiress does have its perks from time to time.

Over the years, our preferences morphed. I prefer to have scheduled meetings with my toys. I don't mind repeats, but anonymous encounters are also thrilling. The club I normally frequent in New York has an incredible anonymous screening process, and they've matched me with some of the most experienced submissives I've encountered. We aren't going there tonight, though. This is a new club to me that came highly recommended by some of the friends I've made in the kink community.

Rendezvous Too opened several years ago and quickly became the top club in New York City. Its offerings are…unique. It has the basics, of course, but from what I've heard, they do an outstanding job of keeping things fresh and staying on top of trends. Last month, they had an Olympic village experience in honor of the games. And before that, an immersive *Titanic* experience. Literally immersive. I heard the lower level's pool was used to simulate the sinking, perfect for anyone with a waterboarding kink. This month's special is femdom, which is relatively tame but perfect for Thatcher's first visit.

Our driver lets us out at the front door, and I take Thatcher's hand. "Are you ready?"

"Are you kidding me? I didn't even know these things existed. Of course I'm ready!" he yelps.

Alright, he's flipped back to excited. That's good.

"I'm excited too. I haven't been here before, and I hear wonderful things—"

"Ooo, are you trying to spoil me?"

"Always, solnyshko." I cup his face, gently at first, then apply pressure with my fingernail, just barely not breaking the skin. "But *do not* interrupt me again. Is that clear?"

"Yes, Ma'am," he says, eyes darkening with lust.

I'm tempted to get back in the car and return to his condo so I can have my boy all to myself. But a bigger part of me wants to share this part of my life with him. Whatever this is between us, I want him to know exactly what he's getting into.

Looping my arm with his, we head to the VIP entrance to check in. As soon as our credentials are validated, a receptionist hands us a brochure with a map of the building and tonight's events, then begins her spiel as she leads us down a hall to a pair of delicate french doors.

"We're about to step into the main auditorium. The standard entrance goes through the bar and lounge first, but VIPs come straight here." She opens the door, pausing for a moment to let us take everything in. And it's a good thing she does.

I've never seen anything like this. The grand auditorium is massive, but it feels intimate as well. They've combined modern style and Art Deco accents with incredible taste. *Maybe I should hire their interior designer.* Metallics, trendy wallpaper, and neutrals blend, with a massive chandelier tying it all together. The auditorium is open to at least five or six stories, and each floor has a view of the stage.

"Wow…" I glance at Thatcher to see him just as awed as I am. "This is *not* what I imagined when you said sex club."

"They aren't all like this, remember? I'm spoiling you tonight."

The receptionist giggles. "Our owners wanted to do something really special with this place."

"Are each of the floors themed?" I ask, unfolding my map.

"Yes of course. Floors two through eight are open to the main auditorium to give an all-inclusive feel. These will be our more popular themes: exhibitionism, bondage, wax play, impact play, group activities, sensory deprivation chambers, and some medfet suites. The ninth through twelfth floors are reserved for primal play, each boasting a different rotating theme. And then thirteen through fifteen are reserved for our elite members."

"And does the chandelier not block the view of the upper floors?"

"Oh, that can be raised and lowered. It's a huge hit for our Phantom nights."

"Phantom nights?" Thatcher puffs his chest, no doubt thinking she means his hockey team, the New York Phantoms.

"*Phantom of the Opera*. The owners are huge fans. At least once a month, they do a spicy rendition of the play, and you never know which man Christine is going to pick. Sometimes it's Raoul. Sometimes it's the Phantom. My personal favorite is when she picks both," she says with a wink.

"Hell yeah!" Thatcher waggles his eyebrows suggestively before leaning in to whisper in my ear. "Can you imagine having two of me to deal with?"

Our tour guide gives us a moment to imagine that nightmare scenario before continuing. "Where would you like to start? Are there any floors that interest you more than the others? Or we can hit them all. The show here starts in thirty minutes if you'd like to wait and watch on the ground floor—"

"Mila?"

A familiar voice cuts off the lady. I turn to confirm, but I would recognize my old friend anywhere. "Riley Lemons? What are you doing here all the way from California?"

"I'm performing tonight!" He smiles, then turns to the receptionist. "That's actually why I came over here. My partner isn't going to make it in time for the show."

"It's about to start! How are we supposed to find someone in *thirty minutes*?" The panic in the poor lady's eyes is stressing *me* out.

Riley looks from me to the lady, then slowly back to me. "Mila? I know good and well you aren't afraid to put on a show. What do you say? Wanna give it a go?"

I freeze, now experiencing a stress of my own. If Thatcher wasn't here, I would probably consider it. He's right, I'm no stranger to exhibitionism and Riley and I work wonderfully together. But…

"I can't tonight. This is my first time coming here—"

"Oh, we don't mind at all if you'd like to fill in," the receptionist interrupts.

"And I'm here with my friend." I cut my eyes to Thatcher, but to my surprise, he doesn't look upset at all.

"Do it! I'd love to watch. I mean, if I were going to watch anyone perform, it would be you! Be spontaneous, remember?"

"Yeah, spontaneous!" Riley seconds.

I glance between the three people, noting their expressions. Hope from the lady, excitement from Riley, and…interest from Thatcher. Well, I already have on my sexiest lingerie, and the stage lighting is perfect.

"Okay," I sigh. "I'll do it."

I can't help but notice, as I leave Thatcher behind and follow Riley backstage, that the excitement that's always palpable before I perform is missing. Instead, all I feel is unease. And all I can think about is my solnyshko.

CHAPTER 30
Thatcher

"PLEASE WELCOME TO the stage, a very special guest…*Miss M!*" The emcee doesn't have to try very hard to rile up the audience, and more people pile into the room by the minute to watch.

Mila slinks onto the stage and scowls at the audience, already projecting a commanding aura and making it clear that she thinks she's better than every single one of them. And she is. In my eyes, at least. More beautiful, more deadly, more…everything. Just more.

"She's here visiting for the evening and has graciously agreed to present with her slave."

Well, he's not her slave anymore, but I guess they have to explain their relationship.

"This useless waif is *not* my slave," Mila growls. It makes sense, so that people in the back of the room can hear, but it's still a disconnect to see her dressed like a sex goddess with a pop star mic on. "He's here because he thinks he can give me an ounce of pleasure. I'm not convinced, but I plan to try my best to torture him until we find out."

With a sharp tug on the end of the leash I now see she's holding, Riley crawls onto the stage behind her. His head is down, and he's naked except for a studded collar with a tag hanging in the center. *Who put that collar on him? What's on the tag?*

Mila positions Riley on a leather apparatus, like a reverse massage chair almost. His ass is in the air, and his legs are spread, but his head is supported as he faces forward. "I refuse to touch this disgusting excuse for a submissive until I've completed a thorough inspection. He needs to be distracted while I examine him. Are there any volunteers?"

Men and women in the audience jump at the chance to take part, and Mila chooses an androgynous person wearing lingerie and sporting an erection. She kneels in front of Riley and speaks too softly for the mic to pick up before he nods, and she rises. The volunteer wastes no time plunging into Riley's mouth and thrusting as Mila pulls on latex gloves.

By the time she's finished with her inspection, I'm speechless. The volunteer came in Riley's mouth and left the stage relatively quickly, but Mila…Mila has taken her time. An entire tube of lube was needed for her to poke and prod her way into Riley's asshole, and the audience applauded when she deemed him "adequate."

He must be loving it, because his dick's been hard the entire time, but I…

"You're doing very well, Riley. What's your color?"

"Green, Mistress."

Mistress? Is that what she likes? She never told me to switch it up from Ma'am, but maybe I…

"The slave is fit to be in my presence, but he was brought to me specifically for punishment. He's been a *very* bad boy and displeased his Master."

Master? Okay, maybe that's whose name is on the collar. Relief floods through me, but I don't have time to question why before an X-shaped piece of furniture is wheeled onto the stage. After Mila secures him onto it, she turns to grab something from the table to the side of the stage, catches my eye, and winks.

I swear I've never seen fire dance in anyone's eyes before, and the beautiful blue I'm used to is almost eclipsed by predatory hunger. She stands tall, her posture Amazonian as always, and brandishes the whip she grabbed off the table.

"This slave is going to *attempt* to atone for his sins by accepting a number of lashes decided upon by himself and his Master. The design has been left open to my artistic interpretation."

Design?

After jolting at the first crack of the whip and resulting scream from Riley, I glance around, embarrassed to have been taken off guard, but it seems I'm not the only one. At least one person next to me flinched, and another submissive nearby got scolded for gasping when they were supposed to be silent.

If I expected any of the measured, moderate entrances into a scene that Mila usually provides, I know better now. She's a master with the whip, her fluidity and grace breathtaking. Every lash blooms on Riley's body immediately, his back, ass, and thighs all pink and then red as she finally breaks the skin.

With the first appearance of blood, she circles the cross to check in before laughing at what she finds.

"This slave is a *whore.* I haven't even touched this pathetic little cock, and it's weeping for me. All because I made you bleed. Do you think this tiny thing is enough to please me?"

"No, Mistress."

"Is that why you let me whip you, hmm? You know deep down that's the only way to be useful to me, don't you?"

"Yes, Mistress."

"At least you know your place. I can't believe you aren't locked in chastity full-time. Your Master and I might need to chat about that. Perhaps that would be better for everyone. We wouldn't have to watch this embarrassing little thing get hard, and you could focus on other tasks instead of thinking about this tiny dick. Would you like that?"

"Yes, Mistress."

She doesn't say anything but continues with her expert whipping, and by the time she finishes, there's enough blood I can barely make out the design, but it's there. It looks like a crest of some sort, made up of lashings of various depths, and I remind myself to ask her what the design was when we're done here.

She and Riley share a loaded look, and both take their mics off before she gently helps him off the cross and presses a kiss to his forehead. The applause is deafening as they exit, and praise for both Mila's skill and Riley's endurance are all around me.

"*She's so lucky to have found a submissive who can take so much.*"

"*Everyone thinks they're a masochist these days until they meet a real painslut. That was incredible.*"

"*It's impossible to find someone who's that good with a whip these days.*"

"*Nobody really enjoys the whip or the cane anymore. All my partner wants is the flogger, which is fine, but where's the real pain, you know?"*

"Hey!"

I startle for the second time this evening as Mila approaches me, much sooner than I expected.

"Uh, hi. Shouldn't you still be with Riley?" I really hadn't thought she'd be finished with his aftercare for at least another thirty minutes.

She rolls her eyes, leaning heavily against the wall and sipping from a water bottle. Her wrist is in a brace, and I wonder if she hurt it with the whip? That's her dominant hand. If her carpal tunnel is acting up and her trigger finger is slow, that could be so fucking dangerous.

"His Master is with him now. He told me before that they probably wouldn't want me back there, which is fine by me. This was a favor to him anyway, and—"

"What was the design?" It's a testament to the energy the scene took out of Mila that she doesn't censure me for the interruption.

"It's their wedding crest. It's a whole thing, but they're getting married soon, and had a crest made with their initials. They're building a house and putting it on everything. As soon as Riley approached me and his fiancé showed me the image, I knew it wouldn't be too hard. Fucking wrist..."

She polishes off her water as I think about the blood she drew from Riley and the gleam in her eye just from holding the whip in her hand. It looked like she was meting out justice for a dark ruler, exacting pain to discourage anyone else from doing whatever the poor soul she was beating had done.

That's what she does, though.

It hits me all at once that this might have been the most Mila I've ever seen. Ruthless, skilled, deadly…I'm not an idiot. Even if I did the obstacle course and the sparring mats with the guys, I know that's not what their job is. Their job is loyalty and enforcement, and the penalty for faltering is what I just watched on stage. *Worse.* For pain, not for pleasure.

I'm not scared of Mila. Never. But if that's what she needs to truly let go, *truly* let off steam…

"You ready to go explore?"

Bright-blue eyes beckon me from my thoughts, and I follow.

Like I always will.

CHAPTER 31

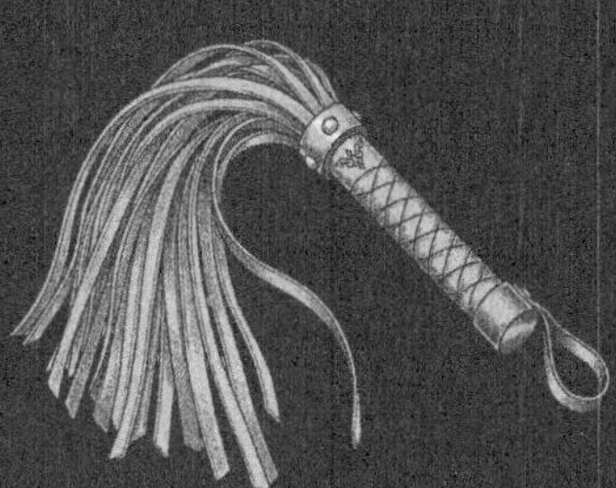

Mila

LAST NIGHT'S EXHIBITION was boring. When I agreed to perform with Riley, I expected to enjoy it at least a little. I used to get such a high putting on a show, and the two of us have had our fair share of performances. We've always had great chemistry, and demonstration requests flooded in from every club we attended.

As forgettable as it was for me, Riley finished twice, and he and his Master adored the way the crest turned out. I don't think the crowd caught wind of my lack of enthusiasm, either. We still put on quite the show, with an invitation to perform whenever we would like at either of Rendezvous' locations. I politely accepted the invitation, but I have no intention of taking them up on their offer. My time is limited, and I only follow through with plans that benefit me.

Plans like the one I originally had with Thatcher.

I would have much rather been up on that stage with him. I would've rather been on any of their floors with him, for that matter. We had the rest of the night to play, but after my exhibition with Riley, Thatcher was…different.

He said he was fine, and we played a bit with a new Shibari rope at an exhibit, but something was off. He deflated after my performance. I wanted to force the truth out of him, but he was such a good boy for me all evening that I never had the chance.

I would've brought it up this morning, but he was back to himself. He had to leave for a team workout, but woke up early and made me breakfast before he left. This time, one suitable for a human and rich in protein. Our conversation, his mannerisms, his humor—it was all normal. I've spent my entire life learning how to read people, and it really was like a light switch.

I'm sure it was just the shock of watching me with another person. We aren't in a relationship, but we are still involved to a certain degree. Sometimes one may think they are okay seeing their partner with someone else, but watching it is an entirely different ball game. Which is fine. One of the most important aspects of an arrangement like ours is honesty and comfort.

"Are you sure you're okay with this? The guys can be a lot sometimes." Thatcher reaches across the back seat to take my hand.

"Yes. I think I'm capable of dealing with a handful of men. You do remember what I do for a living, right?"

"Yeah, but it's men and their women, *and* some of them have children."

"I'll be *fine*."

Jesus, I kill people. I can make it through lunch. Although I'm not sure what's worse between children and the murderers I deal with. Still, I'm excited to meet some of Thatcher's friends, and I guess these are technically some of Teddy's too.

We stop in front of a trendy-looking café, and Thatcher races to open my door before the driver. I laugh as he cheers his victory, allowing him to help me out and lead me to the entrance. The minute he opens the door, my resolve disappears as a choir of hoots and hollers erupts from the back corner of the small room. I do manage hundreds of dangerous men, but this *is* different. For starters, none of my guys speaks unless spoken to.

I glance around at the table and take everyone in, noting as much as possible from their mannerisms to their attire to…the absolutely stunning *fucking blonde-ass women* by their sides. They are all coupled up, and a quick finger check all but confirms they're either married to or engaged to the women beside them. Luckily, only one couple brought their children with them.

Thatcher leads us to the only two empty seats, pulling mine back for me and gaining us another round of oohs and aahs. We're sandwiched between two men, both about the same size as Thatcher.

"Bubba," the one beside me says, reaching out his hand to greet me. "You'll have to forgive me, but Thatcher never gave us your name."

I firmly accept his handshake. "Mila."

"Hi, Mila!" greets several voices from around the table.

"I'm Thatcher's co-captain, but I primarily deal with the defense. This is my wife, Natalie—"

"I'm Milton," the man beside Thatcher says, interrupting *Bubba*. "And this is my wife, Jennifer, and my kids are…" He looks to see the seats where his children once sat to be empty. "Well, I'm not sure where they went but Ethan, Laney, and Martha."

"Hi!" Jennifer leans back and waves from the other side of her husband. "It's so nice to *finally* see Thatcher bring around someone special."

"Very nice to meet you as well. I don't know how special I would consider myself to Thatcher, but thank you anyway."

"Oh, nonsense. He's head over heels for you, doll. You should see the way his goofy little face lights up in the locker room when he talks about you," Bubba adds, as some of the other men chuckle.

"Yeah, he's never acted like that before. Gus, by the way." A large, burly man across from me reaches out his hand to shake.

"It's nice to meet you all. Thatcher speaks so fondly about all of you." *I haven't heard him mention half of these people.* But I'm hoping this will appease them, and we won't have to go around the table individually playing two truths and a lie.

Luckily, the server appears to drop off some appetizers for the table and take our orders. When he leaves, the conversation has progressed past Thatcher and me to the upcoming season. At least, that's what the men are talking about. The women's discussions are primarily superficial about things like shopping, skincare, vacation spots, etc.

I listen in on both conversations, picking up as much as I can about the people Thatcher spends his life with. His friends all seem like good people, however simple-minded they might be. *Oh, to live a life where your biggest concerns were the latest beauty trends and NHL transfers.* Meanwhile, I hold people's lives in my hands. One wrong move on my part and a child grows up without a father.

"Oh hell. Here they come, Sunshine." A chorus of groans sounds from the other side of the table.

Sunshine?

"Oh lord, there's a fucking gaggle of them today."

"Gaggle? A group of bunnies is called a fluffle, idiot."

"Well, Thatcher's been gone for a while, so the bunnies are probably going through withdrawals."

Huh? A group of blonde Barbie-like women titters at the reception podium. There are at least seven or eight, and I know it's almost impossible for them to be identical octuplets, but fuck, they look exactly the same. They aren't too dissimilar to the women around the table, but at least these ladies have an elegance that the Barbie octuplets don't.

"Oh shit, Thatch. The chair beside you is already filled. You don't have an empty seat for them to fight over toda—" one of the men across from us says, stopping when his wife slaps the back of his head. "Ow!"

"Sorry about my husband. Thatcher hasn't ever *brought* a woman to our Sunday brunches."

I smile, but I'm not a fool. I know exactly what the guy was about to say. And Thatcher may have never arrived with a girl, but I'll bet my ass he always left with one. Jealousy floods my mind at the thought of one of those fake-ass women on his arm. If that's what he likes...well, why the *fuck* is he with me? Maybe I have it all wrong, and what I have to offer is just a new exciting flavor for him to try out for a season. *I could take them all out right now. I went light today, but I still have two handguns and twelve blades strapped to my body.*

I didn't realize I was digging my fingers into the seat of my chair until Thatcher lightly pats my hand. "They're being silly. Don't listen to them."

With a forced smile, I nod, but I'm sure he can see the contempt in my eyes, just as I can see the apology in his. *God, I shouldn't even care about any woman he might decide to fuck right now, much less women in his past.* All at once, my feelings hit me like a train. Feelings for Thatcher...ones I should've *never* allowed.

CHAPTER 32

Thatcher

BRUNCH WENT *MOSTLY* well. I was a bit apprehensive about how everyone would react to Mila and vice versa, but she transitioned into the group seamlessly. I've always been slightly envious of my friend's love lives, but never so much as when Teddy left. The two of us were the only bachelors in our group, but we had each other. For the past half year, I've been the only one without a partner, and it's hurt. Today was different, though. I finally had someone there and not just anyone…*the one.* I was on cloud nine. *Until the group of puck bunnies showed up.*

As well as Mila keeps her emotions hidden, I could see how it upset her. Not to mention how different she's been acting since we left. The plan all along was for her to leave early in the morning, but the second we got in the car, she informed me that she would be leaving this evening instead. We then spent the entire drive in silence.

Things haven't been much better since getting back to my condo either. I've never felt so suffocated in a two-story living room with floor-to-ceiling windows in my life. I've tried to start a conversation multiple times, but I'm just met with a "hmm." She won't even *look* at me, and I can't take it anymore.

"Mila, what did I do? Please tell me what's wrong."

She cuts her eyes to me briefly, then looks back up at the TV. "Nothing is wrong."

"Bullshit!" I yell.

I hardly ever raise my voice, and I've surely never raised my voice at Mila before, but it works. I have her full attention at last as she turns to face me, venom lacing her eyes.

"*Excuse me*?"

"I'm sorry to yell, but you're lying to me! *Something* is wrong, and don't you think for a minute I wouldn't notice. I know you—"

"You *do not* know me," she spits. "You know *nothing,* Thatcher Prescott. How could you possibly think a month or so of sex is enough to qualify that you *know* me? You've been nothing more than an escape from the stress of my life. A temporary distraction, that's *all*."

Well fuck, that hurts. But it's not true, and I know it deep in my soul. Our connection is *more,* whether she wants to admit it or not. Yes, the sex is incredible, but the pull between us consumes every one of my conscious thoughts, and even my subconscious dreams. She's the piece of myself I've been missing all my life. The cardinal piece, so intrinsic to who I am that without it, I could never truly exist. With her, I finally have purpose. With her, I'm home.

"I do, though," I whisper. "You know this is more just like I do. No, I have no clue what it's like to be you. Your life is and has always been a contrast to my own, and no matter how many stories I hear about it, I'll never be able to relate. But that doesn't mean I don't care. It doesn't mean I can't see your pain and your stress and empathize with you. I *want* to be your outlet. I want to be your peace, your joy, the light at the end of a dark and stressful day. I would never pressure you for more of yourself than you could freely give, but I'm begging you to stop hiding from this...from us."

Her defensive posture dissipates as she subconsciously leans into me. She would never intentionally do such a thing, but the pull between us is too strong for even her to fight, and I know it. *I feel it.* I take her hands in mine. I risk her shutting off again with the intimacy behind my touch, but she doesn't. "Please, please just tell me what's bothering you."

She sighs. "It's stupid."

"Nothing you think could possibly be stupid."

"The women at brunch made me jealous."

"After that performance you put on last night at the club, you're going to get jealous about women I don't even think I've ever met?"

She rolls her eyes. "*You* told me to do the exhibition! I never would have done that if you didn't tell me to."

"It wasn't just the fact that you were with someone else. It was what you were doing. I don't think I would ever be okay with that, and if that's what you—"

Mila braces herself on my thigh. "Let me stop you right there. Perhaps I haven't explained my role as a Domme well enough. It's my job, my pleasure, to push my partners to their limits in order to give them the most explosive release. That differs from person to person. What Riley likes is different from you, and that's perfectly fine. His extremes don't give *me* a better experience. You have nothing to be jealous of, solnyshko. Believe me when I say, you take it better than anyone ever has."

Smiling, I put my hand over hers. "You never have anything to be jealous about, either, I promise. Those women never meant anything to me. I kept them around for a quick release. It was only ever sex, and even that's become dull over the years. Nothing has or will ever compare to you."

"I know." She smirks. "It wasn't the moment of doubt that's been bothering me. It's that I would even be jealous in the first place. I should know myself better than that. The world I live in is cutthroat, and if I lose sight of my worth, I fear everything I've ever built will crumble. I don't have time for feelings like jealousy or anything else."

Anything else...

"I only want to enhance your life. If that ever changes, let me know, and we'll readjust. I want to *add* to your strength, never take away from it."

She hesitates for a moment to accept my hug, then leans in. "Do you still have to leave tonight, or can you stay?"

"I actually have an early morning meeting. I, uh...confirmed when I was upset. But I'll see you next weekend, right? You're coming to the compound?"

She inches closer, eyes hot with emotions she'll never admit to. She may not even know she feels them yet, but her eyes do. For some reason, this force of a woman cares for me, and I'll do everything in my power to be worthy.

Bridging the gap between us, she has plenty of time to reject my kiss, but she doesn't. The moment our mouths meet, she opens for me. There's an urgency, a passion that sends sparks through my body so deep I feel them in my bones. It's all-consuming, taking the very last pieces of my heart. And when she pulls back, I've never been so certain of my love for her.

"I wouldn't miss it for the world."

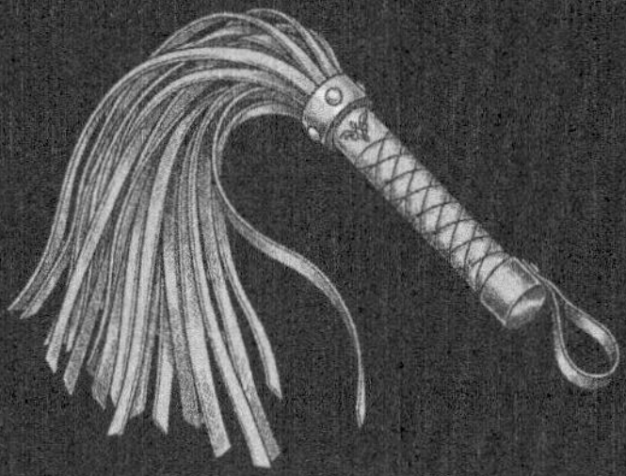

CHAPTER 33
Mila

ALTHOUGH I'VE BEEN dreading this meeting all week, and under normal circumstances I would have enjoyed staying to put Thatcher through his paces…I can't say I'm not a *tad* relieved.

Too many emotions have been swirling in my mind lately. Unwelcome, nasty things that won't do anyone any good. Hopefully, today's trade negotiation can recenter my focus on what matters: shoring up my hold on this Bratva once and for all.

Almost all the pieces are in place, and Misha's going to deserve a yearlong vacation for all the behind-the-scenes shit he's been handling for me. Not that he would ever take it. I think he'd rather chew off his own arm than leave me.

The driver drops my guard and me off at the door of a swanky restaurant, and although the doorman and maître d' are polite, an undercurrent of tension is in the air. It looks like the restaurant has been rented out just for our party, and although it's not unusual for meetings like this, and I've done it many times myself, something seems off.

"Your tables are right this way, Madam, and I hope—"

"Ah, Miss Taranova, I'm so sorry I can't stay any longer. Please know that lunch for you and your men is on me, and eat and drink to your heart's content."

Javier Lopez, the man I was scheduled to meet today, is on his way out of the restaurant in a hurry, albeit seemingly in good spirits. I've wanted to nip any possible animosity between our families in the bud, particularly since his wife is remotely related to the de la Rosa family. With everything that went down between them and Ellie's family…I don't want any needless violence at the beginning of my new reign.

"Mr. Lopez, thank you for coming. I was hoping to speak to you—"

"No need, sweetheart."

Oh, fuck you.

"You're incredibly lucky to have such a man as a future father-in-law, I'll tell you that. He's gotten me to sign off on all sorts of shit today, even deals I'm taking losses on. But it'll be better for all of us in the long run. With him at the helm, you won't have to worry about anything but staying home and growing babies. Lucky, lucky girl!"

Double fuck you.

With that odious monologue complete, he's out the front door, men in tow, a cloud of his sickly sweet cologne threatening to choke me as my anger bubbles to the surface. It takes only a few seconds to calm myself, burying my emotions and tapping into the darkest, hardest part of myself. I barely have time to send a quick text before the person who's just signed his death warrant jovially bursts into the room.

"Mila, darling. Don't stand in the doorway, come. We have much to celebrate and catch up on."

Fucking Zadorov. Of course. I should have known that when Lopez said "future father-in-law," he meant this snake. A quick scan of my periphery confirms that this place is packed with his men, so I plaster a smile on my face and prepare to play a chess match I had no clue was coming.

"Zakhar, it's always a pleasure to see you. Even if I wasn't expecting you today. Do you mind if I visit the ladies' room before we begin?"

With pleasantries out of the way, I signal to my bodyguard to stay behind and make my way to the bathroom. It's a show of trust to go alone, although if any of Zadorov's men think they can take me, I'm not concerned about his plotting at all.

Pulling my phone from my pocket, I swear under my breath to see Misha's reply to my emergency text.

> **MISHA:** Not sure, calling Ace. The plumbers may not have dug deep enough. Neighbors invited us to stay with them in the meantime. We'll have to accept. Can't stay here.

Fuck.

His text would read as nonsense to anyone tapping our phones, but the fact he felt it necessary is concerning. More concerning is what his message means. Ace is our code name for Ivan, and if Misha is involving him, it means he didn't know anything about Zadorov's plan.

Worse is the rest. Basically, we didn't dig deep enough into Zakhar, and he's gotten some sort of upper hand. I'll have to play really fucking nice today to try to figure it out. *Or at least try to live long enough to regroup.* I steel myself and head back into the restaurant.

"There you are, I was about to come check on you. Here, sit down. I'm sure you're wondering what I'm doing here."

"I am curious, yes. Although given how happy Lopez seemed on the way out, I'll admit to being thankful that you've apparently deftly handled a prickly associate for me."

My praise momentarily takes him by surprise, and his jovial facade breaks, shrewd eyes narrowing as he tries to determine my angle. He recovers in a blink, laughing it off and waving a dismissive hand.

"Oh, it was no trouble, my dear. I figured that anything that I could do to lighten your load would be appreciated. I've gotten Mr. Lopez to sign a contract, as you can see here, offering us very generous terms. Much better than you were expecting, I'm sure."

He slides a folder across the table to me, and a quick scan confirms that the terms *are* generous. To the *Zadorov Bratva.* My stomach drops at his slimy smirk. *Fuck, this is about to go from bad to worse.*

"I also made some real strides in other areas that had been vexing you. Here are more contracts with..."

Folder after folder slides across the table, indeed showing that plenty of people who were assholes to me at the negotiation table have been willing to bend over backward to make a deal with Zakhar and the fucking *Zadorov Bratva.* Photos of Thatcher on his way to and from practice chill me to my core, but the final folder is the worst. Nausea and panic flood my senses, and tears fill my eyes before I regain control. These pictures shouldn't exist anymore...*we destroyed everything, I swear.* Fighting the sinking feeling that I can still recall from all those years ago, when I was so little…*shit.*

My position is officially fucked. Every cell in my body wants to fight, to stick a knife in this fucker's eye socket right now and kill my way out of this building. But as many men as I could take down, they'd likely get me too, and I'm smart enough to live to fight another day. Time to put that urge in another neat box and smile.

"I'm surprised by the nomenclature on these contracts, Zakhar."

"Why on earth would you be surprised, dear? If you thought you would keep your name on the outfit once you married Oleg, I'm not sure who ever gave you that idea."

"You and I both know how our last conversation regarding the proposed marriage alliance went. I declined."

"And now, I've given you no choice, you little bitch!" His men perk up as he finally snaps and raises his voice, but a flick of his wrist has them relaxing once more. "Your father fucking knew that a woman isn't built for running an operation like ours, and he saved Thunder Bay from all this bullshit we've been dealing with. Ivan is a weakling, and the harpy he married has put all kinds of nonsense in his head about what women are capable of, too."

"So you're forcing my hand?"

"I'm preventing a war and the unnecessary loss of good Russian men. And I'm doing you a giant favor, dear. We can all see what a toll this is taking on you. I know you'd rather be baking cookies with the children, and this way, that's all you'll be required to do."

"Has it ever occurred to you that it might not be possible for me to give your son children?"

He shrugs like he couldn't care less. "We'll find another dark-haired bitch, and he can knock her up instead. As long as you raise the kid and keep up appearances, it shouldn't be a problem for anyone to look the other way. That might be the best-case scenario, anyway. Keep the weak Taranov blood out of my line. It takes generations to breed that out."

I'm going to end your bloodline. Not today. But soon.

"Well, Zakhar, I don't know what to say."

"You can say 'Thank you, Father-in-law, for solving all of my problems and allowing me to live a soft life befitting a woman.'"

"If you think—"

"I *do* think, pussycat. Your claws are well noted, and your feisty spirit will serve you well in my son's bedroom. Based on what I hear, you'll need it. But for now, in this room, I think you'll find that you're going to do what I tell you to do and say what I tell you to say. And I want to hear you say it."

My chest rises and falls calmly, and I refuse to let the red blush of anger rise from my chest to my neck. My heart is racing, though, and I force myself to take stock of the situation. Each of his men watches me closely, relaxed but ready to riddle me with bullets at one word from their boss. More than a few of them have smirks, enjoying seeing me so humbled. I box this feeling away for the next time I need to be my most ruthless.

"Thank you, Father-in-law, for solving all of my problems and allowing me to live a soft life befitting a woman."

"See, gentlemen, you can teach an old dog new tricks." A chorus of laughter fills the room, but I don't hear it. It's funneled straight into another box, only to be opened when needed. "This is a perfect example of why you aren't fit to lead. No man would have sat there and taken this from me lying down. You'd probably get up on this table and spread your legs for us all if I told you to, wouldn't you? Not like you'd have any choice..."

Please, no. No, no, no...

"But I don't have time for that today. Maybe at the wedding reception. I don't have any further need for you. Take that packet of information and expect a call to coordinate travel and all the logistics. The wedding will be in the Motherland, obviously, so start packing. Now get out of my sight, dear daughter-in-law."

Gladly. With one last look around the room, I ensure I have every single smirking face burned into my memory. Zakhar's right about purging weakness from bloodlines, and I'll do my best to make sure every single one of these fucker's ends.

Soon.

CHAPTER 34

Thatcher

AS DISAPPOINTED AS I am that Mila couldn't stay last night, nothing could bring me down from my high right now. Even though she ended up leaving, we still had an outstanding evening, filled with laughter and orgasms. The best way to spend any day, in my opinion. And after our heart-to-heart, things felt even more intense than usual. Maybe it's the fact that I know deep down she cares about me, or maybe it's just that I've finally realized my own feelings. *Love.* I've never felt romantic love. I always imagined it would feel like a shackle, locking you to someone, but it's the opposite. Being tethered to Mila is a freedom I've never felt before.

I'm in love with Mila Taranova.

I smile at the thought of her as I walk into our practice facility. Just like everything else since my grand realization, the building is somehow…*better.* The air feels fresher, the paint looks brighter, and I'm more excited than ever to put on my skates and play my beloved sport.

"Ayo, look who finally decided to show up today," Bubba yells from the other end of the locker room as I walk in.

"It's the ole loverboy himself."

"Did your lady keep you up late last night?"

"She's way out of your league, man."

The guys mess with me as I make my way to my locker, but I don't mind. I'll take all their taunts. At least I finally have someone for them to talk about now.

Milton walks in as I'm changing my clothes, his grin growing the closer he gets. "Hey, Sunshine! Did you have a gooood night last night?"

"Nah, Mila left yesterday evening. But I had a good afternoon," I say, wiggling my eyebrows.

"Hell yeah! I really like her, and Jennifer is about ready to plan your wedding. What are you guys anyway? Are you officially dating? Exclusive? Just casual? There are so many different terms these days. I can't keep up."

There's nothing casual about the way I feel for Mila. After our conversation yesterday, I would assume we're at least exclusive, but dating might be a stretch. "Hmm…I'm not sure. We are at least *very* good friends."

"Well, you'd better make it official before someone else does."

Gus skates over from his seat and sits in Bubba's seat beside me. "Yeah, that woman is way out of your league, Sunny boy."

"Move, asshole." Before I can respond, Bubba slaps Gus in the head with his stick to scoot him over. "He's right, though. How did you say you met her?"

I hella told you last week exactly how I met her, and you didn't believe me. "Oh, that's Teddy's sister."

"The fuck? Teddy has a sister?" Gus shouts from the other side of Bubba.

"He, um…didn't know about it until he moved to Thunder

Bay." *I really should protect the Taranov family secrets.* "They share a father, but neither of them knew about each other until he passed away."

"I can kinda see it now," Milton chimes in. "Damn, their dad must've been massive. Those are two large humans."

"Hey, don't say that about Mila, asshole!"

"Whoa, I didn't mean any disrespect. I'm just saying it's in the genes. If anything, it's a compliment. You two would for *sure* have some athletic babies."

"You guys are getting ahead of yourselves. It hasn't even been two months since we've been seeing each other or...whatever." *Not that the short time matters at all to me. I would marry her right now if she would have me.*

"Look, all we're saying is that if you're holding out on a relationship because you're afraid of commitment or something, stop," Bubba says, putting his arm around my shoulder. "I know it's a new concept to you, but she's the one. We all saw it, so just trust us and make the woman yours already."

I smile and nod, but it will never be my decision. I only *wish* it were me we were waiting on to be official. Nobody could ensnare Mila Taranova unless she came willingly, so I'll just keep groveling at her feet until she does.

The practice bell rings, and everyone files out, immediately forgetting about my love life. *Thank God.* As always, I'm the last man out. I turn off the lights and make my way to the rink, but I don't get far before Coach stops me.

"Prescott, my office. Now!"

Backtracking to his office, I pop my head in the open doorframe. "Yes, sir?"

"Have a seat, son."

I go through any and every possible thing he could want, but I'm coming up short. *He must have heard about Mila and wants to give me flak.*

I plop myself down as well as I can with my pads on in his small seat and wait for him to say something, but he never does. And the sadness in his expression all but confirms this meeting isn't just to mess with me. "Um…what's going on?"

Coach hangs his head with a sigh. "You're being transferred."

A moment of silence passes as all I can do is blink. "I'm sorry, what?"

"You're being transferred—"

"No, I heard you, but…why? Have I done something wrong? I've really been feeling good about my performance lately, but if you're not happy about it, I can work harder or—"

"It's not, Thatcher. I didn't have a choice in the matter. Trust me…"

"Okay, well…where am I going?"

"Thunder Bay."

Well, at least I'll be with Teddy. That will be nice. And Mila will surely be planning to visit often anyway, so it shouldn't be too inconvenient for her. We can talk about it this weekend and… wait…"When do I need to be there? I'm sure I can get my things packed in a week or so—"

"You leave today. You have a jet waiting for you right now. Housing is already set up with everything you'll need, and your things will be sent to you ASAP."

"*Today*? I can't leave today. I have…and I'll need..." I guess I could leave tonight. If I leave practice now and drive to Mila's, I can see her in time to make it back for a flight. "Okay, I can make it tonight, I'll just—"

"I didn't say tonight, I said *right now*. You have fifteen minutes to pack up your locker. I'll tell the guys. It'll be easier that way."

Fifteen fucking minutes? There's no fucking way. This has to be a joke…right? I wait for a moment, hoping this is some stupid prank, but the look in Coach's eyes tells the truth. The truth is I'm getting on a plane in fifteen minutes to fly over a thousand miles away from the only city I've ever known. From Mila… From my *home*.

"I'll…I'll go get my things…" I say, barely making eye contact with Coach as I get up and go to leave his office.

Silence fills the air until I open the door. "Thatcher?"

Turning back, I think a *tear* falls from his eye. "I'll miss you. And good luck in Thunder Bay. Tell Teddy I said hello."

With a last salute-wave, I say my final goodbye and damn near run to the locker room to grab my phone. *Mila still hasn't responded to my good morning text.* She had an important meeting, but that should have ended hours ago. I'm on the verge of a mental breakdown when I remember that I can always just fly back to see her this weekend. Still, I want to let her know what's going on. I would want her to do the same for me.

I start to text her, but decide to call instead. She said only to call for emergencies, but I think this warrants it. The phone rings once, then twice, before forwarding to voicemail. *Maybe she's dealing with super important Bratva stuff.* I guess a text will have to do.

ME: Sorry to call…got some big hockey news. Call back when you can!

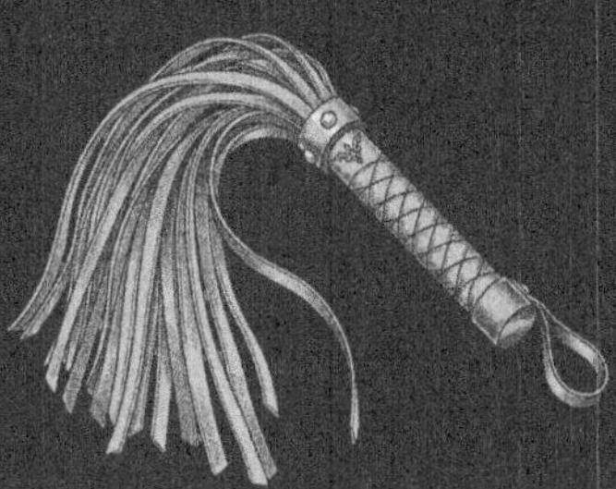

CHAPTER 35
Mila

THE MOMENT THE Zadorovs left, I went into survival mode, locking down anyone who could be at risk. The Thunder Bay compound is under high alert with double the normal security. Teddy and Ellie are on *strict* orders to stay home, with Teddy's only allowance being hockey practice. Even then, he's got an extra security detail with him everywhere he goes.

And then there's Thatcher. *My solnyshko.* He was actually my first thought. I knew the moment I saw his picture in that folder that he had to leave. The compound in New York isn't even safe enough for him. I'm not sure if anywhere in the world would be safe enough for my liking, but Thunder Bay is as close as I'll get. The Taranov branch there might not be quite as large as it is in New York, but thanks to Teddy's union with Ellie, he has the added force of the Santori Mafia.

Sending him away was a no-brainer even though I *know* it's going to hurt him like hell. *If I'm honest, it hurt me like hell too.* But I need him to let go. This was just the first of what will be a never-ending stream of blackmail targeting Thatcher as long as he's attached to me. So it has to end.

While I was arranging everyone's safety, Misha was plotting how to get out of their trap. He's the only one who knows what's going on, and even though I would've preferred to keep it that way, he implored that I go to Ivan for help navigating this… arrangement.

"So what are you going to do?"

"I guess I'm going to fucking marry Oleg. What do you mean? I can't let them hurt Thatcher. Or anyone else, for that matter. And if they spread the word about…what happened…I would lose all of the respect I've earned over the years."

"What about Ivan?"

"Ivan? You want me to tell Ivan about all this? What if he—"

"He's not like that, and you know it. If I'm right about him, and I always am, he will help us. You can't marry Oleg, and you know it. We haven't come all this way for me to watch you be ensnared in such a trap as marriage…"

"Okay, so…Ivan?"

"I've already arranged a meeting. In an hour at his office in the city."

I've just raised my hand to knock on the office door when Ivan yells from inside, "Mila, come in!"

He's had this office in the city for years but started operating out of here more often when I moved into the compound. This is the first time I've met him here, and I have to say, it's charming. It's warm and inviting, yet sleek and professional. The contrast between this floor and the estate tells me that Ivan wasn't the one who authorized the design choices there.

"Please have a seat, dear. You too, Misha. We have a lot to discuss."

We do as he asks, and he slides us both a folio, then opens one himself. At first glance, it looks similar to the one I was handed earlier today, and a quick peek inside is all the confirmation I need. Misha waits for my reaction before opening his, and when I place it back on the desk, he does the same.

Silence suffocates me, and I know I need to say something, but I'm struggling to *breathe,* much less talk.

"How did you get these?" Misha asks, sensing my panic.

"The Zadorov family thought sending these to me would help their case."

"And does it?" Misha growls.

Ivan smiles at me, then looks back at Misha. "It would seem they have gravely miscalculated whose side I might be on. I would never stand for such...abomination. I hope you know that. If I ever found out something like that happened to my daughter, well... Let's just say their lack of judgment just gave us a real chance to finally get rid of them and anyone else they are working with."

All I can do is nod as tears well in my eyes. The kindness Ivan has shown me, *is currently showing me*, it's more than even that of my own father. I've never talked about what happened in

Russia to anyone, and especially not to Igor Taranov. He wasn't a monster like his father before him, but he would have never believed me. He admired me, and I was always certain of that. But in the back of my mind, I knew not to push my luck. His respect would have gone out the window the second I tried to play the victim of abuse. Misha is the only one who has ever known, and that's exactly how I would like to keep it.

Ivan's expression softens as my tears begin to fall. "I don't need you to tell me everything, dear, just enough so that we can cut out that cancer once and for all."

He reaches across the desk with a tissue and waits patiently as I pull myself together. A few calming breaths are all it takes in order to think straight again, and I dive into my past. With my mental breakdown out of the way, I'm ready to do anything and everything to finally give those assholes what they deserve. Every name, every face, every action…I remember them all. And anything I leave out, Misha is quick to include. Ivan takes notes as we walk him through everything from the architecture of the building to the soldiers' strengths and weaknesses.

It doesn't take long to formulate our plan. Ivan is going to play the role of the misogynistic asshole they assume he is, and as long as I can act like a good submissive bride, it should be foolproof.

I'll fly out today with Misha and a small group of our men, just enough so that we don't set off any alarms. Ivan isn't supposed to be coming for several days, closer to the wedding date, but he's going to sneak in by using his wife Blanche's family plane to a nearby country, then cross the border by train.

It's genius, really. The Bratva boss taking a passenger train into the country. Apparently, he knows a hacking genius who changed all the tickets on that route so that it will be filled with

Taranov soldiers. The hacker has also made fake identification for all the men, so that if the train is stopped, there won't be any legal problems. Hundreds of our men will be able to get into the area without notifying the Zadorovs or their allies.

Teddy will then fly over closer to the wedding with Ivan's son, Sasha, posing as his father. Blanche is confident that with the proper makeup, the disguise will be foolproof.

Misha and the men who come with us will have five days to prepare the Zadorov fortress for the takeover. We'll have to gain control of the tech, which Ivan's guy is supposedly helping with, plant weapons throughout for our men when the time is right, and provide several entry points to sneak said men in…among other smaller tasks.

My only task is to behave.

Parting ways with Ivan, we head for the plane where our small group of men waits with an extra suitcase for both Misha and me.

Everything is ready to go, but there's one call I'm waiting on before we take off. So all we have to do is sit and do nothing but…stress.

Luckily, Misha knows my tells. "Did you hear something thud under Ivan's desk when we were making our plans?" he asks in an attempt to distract me, I'm sure.

"I *did* hear something. It was when Ivan said he would fly in with the men—"

"Then he corrected himself and said he and his wife would fly…" Misha raises a brow, smirking. "You don't think…"

"Holy shit! Do you think that was his wife?"

"He doesn't seem like the kind of man who would mess around."

"Damn, Blanche is freaky."

Misha laughs, but before he can respond, my phone lights up with a call from Thatcher. *Good, he got the news.* I decline the call and silence my phone, then turn my attention to Misha. "Are you ready to go back to Russia?"

He takes my hand in his and kisses my knuckles. "Let's do this, moya tsaritsa."

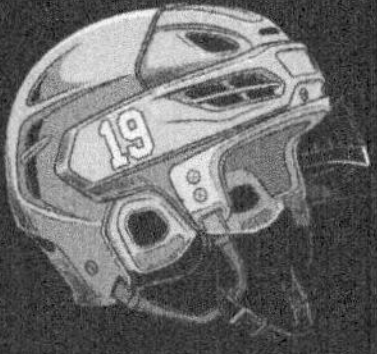

CHAPTER 36

Thatcher

AS NICE A gesture as it was, a private flight wasn't what I needed. At least on a commercial flight, I would have a person or two to talk to, keeping my mind occupied. On top of everything, the Wi-Fi was out, so I really had nothing to do but get lost in my head. My anxiety rose higher with each new hypothetical scenario I created, until I was a sweaty mess. The moment we landed, I checked my phone for any reply from Mila, but again, nothing.

I contemplate calling again, but she has my latest text. She'll call when she can. She's probably just busy as fuck, the poor woman. This is just what life is going to be like with a Bratva boss. And as much as I miss her, as sad as it makes me when she doesn't respond, I'll gladly take this over a life without her completely.

Teddy and the Santori brothers wait for me on the tarmac, and my mood improves immediately. I shake Gabri's hand and give Nikki a half hug before practically jumping into Teddy's arms.

"Wow! This is quite the reception. I expected Teddy, but damn. Do the captains come out to welcome all the new transfers like this?"

Gabri lets out a single chuckle, but it's Nikki who responds. "Only when our brother-in-law practically forces us to—Oww!"

Teddy punches Nickki in the arm, then corrects him. "He means to say, only for the most special transfers."

"Yeah, what he said," Nikki grumbles as he soothes his biceps. "Only for fellow captains anyway."

"Well, thanks, guys. I was rushed down here. Is there some big meeting or practice we need to get to? Or, fuck, I don't even know the address to the condo they supposedly set up for me. Would you guys happen to know any of that?"

Teddy scratches his neck in the way he always does when he's hiding something. "Um, actually, we're going to be practicing in the rink at my estate today. And you're going to move in with me! When Ivan called this morning to tell me the big news, I immediately offered you a room. The estate is way too big anyway, and I've missed the hell out of you. He said he had men packing your stuff to send over, but I went ahead and picked up a few days' worth of clothes and got all your favorite toiletries. Yay, right? We're gonna be roomies."

"Um, sure. Woohoo!"

Ivan?

I suppose if I'm going to do this, I might as well move in with Teddy. The past few days I was alone in my condo sucked after living with Mila all summer. She was busy, but it was nice having people around all the time. Even though this Taranov compound experience won't be quite as enjoyable. As much as I love and have missed Teddy, we aren't *that* close. Not that *anyone* could ever compare to what I feel for Mila.

Ugh, Mila. And if Ivan knows about this trade, surely Mila knows as well…so why is she ignoring me? *That's the real reason*

I'm sad. In any other scenario, I would be *thrilled* to move in with my best friend. And the Thunder Bay Rising Tide is arguably the best team in the league right now. They lost in the finals last year, but that was just due to their family tragedy. And then of course, Teddy getting shot halfway through the series put him out as well. Everyone and their mom agrees that with those three back and healthy, next year's win is a shoo-in.

We file into one of the guy's fancy blacked-out SUVs and make our way to Teddy's new home. *Fuck, Mila's old home.*

I didn't notice it before, but the decor here screams Mila. *No wonder she's stressed out living in that gaudy-ass house.* This is more hers than Teddy's at this point. Even with her absence, living in the house she helped make a home brings me a sense of peace.

The guys lead me through the house to the training facility, and wow. This is so much nicer than the one in New York. In fact, everything is nicer here.

"When did you put ice in?" I ask as we head into a full-size rink.

"Oh, I didn't. Mila had that put in after I started training here." Teddy hands me a bag of practice equipment. "The locker room is right through those doors. I usually let Gabri and Nikki get through before I go in. There are some things you can't unsee."

"You're stupid. I'm pretty sure I'll be fine." I take my bag and follow the Santoris. If Mila designed these locker rooms, I'm sure they are top-notch.

"Whatever, man, but don't say I didn't tell you so!"

"So, how are you holding up?" Teddy asks as I step onto the ice.

"I don't think I'll ever be the same."

"I told you."

"Wait, when did you come in to change?"

"I have my own locker room, silly. I *am* the Pakhan after all, aren't I?"

"You motherfuck—"

"Hiya champ—" Nikki skates up behind me and throws his arm around my shoulders, scaring the shit out of me in the process. "Whoa, down boy! What's got you so jumpy all of a sudden?"

"Ask your brother," I grumble.

I can hear Gabri chuckle from the other side of me as Nikki bends in half, bellowing his laughter. "You get used to it."

When we're all done stretching me as far away from Gabri and his monster…thing as possible, Teddy takes his position in the net.

"Alright, Thatch, you and Nikki are going to take turns going one-on-one with Gabri and—"

"Wait, where's the rest of the team?"

Teddy reaches for his neck again. "Oh, this is just a private practice—"

"We thought it would be better if we broke you in first," Nikki interrupts. "That being said, let's see what you've got."

I take my position across from Gabri and wait for Nikki to drop the puck. He's the best defenseman in the league, and I always dread going against the motherfucker, but my nerves calm the moment it hits the ice. I manage a breakaway and cross over Nikki, but my efforts are for naught as my shot finds Teddy's glove.

Gabri pats my shoulder as he makes his way to the center, where Nikki will challenge him next. "Great try. You've gotten better, Sunny D."

"Yeah, man, what was that? Your speed and agility are wild. You're usually dragging the first couple of weeks of preseason, you know, after all that partying you do."

"Ha. Ha. Ha." I flip Teddy off, then grab the puck. "I spent the summer training with Misha, that's what. That man is *insane.*"

"Don't I know it." Teddy's eyes go blank as he stares into the lights, frozen.

"Um, you good, bro?"

Blinking, he shakes his head. "Yeah, good, sorry. Anyway… How is Misha? I miss that guy."

"Oh, he's doing fine. We're best friends now."

"That's great, especially since…Well, I know Mila can be a lot. Hopefully, she didn't hook you up to her milking machine?"

I choke on my own spit. "Yep, nope, she sure did…didn't—"

Thank *God,* Nikki interrupts. "Are you two going to stop talking so we can practice or what?"

The Santori brothers wait as I skate to the center of the rink. Dropping the puck, I back off to the sideline and watch in awe. I've seen these two play on numerous occasions, but I've never seen them go up against one another. It's like watching a battle of fire and ice as they dance around each other. *There's no wonder the Rising Tide is so fucking good.*

They go for what feels like an eternity until Nikki finally bests Gabri and gets a shot past both him and Teddy.

"Goddamn, Nikki. *Fuck*!"

The brothers laugh as they all skate over for a drink of water. Teddy plops down on the bench first, stretching out his legs. "Yeah, he's a fucking problem."

"Gabri and I have been training all our lives like you did this summer." Nikki slaps my back and passes me some water. "Don't worry, we'll whip you into shape! Just like we are with our ole brother-in-law. Isn't that right, Teddy Bear?"

Teddy rolls his eyes. "Yeah, thanks. Your sister's been loving the improved endurance."

Gabri chuckles as Nikki mumbles, "Asshole."

"How are Ellie and the baby doing?" I ask in an attempt to ease the tension.

You can practically see hearts in Teddy's eyes as he thinks about his family. "They're doing great. She was so excited that you were joining that she and Nonna are currently whipping up a big dinner for us all. I think she said something about your favorite chicken potpie."

"Oh man, I can't wait. Mila had some Michelin-rated chefs in New York, but they didn't compare to Nonna and Ellie."

"You never got around to telling me about how your summer was up there. Nikki's rude ass interrupted our conversation." He cuts his eyes to Nikki, who's sticking out his tongue.

"It was a good time. I got to train and party it up with the guys, and I can already tell Misha's training is going to make a difference in my performance this season."

It was the best summer of my life. The best time of my entire life, actually. I learned a lot about myself and fell madly in love with your sister in the process.

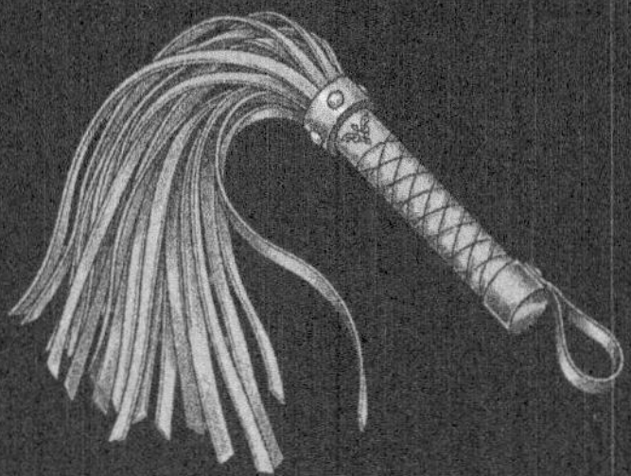

CHAPTER 37

Mila

"I HAVE TO SAY, pussycat, you are a pleasure to be around when you aren't acting like a bitch."

I give Zakhar my best smile and bat my eyes. "I was under so much stress before, but now that you've taken that off my plate, I feel like a completely new woman."

He extends his arm for me as he continues our tour of the gardens. "Yes, you need not worry about all those things anymore. I'll take care of everything from now on. Your only job now is keeping my son happy, but with this new and improved version of yourself, I think you will do just fine."

Thatcher on his knees, gagged, blindfolded. Sweat beading on his brow, his hair ruffled. Every muscle in his body flexed, his veins popping out at his restraint. His substantial cock rock solid and weeping, begging for release.

"You're being such a good boy for me. Just for that, I'm only going to make you wait five more minutes before I sink down onto you. Do you want that, baby? Are you ready to feel my cunt strangling your dick? Will you be able to take it and let me ride you until I'm finished, or are you going to be my good boy and wait for me?"

"Yes, I'm quite confident in my ability to please Oleg. He'll be in heaven." *Or hell, more likely.*

"Good girl," he says, almost losing his life. *Just a little bit longer, Mila, just hold on.*

"Now, I don't know if you remember this section of the garden from your time here. Under your grandfather's ownership, it was rather run down. We decided to turn this into a greenhouse since the sewer line underneath provides such excellent natural fertilization. Many of the vegetables we eat are grown right here. We try to outsource as little food as possible to avoid the risk of poison. America might not be as bad anymore, but it's still cutthroat here in the Motherland."

"Oh, this is lovely. And how smart! I don't know if I would ever think of such a thing. It's a shame Grandfather didn't do the same. His fate might have been much different."

I actually remember every square inch of this godforsaken fortress. I kept tabs on every weak link within its walls so that one day I could exact my vengeance. This wasn't the way I intended to accomplish my feat, but when duty calls…Zakhar might think he's taking me on an innocent tour, but all he's doing is confirming which parts of this place to utilize when we deploy our takeover.

Like this greenhouse, for instance. Zakhar might think he was smart to renovate, but my grandfather kept this area barren because the sewer is one of the few underground entrances into the fortress. By building a structure around it, intruders are harder to spot.

"As you can see, we've added on to the size of the gardens as well. I considered having the wedding here. It's beautiful enough, and having the ceremony within our walls limits the risk of ambush...But your cousin was adamant about having it in a church. And I do agree with his point. This marriage needs to be *seen*. Your grandfather's passing of the torch to me was the first sign of union between our two families, but this wedding... This will do away with any doubt that the Zadorov family is the powerhouse of Russia."

"He wanted to have the wedding in their fortress, but I convinced him to have it in the church. It's a risky move, but his ego won the better of him, just like I assumed it would. He wants the world to know he's finally taken over the Taranov Bratva. Fortunately for us, his ego will be his downfall. With him and his top men out of the compound, it will be much easier to get our men in. And the church I chose is perfect for hiding Taranov soldiers as well. It's technically within his territory, but one of my oldest friends is the patriarch. He's already preparing for us."

"Yes, Ivan told me about how important the church will be to symbolize this union between our families. He was so ready to get out and live his life that he was willing to hand things over to a *woman*. But I think he knew all along you had a match for me, didn't he?" I purr.

Zakhar chuckles, and again, I have to remind myself not to kill him here and now. "Yes, I offered for Oleg to take his place years ago when he started to look toward retirement. I was surprised his own son didn't want the mantel, but to each their own. It's not every day an arrangement like this one falls into your lap. He's lucky Oleg wasn't already married...Speaking of which, have you gotten the dress fittings all settled? I know it's short notice, and well, you're much larger than the average woman here. My mistress recommended we go big so that our seamstress would have as much material to work with as possible."

"That *is your dress?" Misha holds up the monstrosity with wide eyes before losing himself in laughter. "How big do they think you are? Mila, please tell me you aren't wearing this shit."*

"Yeah, it was about six sizes too big. And the extra ruffles add on twice the material too. But yes, asshole, I'm wearing the giant dress with a hundred different places for me to hide weapons. They think they're being funny, but this is the best thing that could've happened...plan A as far as dresses are concerned."

"How many different dress plans did you have?"

"Six," I deadpan, shivering at the thought of plan F.

"Yes, of course the fittings have gone spectacularly. You have the most wonderful seamstress. I'm sure you can see how difficult it must be for me to find clothes that fit properly. I've gone through dozens of tailors, but they all struggle. Gladys did an incredible job, though. I hope you don't mind if she comes with Oleg and me to New York. I'm going to need her, especially for the more *delicate* garments." I wink.

"Of course, pussycat. It can be an extra wedding gift."

"Ivan, what will happen if we succeed? Taking out the Zadorov family, as well as the other heads involved with their outfit, will leave too big a hole, and you know it. If you're retired and I'm running New York, who's going to monitor this? Someone is going to fill that, whether we like it or not. And what if they are worse than the others?"

"We have other family in Russia, dear, and they share the values you and I do. My father and yours had another brother by the name of Alexei. He was the oldest and the heir to the Russian branch. He didn't agree with your grandfather's regime. By that time, my father was already the established Pakhan in New York, and your father in Thunder Bay. Alexei had three sons, and your Grandfather assumed they would make a better choice of heir than their father, but he

needed something temporary. A regent, if you will. Zakhar was young and ambitious and just the strand of evil your grandfather enjoyed.

"He was never supposed to take over this branch permanently, but when your grandfather died, Zakhar sent out death warrants for Alexei and his sons. Alexei turned himself in, but his sacrifice allowed his family to escape. They took refuge with us in New York for several years. I was closer to them than my own siblings. After a while, it became dangerous for them to remain at our compound. They were old enough to care for themselves and all scattered in the wind to different states within America. I kept in touch, though. The three of them agreed to take this role together, in order to rule this branch as more of a democracy than a dictatorship."

"*Extra*? Oh, I have a feeling I'm going to leave with more than enough already."

CHAPTER 38

Thatcher

"AND THIS IS your room!"

Ellie opens the door to reveal a beautifully decorated room in the west wing of their compound. The estate isn't as large as the one in New York, but what it lacks in size, it makes up for in elegance. As fun as the red latex is in my bedroom, and Mila's, it's a breath of fresh air to be staying in more modern surroundings. The soft blues and beige wood give off a beachy vibe, fitting for a city like Thunder Bay.

"What do you think?"

"It's fantastic, but you didn't have to go to all this trou—"

"Oh, don't mention it. We had it fixed up for you as soon as we moved in. It was one of the first changes Teddy made."

I give Ellie a quick hug and kiss on the cheek, then turn my attention to Teddy with the cheesiest grin I can muster. "You were thinking about me, huh?"

"Whatever, man," Teddy mumbles, rolling his eyes.

He never sees my tackle coming, and even if I don't quite get him to the ground, I still squeeze him in the tightest hug I can manage. "Nah, admit it. You were thinking about me."

"I'm going to give you two lovers some privacy," Ellie giggles. "Let me know if you need anything."

The moment the door closes, I plop on the bed, noticing how comfortable the mattress is. This is *much* better than the bed in New York. "So, how's life?"

Teddy lowers down onto a chair beside the bed with a raised brow. "I've been with you all afternoon. I've told you how life is."

"Yeah, yeah, but we were with *the Santori brothers.* It's not like you can *really* get into things with them around."

"Jesus, what kind of things do you think I've been up to?"

"Um, their sister for one—"

"*That* isn't up for discussion with *anyone*...You know I don't kiss and tell—what? Why are you looking at me like that?"

Okay, so maybe I really didn't want to hear the gushy, intimate parts of his and Ellie's relationship and this was all just a setup to tell my best friend that I'm in love with *his* sister.

"Um, well, *you* may not kiss and tell, but I've never been able to spare you any details of my love life, and even though she will probably kill me for saying this—"

"Whoa, there's a *she?*"

"To you in particular—"

"To me in par—huh?"

"Your sister and I are kind of together!" I blurt out, closing my eyes as if that will protect me from Teddy's wrath. He may be a teddy bear, but he's a *big* motherfucker. But after what feels like an eternity of silence, I open them, not to anger, but to a *shocked* expression on my friend's face. "Um...can you say something?"

Teddy takes his time looking me up and down before responding. "You. And Mila. Are...together?"

"Yes. Are you—"

"And what do you mean by *together*? Like, you lived in the same house for a while? You're friends? Wha…what do you mean?"

"Like…We enjoy each other's company and have a sexual relationship and decided recently to give this a real shot."

"*How* recently?"

"Well, we've been…doing stuff for almost two months now. But we didn't decide to give it a real shot until this past weekend."

"I don't mean to sound rude, but does Mila know about this relationship?"

"Yes? Of course she does. I mean, I haven't heard from her in a couple of days."

"Well yeah, I wouldn't assume so since she's on her way to get ma—*fuck*." Teddy's face turns as white as a ghost. "I…I need to go see about, um, Ellie. I forgot she likes, um…foot rubs."

"Wait! Are you mad at me? I know it's your sister, but…but I love her!"

"*Fuck*," Teddy mumbles as he combs his fingers through his hair. "I swear I'm not mad. I always knew you had a crush on her. I'm just surprised as hell that she gave you the time of day. No offense to you, she's just…intense. But look, I really need to get to Ellie's, uh, feet. You've got a mini fridge and a snack bar stocked with all of your favorites. Your bathroom is right through that door and should have all your preferred toiletries. If you need anything, just let us know." He pauses at the door, looking more troubled than I've seen him in a very long time. "I really am happy for you, man. I…I hope it all works out. I'll see you in the morning."

Well, that's fucking weird. I guess it's good that he's not mad at me. Although I'm not sure how to feel about "I'm just surprised as hell that she gave you the time of day." I'm an excellent catch, thank you very much. I mean, in his defense, Mila *is* like…the *ultimate* catch. Okay, in all honesty, I'm also shocked that she chose me.

Nobody has ever really chosen me for me.

Sure, I've had plenty of women throwing themselves at me, but let's be real—I'm a very successful athlete and a trust-fund baby on top of that. Add in the fact that I'm decently handsome, and I'm every gold digger's dream. But if you stripped the money and notoriety from me, not even my good looks would be enough to grab their attention.

I know this because there have been plenty of people in my life who haven't been interested in those things, and they sure as hell didn't care about me. My parents, in particular. So for a woman so incredible to take interest in who I am at my core, well, I don't know if I'll ever completely believe it.

It's why I enjoy submitting to her. I *have* to please her. Deep in my soul, I feel the need to do whatever it takes to be Mila's good boy. It ignites a fire in me to know I've made her happy. Maybe that's why we work so well together. Whatever trauma she's had that's led her to her sexual preferences blends so perfectly with mine.

Falling back on the bed, I check my phone to see if there have been any new messages, but there's nothing.

Why won't you answer my calls?

I want to believe she's just busy, but the longer she stays silent, the more I doubt it's so simple. Fuck, I'm over here worried about her ghosting me when she could be in legitimate danger. Grabbing a pillow, I hold it tight to myself as my tears finally break free. Tomorrow, I'll have Teddy and the new team to keep me occupied, but tonight all I can do is pretend this pillow is Mila. That the love of my life is here with me, safe and happy.

CHAPTER 39

Thatcher

THE DISTRACTION OF settling into Thunder Bay this week has been the only thing keeping me from thinking about Mila. The love of my life who ghosted me as soon as I realized I loved her. *Love* her. Just because she hasn't reached out doesn't mean I love her any less. If anything, this time of no contact has made me realize exactly how much I crave her in my life.

It took me less than one day before I spilled the news to Teddy about Mila and me, and although he didn't believe me at first, he's been supportive. I know it's a hard line for him to walk between being my best friend and trying to cultivate a relationship with his newfound sister, but he seems cool with it, for the most part. I'd never expect him to tell me all her business, or any of it, really, but it would be nice to know anything at all about *why*.

He's let me know she's okay, and that'll have to be enough for now. My days have been hockey, training, recovery, eating, and sleeping. That's it. I'm not sure what I'll do long term, but I've managed to convince myself that Mila will reach out, and all I have to do is wait.

Pathetic. I make another lap around the compound, trying

to use the skills Misha taught me to memorize building layouts quickly. One more right up here and I should be…

"Ah!"

"Fuck!"

Teddy barrels into me, rounding the corner like someone's lit his ass on fire and scaring the shit out of me. He's surprised, as if I'm the last person he expected, and he doesn't seem thrilled to see me. *Surely, someone has trained him not to run his hand through his hair when he's nervous?*

"You're in a hurry," I say, unable to hide my curiosity. He must notice me narrowing my eyes at his obvious tell, because he drops his hand to his side immediately and tries to act nonchalant.

"No! I mean, no. Not at all. I do have somewhere to be, though, so…"

"Somewhere with your passport in your pocket?" Oh God. I'd almost forgotten how awkward he can be. Once he realized Ellie was into him, he became all suave with her. And the Bratva training has made him pretty damn scary to watch in the sparring ring. But this is old-school Teddy. I've caught him in a throwback moment of tension.

"Uh. Yeah, actually. Apparently, I'm being summoned to a big Bratva wedding in Russia. Fucking Rusev lost my invitation, so I've gotta leave now. You'll hang out with Ellie for me, right?"

He's trying to ease past me down the hallway, but even though I'm not quite his size, I can still block him a bit.

"Sure I can, but it's Friday. What about the exhibition match on Tuesday?"

"Coach knows I'm going, and the wedding is Sunday. I'll be back before then. Ivan assured me."

We both realize what he said at the same time. Why the hell am I asking about hockey? Who the fuck cares?

"Is she—"

"I've really gotta go, Thatch. You know I love you like a brother, and I hate to see you in an ounce of pain. Please believe me when I say it'll all work out. I really do think so. But right now, I have a plane to catch, okay? Love you, man."

"Love you, too."

I lean heavily against the wall, staying put for the five or so minutes it takes Teddy to grab a bag and head for the SUV waiting outside the front door. Ellie, looking more pregnant these days, squeezes him for a hug and wipes her eyes when she lets him go. *I don't really think she's been all that emotional lately…*

Maybe she's upset that she doesn't get to go to the fancy Bratva shindig. Or maybe she thinks Teddy will be in danger during this trip. I guess I can imagine any Bratva occasion having the potential to get rowdy and dangerous.

Continuing down the hallway as the sun starts to set, Teddy's locked office door beckons. The keypad taunts me even though I've never been much of a snooper. I wonder…

2…6…6…2…7

The satisfying click of the lock proves that Teddy hasn't changed a bit, and I step into the office, closing the door behind me. Too late, I consider that it might be booby-trapped or equipped with lasers that'll fire poison darts at me as soon as I take a step, but I cross the room to the desk unscathed.

I've been here before, but only briefly. I don't think it's necessarily Teddy's favorite room in the house, and I don't blame him. I wouldn't want to be reminded of the massive weight on my shoulders any more than I needed to be. It does have a sick bar cart in a globe, though, so it isn't all bad.

He's filled in the bookshelves with some of his own knick-knacks, including framed photos of him and Ellie. Some of these look like she's sleeping…*Jesus, Teddy.* Seeing him and Ellie just reminds me of Mila, as everything else does.

Continuing my perusal, I hit the jackpot on a side table near a banquet chair. *A three-wick candle.* Hell yes. I haven't burned a candle since…well, since before Mila. But there's a big-ass tub in my suite, and a candlelit bath might be just the thing I need to relax.

I need a lighter, though, and there's not one in sight. Surely in his desk drawer, though. This is invasive, I know, but I'm a trustworthy guy, and Teddy and I have shared a *lot* over the years. I'll just find a lighter, go enjoy my bath, and go to sleep.

Except there's not a fucking lighter in sight. Just my luck. Sitting back heavily into the giant leather desk chair that Teddy must have made custom, I note how tall his desk is. I would fit under there perfectly, with plenty of room to kneel and please Mila…

Goddamn, I have to get a grip. I'll have a bath without a candle, then drink a bottle of wine and go to bed. Anything is better than…*ooo, shiny.* A golden flash catches my eye in the desk drawer, and pulling it free reveals a thick cream piece of cardstock with gold lettering. It's in Cyrillic, but based on the entwined wedding rings embossed at the top, I can guess this is the invitation to the wedding Teddy has to attend.

Teddy's desk phone rings, startling me, and I drop the paper, feeling like a kid who's been caught being naughty. *Which I suppose I am.* It's the perfect reminder that I shouldn't be in here, and I'm late for my bath. Grabbing my candle in case I find a lighter elsewhere, I bend down to retrieve the invite, realizing it flipped when it fell.

The front text was Cyrillic, but the back…the back is in English, and my candle clatters to the ground as I read every other word, tears clouding my vision immediately.

You… cordially… wedding

Mila Taranova

&

Oleg Zadorov

Panic steals my breath as I pull my phone from my pocket with shaking hands. That fucker better not be on the plane yet. If he doesn't answer my call, I'm taking Ellie to her parents' house and burning this place to the ground. Luckily for the entire Taranova Bratva, Teddy picks up on the third ring.

"Hey, man, we're about to take off. Is everything—"

"*Her fucking wedding? Mila? I love her, and you're going to her goddamn wedding without a single explanation?*" My anger is wild and hot as I lash out, but it dissolves just as quickly into pain, and I can't control my sobs.

"Where are you? How do you—"

"I'm curled into the fetal position under your office desk, asshole. I was looking for a lighter, and I found it—"

"Please don't light any candles—"

"Fuck you!" I scream again, and this is so much better than sobbing that I decide to stick with it, yelling at Teddy until my throat feels like it's been shredded with the same knife as my heart. "I don't care about your plane, but if you don't tell me the entire truth right now, I swear to God, you'll regret it."

I can't believe I've just threatened my Bratva boss best friend, who definitely has more than a few kills to his name at this point, but I don't give a shit anymore. My Mila is marrying someone else in two days in fucking Russia, and I have no clue what's going on.

"I'll forgive that because you're upset and I love you, but do not threaten me ever again, Thatcher. Do you understand?"

His voice is deadly serious, and I sniffle out a petulant yes so he'll continue.

"I don't know much more than you do. I don't think everything is as it seems, and I told you I think everything will work out, but I won't learn more until we land in Russia. Now, I have to go. We're literally about to take off. Everything will be okay. Please take care of Ellie. I'll see you next week."

The service was already starting to spot by the time his goodbye fades away, and I let my phone drop from my hand to the floor. The daylight fades until darkness consumes the room, yet I can't bring myself to uncurl and move from my hiding spot under the desk. I briefly consider that I might feel safe under the desk because that's the first place I was allowed to touch Mila, and I swear I can almost feel her hand playing with my hair.

The pain overcomes me, and I vomit violently onto the rug under the desk, mostly bile since I haven't eaten since breakfast. My first thought is to find something to clean it up, but this is the least of what Teddy deserves for being less than honest with me earlier. In any case, it's enough to get me off my ass because, as miserable as I am, I can't lie here with the stench of vomit.

Trudging back to my room feels like a death march, every step representing another inch away from Mila. Having to think about her in the past tense is the worst fate I could imagine for myself, and if I hadn't realized I had loved her before, I sure as fuck would now. This is heartbreak, and every stupid song and movie about love lost suddenly makes sense.

The funny thing is, she'd be so disappointed in how I'm acting right now.

"*You aren't a quitter, solnyshko. I know you can take it. The reward will be much better on the other side if you keep pushing.*"

That's the problem, though. I *am* a quitter. Anything I managed to endure was only because of her. And this time, she's not by my side. *That's the difference.* I brush my teeth and try to sleep, but it's impossible. I'm haunted by the idea that if the shoe were on the other foot, she'd burn down the world to get to me.

She'd burn it all down without a thought. I know this is true, deep in my bones. I don't know why she's getting married, but it can't be a simple answer. It has to be politics, or blackmail, or...

Blackmail.

Shit. *Shit.* I've been moping and wasting precious fucking hours when it's so goddamn obvious. Mila's in trouble. For the first time in over a week, I have a clear purpose in life, and one priority above all others.

I dial a number in my phone that I haven't used since my playboy days, but there should be plenty of goodwill left over to ensure what I need is ready within the hour.

"Hey, Prescott. Long time no talk. Wanna party?"

"I need a long-haul jet. Range to get to Russia. Ready and in Thunder Bay as soon as you can have it here. Cost isn't an issue."

"Shit, man, consider it done. I have one in Miami that can get to you in no time. But what's the rush? Should I be worried?" He laughs, but I don't return it.

"Not you, man. But someone should be. Someone's got my girl, and I'm getting her back. No matter the cost."

CHAPTER 40

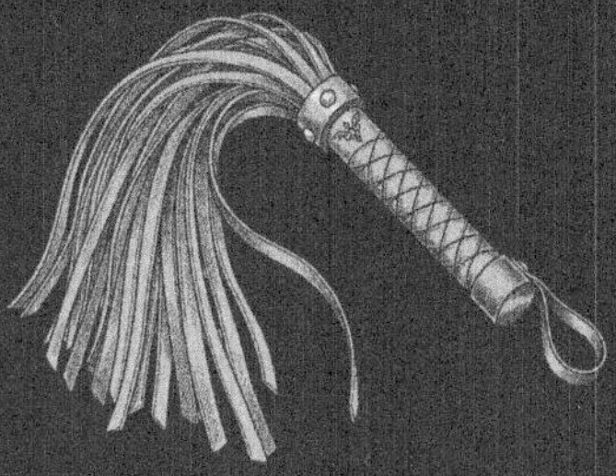

Mila

WITH EVERY PASSING day, I miss Thatcher more. It's been torture to have to ignore him, and I know he's probably spiraling at my silence. Teddy arrived today, and I wanted so badly to ask him how my solnyshko was doing, but even that's too dangerous. We're so close to the finish line here, though, and I just have to make it through one more night pretending to be in love with Oleg the oaf. Between him and his father, I'm not sure who I'm more excited to kill. It was decidedly Zakhar, but every moment I'm forced to stand by Oleg's side, I loathe him more. As I sit beside him with his unwelcome hand on my thigh, inching higher, it's taking everything within me not to take him out right here and now.

"To Oleg and Mila!"

Cheers erupt after the last speech, bringing my focus back to the table of guests. I'm at the head of the table beside my all-too-handsy *fiancé*, with Zakhar and his friends and men placed closest to us. My own men and family are seated so far down, I can hardly see them.

"Everyone is dying to know about the lady who snatched our Oleg up. Tell us about yourself. How did you two meet?" one of the more noticeably drunk wives slurs from a few chairs down.

"Oh, well, I run the—"

"My *beautiful* bride has been helping me transfer things over in New York," Oleg says, squeezing my thigh. "That's how we met, actually. The Zadorovs will be taking over the outfit there and installing me as the Pakhan, so I've been spending quite a bit of time there. My girl was being so kind, helping her cousin get his records in order to make things easier for everyone. Isn't that right, pussycat?"

"Spot on, darling." My saccharine smile must be convincing, because nobody bats an eye, even as I wrench Oleg's hand off my thigh.

The faux story draws the attention of the other women seated nearby, who coo in unison.

"So was it love at first sight?" This time the question is directed at Oleg instead of me.

"Oh absolutely! Trust me, I had no intention of falling in love so easily, but I knew the moment I saw her that she was it."

Oleg drones on as I glance at where Misha is staring back at me. I can't see him well enough to make out his expression, but I know he's furious.

"What are these two lovebirds talking about?" Zakhar says, interrupting his son.

"Oleg was just telling us how smitten he is."

My father-in-law-to-be chuckles. "Oh yes, we're all smitten with our sweet little Mila. I know she's going to make my son a very happy man. Just look at how in love they are!"

Oleg leans down to kiss my head. I do my best to smile instead of cringing, and judging by the women's swooning, I guess my acting skills are still on point.

"See, look at my little lovebirds. These two are going to make me a litter of grandchildren!"

"A litter of heirs you mean?" One of the nearby men laughs. "You're going to need a lot in order to run all of the outfits you've taken over, Zakhar."

Oleg throws his arm around my shoulder and pulls me closer to him. "Don't you worry about the grandchildren. I'm going to put so many sons in my wife, she won't know what to do."

Fuck that shit. I can't stop the visceral reaction to slap the shit out of this asshole. Luckily, his crude language warrants such a response, so I play the bashful bride.

"Oleg!" I gasp, slapping his shoulder way harder than necessary for the act.

Our audience eats it up, breaking out in laughter. His eyes darken momentarily before he remembers where we are and joins along.

"Oh, you'll pay for that one soon, *wife*," he pretends to joke.

But I know he's serious. I know that, given the chance, his abuse would be insurmountable. That's why he'll never get the chance to lay a hand on me, or anyone else for that matter.

Tomorrow. I just have to survive until tomorrow.

The possibility of failure rarely overwhelms me, but with so many people who mean so much to me all here together, I can't help the momentary lapse.

Ivan and Blanche sit, shmoozing the people all around them like it's the most natural thing in the world. I've gotten so close to Ivan in the past couple of months. He's so gentle and fatherly, and didn't have to come here and risk his life. His wife definitely didn't have to. They have children and grandchildren and a million other reasons to live, yet they chose to come help me. If anything happens to them tomorrow, I'll never be able to forgive myself.

Then there are my brothers sitting across from them. To everyone else, Misha looks as cool as a cucumber, but I know his subtle tells. And Teddy's as obvious as day running his fingers through his hair. *I have to get that trained out of him.* Before Teddy came into my life, Misha was the only person I loved. Then Teddy showed up, and as much as I fought it, I couldn't deny the love that my baby brother brought into my life. I would tell myself it's just one more person, but as an extension of Teddy, Ellie and their baby were always a part of that love as well. If anything happened to them…well, I wouldn't want to continue living.

At the thought of my own demise, my mind goes to Thatcher. It would kill him to lose me. It's a realization I've had recently, and one that's added pressure to my already overloaded list of responsibilities. Of everyone I hold dear, nobody holds a candle to Thatcher. Not even Misha can compete with the love I have for my solnyshko. I have to stay alive for him.

Fuck, more than that. I have to stay alive for *me.*

I've always had something to die for, but for the first time in my life, I have something to *live* for.

My determination finds me again, washing away any doubts of success tomorrow. It *has* to work. And I refuse to allow anyone I love to perish in the process. We'll take our territory back once and for all, burning anyone and anything that stands in our way.

CHAPTER 41

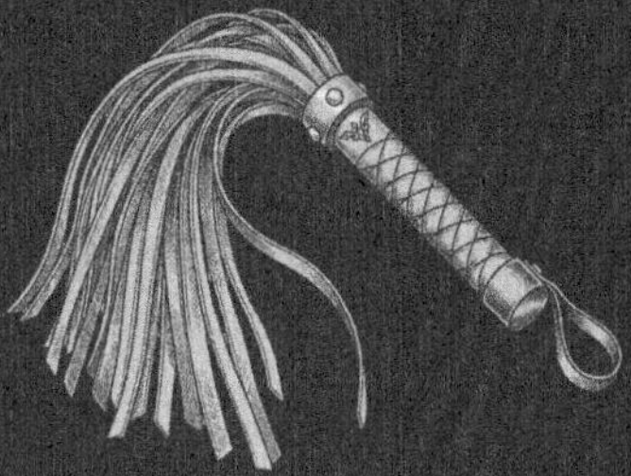

Mila

IF I EVER pictured planning a wedding for myself as a little girl, which I didn't, basically none of this would have been in my vision. Not this gaudy dress, not this brutalist church, and certainly not the oaf at the end of the aisle. I can't say that I wouldn't have pictured the blackmail, since that's such a huge part of our lifestyle, but I would have imagined myself as the blackmail*er,* not the blackmail*ee.*

The very few things I have control over, though, are precisely as I would have wanted. My closest friends and family, small circle that it is, are here to support me. The "wedding lingerie" I've chosen, completely concealed by this monstrosity of a dress, is perfectly tailored and makes me feel like a queen. And, hopefully, everything will go to plan.

"Come in!" A knock interrupts my reverie, and since very few people know where I am right now, I feel safe letting whoever it is in. That, plus the fact that Misha hasn't been more than two feet away from me since we arrived in Russia. *Not even when I went to the bathroom.*

"I've seen it all, moya tsaritsa. Don't you recall when you tried to sever your femoral artery in South Africa, and I had to hold pressure on it for four hours before we got to a hospital?"

Since our plan was finalized, he's calmed down, but I know him well enough to see the turmoil underneath his facade. Hopefully, he can have plenty of the one thing that soothes him soon enough.

"Mila, darling, you look...dreadful."

Blanche and I have become fast friends recently, and although I don't think I view her as a *motherly* presence, she's a badass. Maybe a cool aunt.

"Thank you. I *feel* dreadful."

"You know, this dress looks remarkably similar to my own."

"Oh? And you think it's—"

"Dreadful? Absolutely. I didn't have much choice in mine. A little old lady picked it out of her stock in a tiny town, and we eloped with zero time to plan. In any case, it was a happy day, even if I hated the gown."

"Hmm." I don't know what to say to that, since today is highly unlikely to be happy at all.

"Well, I didn't come here just to insult your gown. Although I'd be remiss not to mention that you look beautiful, dear. So much so that even the gown can't dim your radiance. Your hair, in particular, is giving—"

"Warrior queen," Misha pipes in, proud that someone noticed his handiwork. The crown braid around my head is much more intricate than I usually wear, but then again, it's not your wedding day very often. He's had to braid my hair for years, especially early on when I wouldn't let anyone else close enough to touch me. This is his best work yet, I think.

"Yes," Blanche agrees. "Very warrior queen. But as I was saying, I did come bearing a gift." She rummages through her purse before pulling out a pair of sapphire earrings. "My late husband gave me these when we found out our second child was going to be a boy. It would be an honor if you would wear them today. Ivan is very fond of you, and I hope that we'll get to spend more time together and introduce you to more of our family. I've already had Christmas stockings made for you and—"

Misha must notice the emotion clouding my features, and he jumps in to save me just as I thank Blanche with a tight hug. "Well, it looks like it's time to get this show on the road. Ready, moya tsaritsa?" He holds out a hand and my bouquet, ready to walk me down the aisle and hope everything goes to plan. Every second of time and inch of space in the church has been accounted for, and as long as there are no surprises, I'm confident of our success.

No surprises, and we might just make it out of here alive.

"I'm ready, moya sila."

"This really is the ugliest church I've ever seen in my life," Misha whispers as we stand in the vestibule, waiting for the music of my processional to begin. "They couldn't have added a single pane of stained glass? A hint of gold?"

He's not wrong. This is a post-Soviet brutalist eyesore, all concrete and sharp angles. It's going to be easier on my conscience to destroy, though, so that's a point in the ugly church's favor.

"You know, moya tsaritsa," Misha begins, and I hear a rasp in his voice.

"No! No, Misha. None of that. Don't tell me that you love me and that the life we've built for ourselves is more than you could have imagined. Don't remind me of our escapades running around as barefoot children or getting high as scrawny teenagers. Don't mention how much I've grown, or how proud you are of how I've never let anything extinguish my fire."

He sniffles, but I fight through.

"And I won't tell you that I love you too and would be dead without you, or a husk of myself at most. That every bar fight and late night have been more vivid with you by my side, and that your presence is why I was able to continue when I wanted to stop so many times. I'm not telling you any of that shit because one day, you're going to have a wedding and we'll get to say these things for real. Today is not that day."

He snorts and laughs, only once. "Alright, moya tsaritsa. I won't say any of that, and you don't either." Passing me the bouquet, heavier than before, he offers his arm as the music swells. "I will tell you that you have lipstick on your teeth, though."

Before I can find a mirror, he laughs again, and the doors to the church open, revealing hundreds of stony-faced Bratva cousins, here to try to gain favor at the event of the year. *They might not gain favor, but it should certainly be a show to remember.*

As we begin our processional, I note that all our men are advantageously positioned. Hopefully, none of them flagged on Zadorov's watch list, although they're all wearing minor facial prosthetics to try to avoid recognition software.

Oleg stands at the altar like a conquering hero, and I smile. To anyone else, perhaps it seems like I'm happy to be walking to my fate with this man, but it's the thought of slitting his throat that fuels my grin. Zakhar is in a place of honor at the front of the church, looking like the cat that got the cream. *Or the man who foolishly thinks he's staged a successful coup.*

When we finish our trudge up the aisle, Misha hands me over to Oleg, who places a slimy kiss on the back of my hand as we turn to face the priest. As the traditional ceremony begins, I tune out my surroundings and turn inward to begin opening my boxes. Some are old friends that I've relied on over the years to survive early on and thrive more recently. Others are new, ready to be tapped into for the first time.

With only a few more aspects of the ceremony remaining, the first of our men should be arriving soon, taking their places on the roof and in the crypt underneath our feet. Then the cavalry can arrive, if everything is timed correctly.

Bang!

The heavy doors of the chapel are thrown open, and the collective gasp of the guests is drowned out only by the clacking of hundreds of guns being cocked to be pointed at... *Thatcher?*

"I object!"

Oh *shit.* Either he doesn't notice the danger he's in or he doesn't care. He slowly walks up the aisle, voice echoing throughout the church even as he sniffles.

Oh, solnyshko.

"That's *my* woman, the love of my *life*, and you can't fucking marry her! She belongs with me! Mila, don't do this!"

Thatcher's heartbroken gaze locks onto me, and I swear I can hear my own heartbeat for a few moments.

Then all hell breaks loose.

CHAPTER 42
Thatcher

"THAT'S *MY* WOMAN, the love of my *life*, and you can't fucking marry her! She belongs with me! Mila, don't do this!"

There. I've said my piece. Now, regardless of what happens, I'll know I left everything on the table, and there's no room for regret. Except I'm in the middle of this goddamn church with hundreds of people staring at me, and…*guns*?

Oh, *fuck me.* I've barged into a giant Russian Bratva wedding uninvited? But why weren't there guards at the door? I didn't see a soul outside. I just walked right in.

Maybe I should apologize? Ask to speak to Mila privately? That's it, I'll just beg her to hear me out one-on-one, then…

The world goes hazy as smoke fills the chapel. My ears are ringing, and it's fucking pandemonium in here. Gunshots, explosions, and general sounds of destruction rattle the glass of the windows, and I drop to the ground behind a pew.

My instinct is to hide, not fight, and as a bloody body falls over the pew next to me, bile rises in my throat. I'm not making it out of here alive. And Mila…

Fuck! Mila!

I scramble for the far end of the pew, avoiding the aisle where the most action seems to be, based on the screaming. I have to get to her, but I'm fighting upstream from the crowd heading for the exits. *And stepping over more bodies every minute.*

The smoke is clearing now, and I focus on the front of the church, hoping to steal a glimpse of a puffy white gown. Or maybe she's escaped already, and I can at least rest easy or die happy knowing she's safer than here.

Before I can decide whether to try to get closer to the altar or to cross and make sure I haven't missed Mila on the other side of the aisle, I see her. She's in white, but it's not the poofy gown from earlier. Only the bodice remains, ripped and stained with blood that doesn't appear to be hers. At least not with the way she's moving.

She's *terrifying.* Her bodice may be white, but she's wearing black tights strapped with knives. Either she knew something was bound to happen today or she's always prepared. Knowing her, it's probably both. Moving closer to the front pew, she's evading capture and leaving chaos in her wake. Nobody's shooting at her, though.

They're sure as shit still shooting at me, and I duck as a bullet passes close enough that the wall where it hits sends debris into my face. Something's in my eye, and I fall to the ground as the sound of the fighting escalates. *Fuck,* I'm not sure how I can get out of here.

"Get *up,* solnyshko!"

I can barely see, but only one person has ever called me that. My savior wrenches me up from the ground and immediately lays into me.

"What the fuck is wrong with you? Were you planning to lie on the ground and die? I know how strong you are. Even if your eye doesn't work, your legs do. Up!"

The sniffle escapes before I can help it, but I'm just so goddamn happy. That's *my* woman. If she thinks I can get up, I can.

"Do *not* cry right now, Thatcher." She moves us toward a side door I hadn't seen, hidden behind a recess near the front of the church.

"Well, pardon me for being happy to be rescued by the love of my life minutes after I found out she was marrying someone else! What the actual fuck, Mila?"

"You have to be fucking kidding me." She drops my arm to reload her handgun, then shoots someone blocking us at point-blank range. Lifting me over the body like a toy, we continue. "This is really not the time to—"

"I think it's the perfect time. I fly to Russia thinking there's no way the—"

I'm interrupted by an idiot who thinks it's a good idea to try to engage me in hand-to-hand combat. Mila deftly parries his knife away from me, then adds one of her own to his heart, kicking him away and pulling me again.

"It's a ruse, solnyshko. Fucking hell. You think all this is happening because you interrupted the wedding? No, these are my men taking out the head of the snake once and for all. It was planned, and the marriage was never going to be legal, so for God's sake, let's move."

"You don't—"

She shuts me up with a harsh, hot kiss, reclaiming me as thoroughly as if we were standing at the altar ourselves.

"I love you too, by the way. Now please, *please* follow my lead so I can get you out of here."

"Me? You mean us, right?"

"This is my fight, solnyshko. Mine and Misha's and Ivan's. Blanche is somewhere with a machine gun, fighting for our side of the family. Teddy's here too, hopefully sticking close to Misha. I'm not going anywhere."

We stand for a tense few seconds, and I feel like I'm on the verge of a breakdown. I *just* got her back, and she loves me. Me! And now she wants to stay in the midst of this battle…I want to kidnap her. Hide her away from the world so she's safe. But that's not Mila. People should be hiding from her.

"I'm not leaving you," I whisper. As much as I wish my voice was stronger right now, I'm terrified. "I *refuse* to leave you, even if I can't necessarily help."

The flash of indecision in her eyes makes me think she might force me to leave, but finally she sighs and pulls me back toward the front of the church. She plops me down behind the altar, unleashing a hidden latch and pointing at the door she's just opened in the side.

"This is bulletproof and fireproof, so please stay in here. I'll come for you, Thatcher, I swear. Promise me you'll stay?"

"How the hell did he manage to fall asleep in there?"

"Well, I imagine it was pretty muffled, and he had a long flight."

"Yeah, party foul, by the way, man. Leaving him with *no* explanation at all? Poor Sunshine."

"Hey, you gave me barely any warning! My pregnant wife was my main concern, not that I don't love Thatcher like a brother, but—"

"I can see why you're so smitten with him, dear. He's a fine specimen. Ivan, he reminds me of our pool boy, don't you think? Just with less hair down there—"

"Wake up, solnyshko. Float out of your dreams and come back to me."

That voice, not grating like the others, makes me want to try to open my eyes. My neck hurts, and I don't know where I am… am I naked?

Fully awake now, I try to stand, only to whack my head on the top of whatever oven of a box I'm in. I can see Mila through a small door, though, so I do my best to crawl through, basking in her smile and the fresh air once I'm out.

I plop down on my back, stretching all my muscles that have been bunched up for what must have been hours, and remember where I am. *Shit,* I slept through the entire end of the battle? Based on Mila, Teddy, Misha, Ivan, and Blanche all staring down at me, things must have gone in our favor.

Everyone seems to be holding back laughter, though, and Blanche's eyes are focused far south of my own.

A breeze tickles a *very* sensitive spot just as Teddy speaks up. "Thatch, brother. Why the hell are you naked?"

CHAPTER 43

Mila

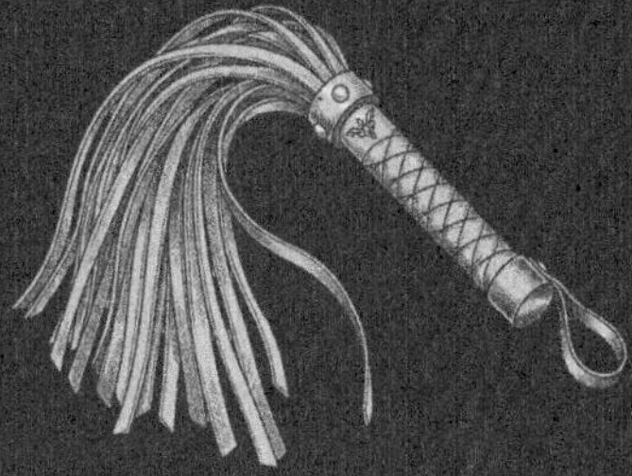

GRANDFATHER'S OLD OFFICE may look different after Zadorov redecorated, but the same ghosts haunt it as when I was a child. The walls are a different color, but they suffocate me as if no time has passed. The only difference now is that I'm sitting behind the desk instead of, well…

I feel his presence before he even makes a noise. "Come in, moya sila," I call, still looking down at the cluster of paperwork spread out in front of me.

He does as commanded, plopping down in the chair across from me and kicking his feet up on the desk.

"Is it bad?"

While I've been locked in Zadorov's office for the past twenty-four hours, doing my best to sort out the mess he's gotten the once-powerful Taranov Bratva into, Misha has been dealing with the more tragic aftermath of our takeover.

"It's not as bad as it could've been. Less than twenty—"

"And their families?"

"All taken care of with enough money for this life and the next."

"Good. How's Thatcher?"

Misha chuckles and grins for the first time since yesterday. "He's milking the shit out of all of this. He's got every old nurse in the place babying him. You're going to have your hands full with that one. I'll tell you that right now."

The mention of Thatcher brings a stabbing pain in my chest that I can't seem to fight. There's so much I need to tell him, and I'm not sure he'll stick around when he finds out.

"What about you? Have you been able to sort anything out yet?" Misha asks, bringing me back to the moment.

Rubbing my temples, I finally look up. "No, and I don't think I'm going to anytime soon. This takeover was more than any of us expected, and it's going to take months of effort from Ivan, our cousins, and me to get our outfit back on track. Can you imagine what my father would think of me now? Not only am I running the largest branch in the States, but I'm heading up a massive cleanup in the Motherland. I'm sure he's rolling over in his grave at the thought of his *daughter* taking on more than he ever did."

Misha scratches his neck, then slides a folder to me. "That's actually what I came in here for. You see, Ivan's hacker guy has been working on gathering all the digital intel for him and when he came across these files, well, look for yourself."

I never know what to expect with Misha, but I would have never imagined this. It's page after page of conversations between Father and Zadorov going back and forth about my place as the leader of the Thunder Bay branch, spanning *years*. I'm trying to make sense of it all, but the more I read, the more hazy everything becomes.

"What...what is this?"

"Read it—"

"I can't!" I hiss as my eyes begin to water.

Misha smiles lazily, any ounce of teasing gone as he softens his voice. "He always wanted you to take his place. It was Zadorov fighting it all along. He started years ago, trying to get your father to agree to a marriage between you and Oleg, to no avail. After years of Igor turning him down, he pulled out the big guns. First with Teddy. I'm not sure how he found out about your brother, but even that didn't shake your father."

I flip through the papers and do my best to focus on the conversations about my brother. God, Father really basically told Zakhar to fuck right off.

"Tell the board I have a son. I couldn't care less. My daughter has more balls than you and your pathetic son combined. If Mila wasn't the best man for the job, I wouldn't be leaving her my legacy."

"God, did he even know about Teddy before then?" I ask under my breath.

"Unclear, but it didn't sway his decision either way. It wasn't until, well. Flip to the back."

I do as he asks, only to find the same pictures Ivan and I received as blackmail last week.

"He knew?" I whisper.

"He knew…"

Silence fills the room as I read through the final messages in the folio, and Zadorov's final threat.

"She marries Oleg, or these get sent to every member of the Taranov board."

I never told Father about what happened to me in Russia. He seemed to respect and cherish me, but I assumed that admiration would only go so far.

"Under no circumstances will Mila ever marry your son. Teddy will be my heir. And with Mila no longer in charge, nobody will give a damn about those pictures. All you will do if you ever release

them is bring a war upon our outfits, one you will undoubtedly lose. Thanks to my daughter's genius, our branch has and will continue to outperform yours in every respect. The only reason you aren't already dead is because it would set off a war between our families and cause the death of too many Russian men. But if you ever threaten the ones I love again, I will not be so generous. Do I make myself clear?"

"The ones he *loves*?"

"I would say he loved you very much, moya tsaritsa."

Tears are falling freely down my face at this point, and Misha can't help his tears, either. I allow myself a moment to let things sink in, to *feel*...Until a familiar knock sounds from outside the office.

"Come in, Thatcher," I call out as I straighten up in my chair and wipe my eyes.

My sunshine boy strolls in, brightening the entire room with his smile, stopping only when he sees the redness from Misha's and my tears. "What's wrong? Is everything okay? Are you alright?"

Misha stands and pats Thatcher on the shoulder. "I'll leave you to it."

"What's wrong?" he asks, still somehow brightening the room, even with concern on his face.

"Um, why don't you sit down. I think you and I need to discuss some things before we take this...*thing,* between us any further."

"This *thing* being love?" He does as I ask and slowly sits in the chair Misha was just in. And if this conversation is anything like the last, we are in for an emotional ride.

"Yes." I chuckle. "This thing being love. I do love you. Truly, I do. But this isn't a gentle life I live, and well...love is hardly ever enough but certainly rarely in the position I'm in."

Thatcher's brow creases in confusion as he stares into my eyes.

Into my soul, more like. "I don't care about your job. I think it's badass—"

"This isn't a job, Thatcher, it's my *life*! You may not care now, but you will. I'm not like Ivan or Sasha, who met the love of their life and found a way out of this life. There isn't an out for me, and even if there were, I wouldn't take it. *This* is my first love. I'm not saying I don't love you, solnyshko, because I do…so, so much. But you will always have to deal with the demands this life makes on me. The mental energy alone is hard, but the time I'll have to spend away. Even living together would feel long distance. Is that really the type of relationship you want to have for the rest of your life? I mean, I'm not trying to rush into marriage or anything, but you don't exactly get to just walk away from the Bratva with the information you would have as someone so close to me. And not to mention the *danger* of it all. You would be the first place my enemy would go to get to me."

"I don't care about any of that. I thought I made myself perfectly clear when I interrupted your *Bratva* wedding!"

"Yeah, that was dumb. You can't do things like that anymore. You could've gotten us both killed! See, it's things like that—"

"Yes, yes, I know it was dumb, and I swear I'll never do anything like that again, but I couldn't lose you. I refuse to lose you. If my life is the price for your love, so be it, because I swear to God, it's not a life worth living without you."

Our heavy breath is the only sound in the office as we get lost in each other's gaze. I want to say okay. I want to move on and make peace with the fact that two other living people know what happened to me all those years ago and be done with it, but I know I can't.

"It's not just that, is it? There's something else…"

"I…I can't have children."

Thatcher pauses, and his already soft eyes never leave mine. "Is that…is that something that you wanted? Because from my standpoint, Mila, I can tell you that you're more than enough for me. We can be the most fun aunt and uncle to Teddy's kids, or if you want to be a parent, we can adopt. But for me, I'm fine without children of my own. I just want you."

"No, I'm at peace with it now, and I love my life without kids. It's *why* I can't have them…"

My good boy sits and listens to every word as I tell him about what happened to me all those years ago. As I tell him *why* I left Russia. Something I've never done. Ivan found out through photos. Misha was there when it all happened. But I've never actually spoken the words.

I didn't move to Thunder Bay until I was a teenager. My father thought he was doing me a favor by not bringing me over. He was growing Thunder Bay's outfit at the time and thought it was safer for me back in Russia, so I spent my childhood living in my grandfather's house. I was raised to be a particularly special kind of killer. One as deadly as any soldier, who could charm men to their demise as well. My physical training took place with the other men but the, um… intimate training was behind closed doors. At the hands of, well… Grandfather. I didn't know any better of course, this was all I ever knew. Until I got pregnant. I was late to get my period because of the training, and when I did get it, I was too scared to tell anyone. But eventually, I couldn't hide my growing stomach anymore. Grandfather was beyond angry and had me sent away to get rid of the baby immediately. I didn't know it at the time, but he ordered they give me a hysterectomy as well, so that no other accidents would ever happen. The pain was unreal. I never wanted to be a mother, necessarily, but to have my child ripped out of me against my consent was devastating. I was curled up in the fetal position, crying on the floor, when Misha found me. He's the only person I knew I could trust beyond a shadow of a doubt. So I told him everything. He was appalled. He held me as we both cried together, then helped me get my revenge. We waited until the time was right and got rid of Grandfather in the way he personally trained me to, with seduction and poison. After that, we hightailed it to my father in Thunder Bay and never looked back...

Thatcher stands and rounds the desk, squatting in front of me so that we're eye level. He rarely ever touches me without my permission, but he kisses me without hesitation, and I allow it. In fact, I welcome it. For the first time in my life, I feel safe as a man holds me romantically.

"Mila Taranova, my love for you is more undeniable than the sunrise. My heart has belonged to you from the moment I met you, and there is *nothing* you could do or say to ever undo that. I am *yours*. And I don't care about what you've done in the past or what you'll do in the future, as long as you're mine. You are the bravest, strongest, most incredible person I've ever known, my love. Let me take care of you as you take over the world. Let me sit and watch as you rule, knowing that I bring you peace and joy in your darkest days. Let me be that man."

A million thoughts race through my mind. But all of the reasons I've never allowed someone close to me before pale in comparison to the overwhelming *need* to let this man love me.

"Okay, solnyshko."

"What does solnyshko mean, anyway?

"It means little sun or sunshine. And you are, Thatcher. You are my light, my everything, and I would be honored to be yours. In this life and the next."

CHAPTER 44

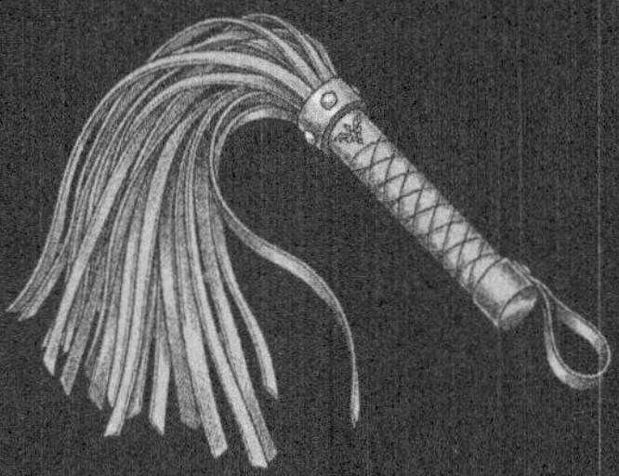

Mila

"HAVE YOU ENJOYED my hospitality?"

They're relatively well-trained, I have to give them that. Or at least Zakhar is. Oleg, for all his blustering ego, has tried to appease me in any way he can think of to save his life. Or to ease his passage from this world. Unfortunately for him, neither of those is on the table.

Thatcher kneels at my feet, warm cheek against my thigh, soothing me as I confront two men who have been trying to take me down for longer than I've been aware of their existence. The catharsis I felt finding out that my father knew every terrible secret I held and loved me anyway has congealed into a cold, fixed hatred that needs to be purged from my soul once and for all.

It isn't lost on me that my closure regarding my parents' unconditional love is much the same thing Thatcher's been seeking his entire life. Although I don't anticipate the same bittersweet ending for him as the one I've received, it'll be my goal to love him enough for two parents as long as I draw breath. Perhaps he'll find peace calling me "Mommy" one day, although he's already been rebuffed from trying to call Misha "Daddy."

"You can fuck yourself, you whore." Oleg spits as far as he can, which isn't very, and falls victim to a coughing fit from the blood draining from his split tongue into his lungs.

"I think that's enough out of that one, moya sila." On my command, Misha grabs the cautery knife, which is one of my favorite toys, and ensures that Oleg Zadorov will never insult me again. He passes out from the pain, and I shrug when Misha wordlessly asks if he wants me to revive him. He can rest for a bit. I really don't care.

Thatcher's hair is soft beneath my fingers, and he relaxes even further into me as I scratch a path to the nape of his neck. He could be asleep, and I hate to leave him, but I've grown weary. It's time to end this chapter.

"Solnyshko," I whisper, scratching a bit harder to try to get his attention. "I need to get up, my handsome boy."

With a grumble, he does as he's told, taking my chair as I stand. He doesn't have to stay for any of this; he didn't have to be here at all. But my solnyshko made it clear that he had no plans to leave my side, and if I wanted him here, there's nowhere he'd rather be.

With Oleg unconscious, Zakhar is the unfortunate recipient of my full attention. He can't spit on me, thanks to the mask in place over all but his eyes, and the defiant loathing there is delicious. Pulling a simple wooden chair in front of him, I turn it around and sit backward, resting my chin on my hands and eyeing my prize.

"You've been very bad, Zakhar."

His eyes flash as I chuckle.

"You hate that, don't you? You think you should be *Mr. Zadorov,* or *father-in-law,* or *sir,* or *Pakhan.*" I can't help but spit the last title, the one that he came so close to taking from me. "Unfortunately for you, I won. You're nothing, mere minutes left to even exist as *Zakhar* before I erase you and your name from everywhere I find it. Yet you still sit here hating me. Even though I bested you."

Misha's puppy dog eyes finally get to me, and I wait while he impales Zakhar's feet into the floor with six-inch spikes through each toenail. He talked so much shit for weeks about *me* being the one who needed to let off steam. If he's this desperate to satiate his blood lust, maybe *he's* the one who needs a plaything. *As a matter of fact...*

"Mmrmph!"

Oleg interrupts my train of thought, finally waking from the shock of having his tongue hacked off. He can't speak anymore, but he certainly can wail and annoy the fuck out of me. One of the benefits of Zakhar's mask is that he can't make a peep.

"Moya sila, I think I'm done with that one if you are."

The shot is immediate, Misha's patience with whiners as thin as my own. Zakhar barely reacts, likely due to both a lack of paternal sentiment toward Oleg and a rapidly waning grip on reality.

"As I was saying. You hate me because you think you deserve what I have, just because you're a man. For *years,* you've plotted against me, stabbing my father in the back in the process and—"

For the first time, a word catches in my throat, but I push through. I refuse to allow this scum to have the pleasure, even at the end of his life, of knowing just how much he affected me. Just how hellish it was to live with the thought that my father had lied to me and betrayed me. Countless tears, *years* of a constant pit in my stomach at the thought that not a single person aside from Misha had ever loved me. Only a beat passes, and I continue.

"And if your stupid little schemes, the deal with the syndicate, all that bullshit you were sewing in Russia…if all of it had worked, maybe you would deserve the title I hold. As it is, I keep my promises. You'll be nothing. Nobody will remember your name or think of you at all."

This reminder finally seems to sink in, and the man who tried to take everything from me senses his pending death.

"While you're…well, let's not say resting in peace, hmm? Perhaps resting in pieces…I'll be here. Enjoying every day with people who are *actually* loyal to me, and running this Bratva the way my father taught me. I'll be the Pakhan for long enough to keep an ear to the ground, and if I hear one fucking *hint* of anyone associated with you stirring up trouble, they'll be with you in hell in a heartbeat. I hope you told everyone never to come near me if you failed. I won't be waiting for them, because I have better things to do, but I'll certainly be ready."

The confusion is clear in the last pitiful whimpers of the asshole whose name will never be spoken again as Misha and I move back into the anteroom to grab Thatcher and leave. Thatcher, who's…asleep?

"He, uh…passed out when I drove the first nail in, I think. After the church, I thought he might be desensitized enough, but—"

"My poor solnyshko," I murmur, pushing the hair out of his eyes. He's not ready for *all* this life entails, even though I know he's going to fight like hell to stay with me as I finish the cleanup in Russia. The scheme that's been lurking in the back of my mind moves to the forefront, and for the first time, I can see a solution that will benefit all parties. *Even if they don't see it that way initially.*

Another whimper from behind us as Misha hoists my sleeping love into his arms finally pushes me over the edge, and my bullet finishes the job before I have time to think.

"Moya tsaritsa, I thought you had a whole thing planned? Just enough calories not to starve, healing him with nurses who were going to pretend to plot with him just to betray him?"

Misha's right, I did have an elaborate plan to extract every molecule of pain before offering the sweet release of death. As we head toward the house, all I can do is shrug.

"I hate whiners," I explain, and both of us laugh, causing Thatcher to stir before settling again. "And, moya sila, I didn't feel like dwelling in that room with a dead man any more than I had to. There's too much to do, to waste time like that."

Finally, we reach the doors to my room, and Misha puts Thatcher down on the bed without another peep.

"So, a long to-do list, huh?"

"Well, you said it yourself. I have three favorite pastimes. One I think I've had my fill of for a while."

Thatcher groans and makes grabby hands, so I put a pillow in his arms until I can join him. He rolls over, content for now, and Misha's eyes are full of mirth but also understanding.

"The other two…I think I'm really just getting started."

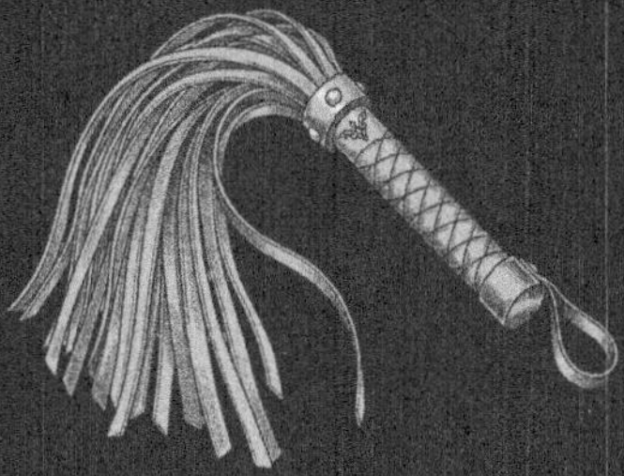

CHAPTER 45

Mila

"YOU'RE MUCH QUIETER tonight than the first time we attended. Are you feeling okay?"

Thatcher's head is in my lap, and I relish each of his delicious moans as my fingernails scratch his scalp. He's been needy, and I've happily obliged him in every way I know how. Well, every way except one, but I plan on changing that tonight. Hopefully, I haven't misjudged things.

He finally sits up and stretches, then turns to face me in the back seat of the car with a sly grin on his face. "I think if you look a little closer, you'll find that I'm feeling more than *okay.*"

A glance down proves that he's fine, physically at least, and I can't help but chuckle. "Alright, you're *great.* But really, any last-minute thoughts or nerves?"

Thatcher turns to the window, watching the city speed by, and places his hand on my thigh, palm up in invitation. This is a gesture he's picked up recently, a silent plea for my attention and touch, and it melts my heart a bit more every time he does it. I happily oblige him, and he squeezes my hand before turning back to me.

"I'm excited. Definitely a little nervous, but more anticipation than anxiety. I haven't been able to think of anything else all day. I…I hope I live up to your expectations."

"Oh, solnyshko." *My sweet boy.* "There's no way you won't. Just keep your manners in mind and remember to ask me discreetly if you need help or want to ask me a question. You'll be perfect for me."

And I have no doubt that he will. He looks sinful, dressed for the first part of our evening in an outfit I've had custom-made for his perfect body. Thatcher isn't hairy and brutish like many of my men, tattooed and scarred. He's unmarked, chiseled to perfection like my own Apollo. The outfit I've chosen for him tonight accentuates his abs while still showcasing to anyone who dares look at him that he's *mine.*

His suit pants are tailored tightly to his ass, showing off how hard he works on and off the ice. Suede loafers add a bit of flair, and pride surges through me to think of how pleased he was to see *my* crest embossed in gold fabric on his shoes. His suit jacket features subtle gold accents and is open to reveal my favorite feature of the outfit.

Rather than a pristine white dress shirt, Thatcher's jacket falls open to reveal his washboard abs, perfectly accentuated by a harness. A *custom* harness loops around each shoulder, underneath each pec, and then bands twice across his trim waist. I don't think he's noticed the missing attachment.

"You look like you're going to eat me alive. I can't wait."

I snap my mouth shut. I've been ogling him for so long that we're already pulling up to the venue. Pinching Thatcher's cheeks together into a pout, I relish the heat in his eyes before pulling him in for a brief, hot kiss. "That's exactly my plan, solnyshko."

"You must come see us soon."

"We'd love to have you for another exhibition. My pet's been asking for your whip for years."

"Any time, we can reserve a stage for you!"

Fuck me, I hope my plans for tonight make it clear that I'm off the market for play with anyone else these days. *For good.*

"Thank you all. But I think it's obvious why I'll be staying in more often. As you can see, I have exactly what I need at home."

And I do. The appreciative sigh that the group exhales echoes what I've heard constantly in the hour that we've been here. Everyone is basking in Thatcher's golden glow and complimenting his behavior.

He's exceptional, just as I knew he would be. When we talked about how tonight would play out, I wondered if he would enjoy the dynamic as much as he thought he would. He knows himself, though, and I never should have doubted him.

"I don't want to have to talk to people and schmooze. I just want to be able to take it all in and relax. You'll know if I need anything. It's exhausting going to all the media events for the team, and even though I enjoy meeting people, I really don't want to at the club. It'd be nice to just exist and..."

"And?"

"And let you take care of me."

His honesty and his precious blush earned him multiple rewards that night, and he's well on his way to having another gold star for his sticker book based on his behavior here. My rules were simple: keep physical contact with me all evening, look around as much as you'd like, but don't make eye contact with anyone, and don't speak. He's been perfect, standing demurely behind me as we made our rounds through my acquaintances and never moving his hand from me once. I've been working on accepting touch in increasingly intimate situations, and it's been comforting to have his warmth on my hip all evening.

Finally dodging the last chatty fan, I lead him away from the group of fans who had gathered around us and head for our dressing room off the main stage. Feeding Thatcher bits of fruit and checking in to make sure he's still feeling well helps me settle further into my Domme headspace. It'll be our turn soon, and for the first time in a very long time, I'm apprehensive about being in the spotlight. I feel confident that he'll be thrilled and fulfilled, but—

"Miss Taranova? Are you ready?"

The interruption comes at the perfect time, forcing me out of the last thoughts I'll have tonight that aren't solely focused on Thatcher and his pleasure. Calm washes over me as I stand before him, running my hands through his hair and pulling his gaze to mine. His dreamy, glazed eyes show me just how floaty he already is, and I can't wait to show everyone how much he means to me.

"Well, solnyshko? Are we ready?"

"Yes, Ma'am."

CHAPTER 46
Thatcher

THE JUXTAPOSITION OF feeling alone on an island with Mila, even while I can hear the crowd murmuring, cheering, moaning, even *fucking* as they watch us on stage, is more than I could have ever imagined. When we discussed my goals for our exhibition, I told her I'd like to be pushed out of my comfort zone. Playing hockey in front of tens of thousands of people stopped making me nervous years ago, and I wanted to experiment and find out if I'd like being stripped down on stage and tortured in front of a crowd.

Walking out mostly clothed, in the suit and harness I'd been wearing all evening, I felt like a god. Mila was showing *me* off. Me! I was the one, out of everyone on earth she could have chosen. She just wanted me. All night, she's been refusing invitations left and right to come to other clubs or play with other submissives. *She doesn't need anyone else,* she said. *Why go out for hamburger when she has steak at home?*

I've been on cloud nine since she pissed off a pushy couple with that comment, and now, as strangers get off to *us,* I feel high. Everything except my harness was slowly removed while

Mila narrated and displayed my best features to the crowd, and the jealousy I could see as she described me as her favorite toy was intoxicating.

"Look at them, solnyshko. They all wish they were you right now, reddened by my flogger and with my plug in their ass. Or they wish they were on their knees before you, tasting this beautiful cock you have."

Mila emphasizes her teasing words with five fast strokes of my archenemy, her custom cock sleeve, and I have to strain every muscle in my body not to come. I continue scanning the crowd, following her rule that I have to *watch* everyone watching me, and shake with effort as a woman being spit roasted between two men catches my eye.

It's been harder than being blindfolded, by far, to ignore the visual stimulus of a room full of live action porn and fight the urge to come. I've gotten much better at controlling myself and knowing my limits since Mila started training me, but *fuck,* it's a nightmare tonight.

"You're being such a *good boy* for me, Thatcher. Turn around and show everyone how pretty your ass looks when it's bright red."

My hands are fastened above my head, but my feet are free to shuffle myself 180 degrees and display my back to the crowd for the first time since I spun while undressing. The appreciation is palpable as they notice how thoroughly Mila's reddened me. She moves to face me, gently running her claws down my abs and making my cock twitch again, wanting nothing more than to sink inside her.

"Do you want to fuck me?" she purrs.

"Always, Ma'am."

"How do you want to?"

"However you want, Ma'am."

"No, solnysko. I mean it. I want to know, in your deepest thoughts, with no limits, *how do you dream about fucking me*?"

Suddenly, I'm more focused than I have been in hours. It doesn't take any time at all to have an answer for her.

"You on top of me, staring into my eyes while I thrust up into you, and I…I'd touch you. I'd want to tangle my fingers in your hair, run my fingers across every inch of your skin, pull your forehead to mine, kiss you, come inside you—"

I'm cut off by her lips on mine just as she clicks on the vibrator deep inside me, and the surprise throws me over the edge of my release. Coating her corset in my spend, she laughs darkly as she walks around me to face the audience again and guide me to do the same.

"Well, well, well. It looks like my toy enjoyed his prostate stimulation a little too much." The crowd laughs, and I feel my face flush as my dick starts stirring already. I don't know why the degradation turns me on, but I'm almost ready to go again.

"I'm sorry, Ma'am."

"Don't tell me you're sorry. Look out there and tell *them* that you're sorry for ruining their show. And make eye contact. I want to believe your apology."

I do as she says, scanning the groups of people still in the throes of their own pleasure, noting the lustful, dazed eyes of submissives like myself and the proud gazes of their masters. "I'm sorry, everyone, for ruining your show."

Words of encouragement flitter through to the stage as Mila pats me on the ass and finally releases me from my overhead bonds. "That's a good boy. Now, on your knees. You have a lot of cleaning up to do."

Hours must have passed by the time I feel myself fully re-engage with reality. Mila has pampered me in our suite backstage at the club, tending to my sore ass and feeding me fruit and honey while murmuring sweet nothings in my ear. Our exhibition was more meaningful than I could have ever hoped for, and I feel so proud that I'm hers. Finally, lying on a couch as limp as a noodle, I register that she's stopped the rhythmic scratching of my scalp and stood from her place seated behind me. As she moves to a table at the side of the room, she clears her throat.

"Thatcher...*solnyshko,* I..."

When she crosses the room back to lower herself onto two knees in front of me, I can see the tears in her eyes. "What's wrong?"

A watery huff is the only answer I receive, but then she reassures me. "I'm fine, my love. Better than fine, actually. I have something I'd like to give you. I'm just finding myself surprisingly nervous."

Oh. I mean, I know our dynamic is odd, but I still thought I'd propose. I have a kickass idea for our rings that involves a secret poison vial and...

"It isn't a ring, I promise," she says, winking and laughing again, less watery now, at how I relax. "But in some ways, it's just as important." She hands me the long velvet box, and I open it immediately, marveling at the *two* collars inside.

"Wow—"

"I love you," she interrupts. "I love you, Thatcher Prescott, regardless of what course our sexual relationship takes. You could tell me right now that you never want to repeat tonight's performance, and I'll happily give up the stage for life. Submission is a gift you give me freely, never my expectation of you. It's something I love about you, but it isn't why I love you."

Well, *fuck*. Now I'm the one sniffling. My eyes are flickering a mile a minute, back and forth between Mila and her earnest expression and my two new accessories. One is so luxurious I hesitate to even consider it a collar. The chain itself is thin and black, with gemstones shining every few links. It's something that I could wear anywhere, even on the ice, and nobody would think anything of it.

The *collar* is unmistakable for anything else—wide, shiny black leather with intricate engraving across the entire band. A solid, thick O-ring rests at the center, and I sense a matching leash or two must be around here somewhere. Before I can say I love them or ask for details, Mila continues.

"Your acceptance of one or both of these doesn't have any effect on our relationship, like I said. I love you—"

"I love them," I interrupt, and she looks so relieved I might even escape punishment for my poor manners. "I love you more than anything. And I'd be honored to wear your collar. During scenes, and outside of them."

There's more to be said, but for now, the adrenaline of emotion washes over us both, and the predatory gleam I love so much returns to Mila's eyes.

"In that case, solnyshko, I think you need a reward for being the *best* boy."

Imagining myself lying at her feet or being led by my leash, I happily move to kneel, but she stops me.

"Oh no, Thatcher. You told me exactly how you wanted to fuck me, and you've earned it, love."

Oh *shit.* She can't really mean…"Hands?" I can't even form a sentence, I'm so shocked. She slowly undoes her braid, long black waves falling down her back like silk. She pulls my hands to her scalp, and I gasp at how soft her hair is.

"Yes, hands. You can touch me wherever you want. And—"

"And?" There's more? What did I even wish for? I was so floaty on stage that I barely remember.

"And you better be ready to fill me up, solnyshko. I hope you've had enough rest."

EPILOGUE

Misha

AS I WAIT for Mila to join me for tea, I can't help but think about how crazy the past two weeks have been, even by our standards.

Coming back to Russia was the last thing I expected to happen this year, but here we are. When Mila and I fled all those years ago, I didn't think I would ever come back. To be honest, I hate it, but if this is where Mila has to be for a while, this is where I'll stay. I know she has Thatcher now, but after the news about her father, she's going to need me more than ever.

We've gotten a lot done in the week that's passed since everything went down at the fake wedding, but it will take months to sort everything out. The good news is that Alexei's sons seem like genuinely good men. Plus, Ivan and his son, Sasha, both agreed to extend their help a while longer as well to fast-track the takeover.

I feel Mila before I hear her walking toward me. God, I've missed her. Even with all hands on deck, it's been so chaotic that we've barely crossed paths. This has been the least I've seen her in as long as I can remember. I turn to her with a smile that I can't fight, but the look I'm met with is anything but happy.

"What's wrong?" I ask as she slowly lowers herself into the seat next to me.

She takes my hand, and I swear tears are welling in her eyes. "I'm sending Thatcher back to Thunder Bay."

Oh, phew.

Relief floods me at the mention of Thatch. Their attachment is new, but it's strong, and I know for a fact that she's struggling with emotions she's never allowed herself to feel before. It makes sense that she would send him back to the States and that she would be sad about it.

"I know it's hard, moya tsaritsa, but you know that's where he will be safest, and you'll be so busy flying back and forth between New York and Russia that he would probably barely see you staying at either place. He's got his season coming up anyway, and he'll have Teddy and the Santoris there—"

"And you," Mila whispers.

"Excuse me?"

Surely, she didn't mean that. I'll be either with her as she goes back and forth or holding things down for her while she travels.

"You're going to go with him, moya sila."

Where's the hidden camera? Mila has never been one for pranks, but who knows, maybe Thatcher has rubbed off on her. To my dismay, nobody jumps out with confetti.

"What are you *talking about*? I can't leave you here to deal with this by yourself—"

"I won't be by myself. I have Ivan, Sasha, and our new cousins to help with things. They're all incredible, and I know—"

"But I can't leave you..."

Mila cups my face. "Of course you can. It's going to be different, I know. Trust me, I'm not looking forward to this either. I hate it. You're as much a part of me as myself. But I *need* you to watch after Thatcher. And, well, you can't stay in Russia anyway."

"What do you mean I can't stay in Russi—"

"You took the virginity of *all three* of the prime minister's daughters, Misha? Really?"

I grimace at the mention of the PM. "Hey, that was a long time ago! I'm a completely different man now."

"Well, he won't work with us as long as you're here. So if you can't stay with me in Russia, you might as well go protect my heart in Thunder Bay."

"I don't know *how* to leave you, moya tsaritsa."

Mila's tears are falling freely at this point, as are mine. "I don't know how to either, but I think it's time we both learned. Falling in love with Thatcher made me realize how much I've been missing all these years. You and I have put our hearts on hold for the sake of the Bratva, and in doing so have sacrificed *decades* of happiness. I thought love was a weakness, Misha, but I was wrong. I was so wrong. It's a *strength.* I should have known. All these years, I considered you my greatest strength and you're the only person I ever truly loved...until Teddy and Thatch." She pauses, resting her brow on mine. "We will always have each other, moya sila, but it's time for you to set out on your own adventure. It's time for you to find your heart, like I've found mine."

We stay still in our embrace for what feels like both an eternity and only a moment as we relish the last moments of our time together. I know I'll always have Mila, just as she'll always have me, but something about this seems like a finality. Like the life we've known as long as we can recall is about to change forever.

I could say no. I could turn her down and refuse. I could beg and pray she lets me stay by her side, like I always have been. But I'll never have it in me to deny my queen anything she asks of me.

Sitting back in my chair, I give her my best attempt at a smile. "When do I leave, Boss?"

EPILOGUE 2

Mila

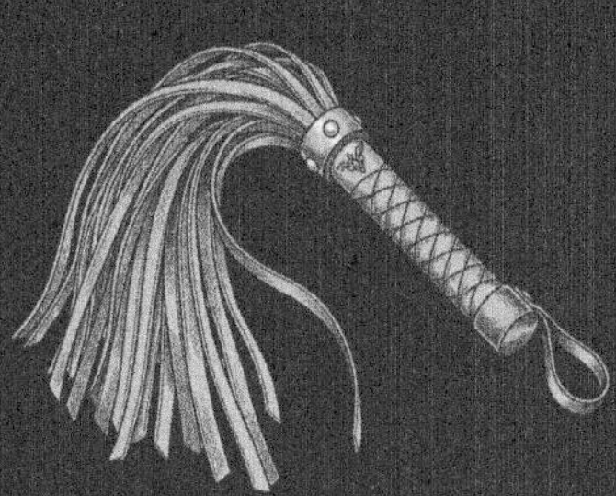

"OH! I'M NOT an expert, but—"

"It's a mocktail," Ellie explains. "You might think that the stereotypical pregnancy cravings would be enough for this baby, but no. Instead of wanting chocolate or pickles, *all* she's wanted is *gin.*"

"That's my girl!" Ellie's Nonna fist-bumps the air in solidarity with the apparently aspiring lush baby, but her gaze remains steadfast on the ice. Warm-ups are well underway, and with her binoculars, I'm sure she's seeing *plenty.*

Ellie's mom, Giulia, returns from the bathroom, wiping her eyes. The Santori family has been through a lot recently, but the baby on the way has brightened everyone's spirits.

This is Thatcher's first game with Thunder Bay, and the only one I'll be able to catch for a while. My visit back to the States is short and packed with the tedium of handling as much New York business as possible while I'm here. Digging up the weeds in Russia has been, and will continue to be, a challenge, and I'm relying heavily on Misha and Teddy to take care of Thatcher in my absence.

After the pre-game video, featuring frothy waves projected onto the ice and culminating in a maelstrom at the center, the team's music starts as a spotlight shines for the announcement of the starting line.

"Number 34, Nikkkkkkiiiiii Sannnntorrrriiiiiiiiiiii!" The crowd chants Nikkie's name as Ellie wipes her eyes, pulling Nonna and Giulia in for a tight hug. Her dad, Dante, is watching from a seat in the rafters tonight, leaving the box to us for a girls' night.

"Number 12, Theodore Taranov!" If anyone associated with the team asked any questions about Teddy's name change, they must have already been forgotten.

"Your captain, number 8, Gabriele Sannnntorrrriiiiiiiiiiii!" Even though I only spent a limited amount of time with Gabri, the eldest Santori, it's clear that the past few months have taken a toll. I can assume, from experience, that he's been stepping up more to help Dante with the business. Managing that as well as a hockey career would be enough to make anyone scowl.

The spotlight transforms into a warmer golden hue as a new projection appears on the ice. Another wave, this time brighter, with a rising sun in the sky behind. Teddy told me the team was planning something special for Thatcher's first game, especially since he's already stolen the hearts of all the guys.

Not that I'm surprised. That's what my solnyshko does. My Rising Tide jersey proudly displays "Prescott" across the back, and after teasing him that I'd never wear a man's name, I can't wait to show him later. If he's very good, and I'm hoping he is, he might get to be fucked by me tonight, wearing the jersey and nothing else.

"And now, by popular demand, new to the Rising Tide, is number 19...Thatcherrrrr Taranovvvvvv!"

The roar of the crowd and the gasps of Nonna and Giulia are drowned out by Ellie, squealing and hurrying to pull me into a tight hug.

"Teddy told me, and it was the worst secret to keep. Well, not the worst, but still. He and Thatcher were both so excited! And I'm supposed to give you this, but he said to only read it when he's *not* on the ice. I think it's the name change paperwork. He said, and I quote, 'Tell her when I'm out there, I better have her full attention, or I'll be very sad, and I'll do the puppy dog eyes.'"

It's hard to keep the tears from falling, but I manage it until the anthem is over and the men skate out for puck drop. On his last warm-up skate around the ice, Thatcher speeds past our box and points at me. If he were anyone else, I'd doubt that he knew exactly where I was, but Thatcher can feel me from a mile away.

My tears spill over as he points at me, then to the back of his jersey, and finally to his heart before locking in for the puck drop. Ellie's wink as she pulls me down to the seat next to hers is fortifying, and I've just composed myself when Thatcher breaks away.

He was deep in his own zone and intercepted the puck with a head of steam. Defenders try to get an angle on him, but every stick falls short in the face of his speed. By the time he reaches the blue line, he's slicing through as if the puck is attached to his stick, control and precision in every inch of his movement. Only the goalie remains, and with a split-second freeze, the puck soars into the back of the net.

God, he's glorious. Watching him skate at the compound, I assumed he was showing off and putting in maximum effort to impress me. It's clear now that it was only a tease. This little shit was being *modest* and not showing off at all. He celebrates with the team before skating across the ice to Teddy, who's come out farther from the crease than usual. The crowd roars as he picks Thatcher up and spins him around in a circle before headbutting him and sending him to the bench.

By the time the third period starts, I'm exhausted. With every moment, I'm more invested in Thatcher's skating and his stats. My skill in noticing when he starts to tire at the end of a shift is improving, along with the little ways he gets sloppy when he's frustrated. The most amazing part of watching him, though, is the sense that he's a little boy flying around on the ice with his friends. His joy is infectious, and when Teddy's grandma Muriel arrives, cursing about her taxi getting into a fender bender, she fits right in. After the Rising Tide secures the win, we all file down to the lounge near the locker room to wait for the team.

"You know, I consider Thatcher to be my son just as much as I do Teddy," Muriel says quietly, standing with me to the side as the Santori family makes their rounds. "That boy is so special, with so much love to give, and it's absolutely killed me all these years to see everyone take advantage of him."

"He's wonderful," I agree. "He's shown me so much—"

"And his parents! Those fuckers don't know how lucky they are to have a child with such a joyful spirit, I'll tell you that. How he managed to come out of that situation with such a good head on his shoulders, I have no idea."

"Yes, I have quite a few things I'd like to tell them if I ever—"

"He's *not* a pyro, you know! No matter how many fires he's started, they've all been accidents! I don't care what the firemen say. They're biased—"

"Wait, how many fires?"

"Whoa, Grandma Dubs! Sounds like you found the champagne fountain in the suite."

Thatcher picks Muriel up and squeezes her in a tight hug, but his eyes are loaded, and only for me. As soon as she pinches his cheeks and tells him how proud of him she is, she moves to join the Santoris and leaves us alone.

"I hope you're not mad that I—ooomph!"

The force of my embrace nearly takes both of us to the ground, but Thatcher recovers just in time to hold my thighs as I wrap my legs around his waist and thrust my tongue into his mouth. There will never be a way to tell him what tonight *truly* meant to me, but as soon as I can get him home and get these damn pants *off*...

"So you're not mad?" His laugh is watery as I pull back to press my forehead to his.

"I'm *so* not mad. I can't believe you pulled this off under my nose, though. Even from Russia, there's not much that you do that I'm not aware of—Misha. That little *shit.* The two of you conspiring against me is a sign of the end times. You can't make a habit of it."

Swaying us back and forth, no sign of my weight being a problem for him to hold for as long as I want him to, he throws his head back in a bellowing laugh. "We'll try to limit our collaborations for the good of humanity. *But* Teddy was also involved. "So please feel free to direct some of your wrath to him." He's using the soft voice that I know is only for me. It means he's saying exactly what he thinks, even if he was taught his whole life that what he thought didn't matter. Like what he did didn't matter.

"I'm overjoyed. It's impossible to process right now that you did this for me, but I'm so proud to see my last name on your back while you annihilate another team. It really does something for me, actually."

"Oh yeah?"

"Mm-hmm. Although now that you mention it, I might be just a *little* mad."

He picks up on my teasing and takes us out of the lounge, finding an alcove with a wall to press me up against. "Why are you a little mad, my love?"

"Well, see…I had plans to reward you that included me wearing nothing but this jersey with your name across it. But since you changed your name, my jersey's obsolete."

His eyes darken, promising that the adrenaline after a win will be something special, and I can't wait to reap the benefits.

"I'm sorry about that. Is there any way I can make it up to you?"

"Hmm, what a good boy, ready to make amends. I'd like the jersey off your back. Perhaps a clean one, not the one from the game tonight. But I want to wear *our* name across my back while I fuck you. Does that sound like something you'd be interested in?"

The promise in his eyes is deep and true as he answers immediately.

"Yes, Ma'am."

ALSO BY T.K. DRAKE

Check out our other books at Amazon.com!

Stay in Touch!

Be the first to know about T.K. Drake's new releases and receive exclusive content!

Tkdrake.com

Instagram: @tkdrakeauthor

ABOUT THE AUTHOR

T.K. Drake is a dynamic duo of best friends who couldn't find the perfect romance novel and decided to write it themselves. As only children, they spent their childhood entertaining each other with elaborate stories and games. Reuniting as adults has inspired them to unleash their creative energy into contemporary and dark romance, bridging gaps in the genre and writing books they longed to read. Based in the Southeastern United States, when not writing they are usually reading, lounging on the beach, or planning their next international vacation.

Made in the USA
Coppell, TX
01 July 2026

83240521R00194